MISS HONEYFIELD
AND THE
DARK DUKE

A HISTORICAL REGENCY ROMANCE

Originally Titled *The Dark Duke*

AUDREY ASHWOOD

Miss Honeyfield and the Dark Duke

Originally Titled *The Dark Duke*

(LARGE PRINT EDITION)

Copyright © 2019 Audrey Ashwood

ISBN: 9781793869470

They say he has a black heart.

They say he is cold, unscrupulous, dangerous.

They say he killed a woman out of jealousy.

Robert Beaufort, the Duke of Scuffold, has returned to the castle of his forefathers. To be seen with him means the ruin of any woman's reputation. When Miss Minerva Honeyfield stumbles upon the duke in an enchanted glade deep in the forest, it is too late to heed her aunt's warnings.

Her indecent encounter is the most exciting event that has ever happened to Minerva – and also the most dangerous one. Despite knowing that the man is ominous and menacing, Minerva is unable to shield herself from her fascination with the Duke of Scuffold.

While Minerva struggles to resign herself to longing for a man who will destroy her name and possibly even threaten her life, her mother falls into mortal danger – and all indications point to the dark duke.

Has Minerva truly lost her heart to a ruthless murderer?

PROLOGUE

*T*he Duke's Secret by M. H.

Lady Marianne de Lacey was of exceptional beauty and innocence, which immediately aroused the desire to possess her in everyone who saw her, much as someone would want to call a precious piece of jewellery their own.

MINERVA HONEYFIELD FOLDED her hands prudishly in her lap and lowered her gaze. Her tea cup sat beside her on a side table, and the tea was cooling almost as quickly as the rather uncomfortable atmosphere in the sitting room.

Mr Giles Meade sat across from Minerva and her mother, a crumb-scattered plate bearing witness to his enjoyment of her mother's skills as a host. Mrs Honeyfield loved pastries and fancies, and the household's cook was a mistress of her craft. Her cakes, tea biscuits and fluffy crème-filled rolls had become quite famous amongst the London crowd. More than one guest had tried to win over their cook – unsuccessfully, as Minerva's mother never tired of recounting.

"Minerva," her mother's voice interrupted her thoughts. "Mr Meade was kind enough to invite us to a concert tomorrow evening. Will you not give your answer?"

Beneath her mother's warm tone of voice Minerva sensed a warning she did not dare to ignore. "It would be my honour to attend," she replied obediently and gave the wealthy young man a smile. If one took into account that he was one of the richest bachelors in London, and that he was someone who enjoyed great popularity amongst her friends, then her words were certainly not a lie. In fact, so far only Minerva's dearest friend Georgiana Bancroft had managed to show herself off to the Beau Monde seated beside Mr Meade, in his magnificent carriage. Georgiana's mother had been extraordinarily determined (and rather scrupulous) to bring Mr Meade and her eldest daughter together on that sunny afternoon. Unfortunately, her happiness was only short-lived, as Georgiana had failed to retain Mr Meade's interest for any longer than the carriage ride had lasted. Georgiana, on the other hand, had told her friend how relieved she had secretly been that the man was not interested in her, since, in a well-hidden corner of her heart, she longed for something entirely different – as did Minerva herself.

Did it mean something that Mr Meade had taken Georgiana on a ride in his carriage and had invited her to a concert? Perhaps he was testing Minerva's public suitability as the future Mrs Meade. He could not guess that Minerva had already decided that he did not meet her standard of what a suitable husband should be.

Both Minerva and Georgiana had agreed about what this mysteriously different *thing* was that a man must have, in order to qualify as a candidate for marriage. He did not need to have a title, nor was impressive wealth necessary. No, for Minerva and Georgiana a man had to have something much more valuable. Personality – that was the word mentioned most often during their conversations. Every now and again, it would be topped by "charm". Both agreed that good looks were inevitably associated with those two qualities. A gentleman with charm always looked good. However, both young women agreed that they would not accept a good-looking man without charm. There were too many men in their social circle, a prime example being Mr Meade, who trusted that their pleasant appearance would secure a fitting bride.

Some of their friends, who were not fortunate enough to be able to see beyond striking, masculine features, also mistook the clinking sound of coins and guineas for personality.

The most important characteristic that Minerva was looking for in a man had little to do with appearances or money. She believed that the man who would one day earn her heart needed a generous personality, almost to the point of liberality. After all, Minerva did something that – despite all the progress of her time – was considered scandalous for a woman of good breeding: she wrote. Not letters, but novels. And, she was not planning to stop, merely because she married, and her husband would not tolerate it.

"Please do excuse me, I think it is time I took my

leave," Mr Meade announced and rose rather laboriously from his chair. Of course, her mother had offered him the most comfortable seat in her eyes but did not realize that the Lord was proportioned differently than she was.

Sighing internally, Minerva allowed Mr Meade to sketch a kiss onto her fingertips, before he took his leave. He also gave her a look from beneath his lowered eyes, which he probably considered a very soulful one. Minerva watched him through the parlour window, as he left the house. His bouncing stride and his posture spoke of success and expectation. His next step, following the concert, would be just as obvious as today's visit, which had not been made to assure himself of Minerva's qualities, but rather to win her mother's favour. Immediately after the concert, she knew, he would request to speak to her father, to discover, discreetly, just how much her dowry might be worth. He would have heard the rumours already – her father was a successful and wealthy man and she was his only child. Mr Meade was not at all different from all the other young (and not so young) men who had asked for her hand in marriage. For all of them, marriage seemed to be a mere business transaction, one that had to be successful right from the start, since it was impossible to change (or step down from) the negotiations once a certain point had been reached.

As soon as Mr Meade had departed, her father joined the two women in the parlour. "I hear that the young gentleman came to visit you and pay his respects," he said while looking at his wife questioningly. Minerva's mother nodded and made a noise, which could only be considered a happy sigh. To draw out the inevitable, Minerva picked up her cup of tea and pretended that she was drinking. In truth, her throat felt tight, and she found it hard to breathe.

As certain as she had been just a short while ago, she now felt more fearful. It was one thing to review a marriage candidate and to be absolutely sure that she would never give the man her hand in marriage. It was a different thing to communicate this fact to her parents.

"He is such a pleasant young man," her mother began. "His manners are magnificent. He is so very polite… and modest." She was probably thinking, as Minerva was, of the previous candidate. His manners had been far too intimate and familiar, even for her mother's liking, whose despair seemed to have blinded her to the faults of the courting gentlemen.

Her father had not yet given up hope, as his next words showed. "Marvellous. Then I assume that we can look forward to a wedding quite soon." He opened the newspaper noisily and hid behind it, hoping that there was nothing more to say regarding the subject of marriage.

"I will not marry this man."

There, she had said it.

The spoon clinked softly in her mother's tea cup. Her father's newspaper rustled almost accusingly, as he held the pages with more force.

"Yes, you will," she heard him say from behind the protective paper wall.

"I cannot marry him," Minerva objected.

How was she supposed to explain to her parents that Mr Meade would never ever allow her to write her novels? And even *if* he did lower his standards to the point where he would allow her quirky little "hobby", then a mere toleration of her passion was far from what she desired in a husband. She needed to write in the same way as she needed air to breathe! Imagining stories, creating people, and sending them into bloodcurdling and dangerous situations – all of that was so much more than just a pastime like knitting or embroidery. "I do not love him." Her parents understood this argument better than any other thing she might have said about things that were denied to women.

Her father's reaction was to grip the newspaper even tighter. Her mother looked at her anxiously and raised her eyebrows as if to warn her.

"You will learn to love him," Chester Honeyfield grunted. "When your mother and I married, there was no talk of any sentiments. Now, we are as happy and content with each other as anyone could ask for after twenty-one years of marriage."

She avoided looking at her mother and focussed solely on the loud throbbing of her rebellious heart.

"Mr Meade does not love me either," Minerva said, acting as if she had not heard her father's argument. "He sees me as nothing more than a pretty little bug. He is looking for a woman who will run his household and sit by his side and smile whenever he is at a social event."

The newspaper sank into her father's lap and revealed the face of an outraged man, who had reached the end of his patience. For a moment, Minerva almost wanted to give in, just so her father would calm down. However, they were talking about her life! She was not willing to give up so easily. "He doesn't love me, but rather the *image* he has of me." Instinctively, her hands smoothed her hair. Her long pale-gold hair showed its natural curl, even when tied back as now, and when unbound, it reached down the entire length of her back. Her face was delicately proportioned and her skin creamy and without blemish. Her well-defined cheek bones prevented her face from looking overly perfect, so that the effect was not that of a porcelain doll, but of a living, breathing woman. In fact, anyone who knew Minerva well also knew that the slight set of her jaw was a good indication of the independent mind that dwelt within. Her eyes reflected her nature, as their unusual light blue-violet colour was tinted here and there with a steely grey, which seemed to change with her moods, just as a blue sky changes from bright to forbidding at the approach of a storm. Her previous suitors had not only praised her eyes, but her immaculate complexion, and her gracious movement, which never seemed to lack in elegance. One of them had even complimented her on her feet and the daintiness of her limbs. At least her mother had agreed with her on that one's unsuitability.

"For once and for all – I will *not* tolerate my daughter marrying a man who will spoil her. You need a firm hand and not some aesthete who will tell you everything you *want* to hear. You need a man who will teach you obedience and refinement – qualities you are currently lacking."

"But…" she began.

She had actually wanted to tell him that he was right in regards of the aesthete. Of course, her future husband should also be smart, educated and eloquent in his use of words, but by no means should he be a man who would agree with everything that she said.

Her father laid down his newspaper and rose from his chair.

"I will ask you one last time. Will you marry Mr Meade?"

She shook her head and immediately searched for her mother's clammy hand to reassure her.

Her father was not only angry – he was completely outraged. Now she would have to muster up all of her courage and remain as steadfast as she could. "I would rather die than to take this oaf as my husband!" Her words did not sound as certain as she would have hoped.

"In that case, I shall take you by your word," Chester Honeyfield replied. "You *will* marry Mr Meade, or..."

"But he is so incredibly boring!" The words burst out of her, uncontrollably.

Her father looked at her with a shrewd gaze and smiled. "Oh, so that is the reason why." He looked strangely satisfied, which scared Minerva even more than his rage had. "I will show you what the word 'boredom' really means. Tomorrow morning, I will send you to your aunt in Scuffold, and you will remain there for as long as I see fit. The only books you will be allowed to take with you are those two over there." He nodded towards the reference books for female behaviour. The advice found in those manuals constantly left Minerva feeling unworthy, as if she were some imbecile – and this only because she had been born a female. So, she had limited her reading of the two books to a necessary minimum and preferred to indulge herself in other books that were much more exciting. She remembered very well the moment she had opened

"The Castle of Otranto" for the first time and read the first few pages. Even her memory of it caused her to shiver, half with anxiety and half fascination, as she thought of the events and adventures that had befallen the innocent heroine.

Her mother placed her teacup back on its saucer and almost simultaneously, Minerva and her father looked over towards her, to see how she was taking the surprising news. Minerva realised, disappointedly, that she would not receive any help from her mother, who only looked at her husband with an expression of surprise on her reddened face, before she rose from her chair. "I shall call for her things to be packed immediately," she said and swept out of the room.

Minerva swore to herself that she would never become like her mother, who obeyed everything her father commanded mindlessly and never objected to anything he said. She had to try to persuade him, one last time. "Papa, please do not forget that the season is not over yet. How am I supposed to find a husband if you send me out into the country now? Nobody will be there!" That final sentence sounded more pleadingly than she cared for. For a short moment, it seemed as if her father could be softened, but then he shook his head and buried it behind his newspaper.

He had rendered his verdict and Minerva would have to follow his orders. She promised herself that she would never marry a man whom she did not love. She really would much rather travel out into the country in the midst of the season and, once there, die a miserable and lonely death.

CHAPTER 1

*L*ady de Lacey had lost her husband in a tragic way, and with it, she had also lost all of her wealth.

MINERVA HAD NEVER BEEN to Scuffold before, and she had only met her aunt two or three times, when her father's sister had visited them as she travelled through London. In Minerva's memory, she was a heavily-built woman, almost half a foot taller than her husband, who had always brought Minerva a small gift when she had visited. The older Minerva had grown, the less fitting those gifts had seemed. The last one had been a glass jar of honey, and Aunt Catherine had enthusiastically praised its healing qualities. She had even gone as far as describing the very last detail of her own various illnesses and the amelioration through the sticky juice, until Minerva had felt herself taken ill from the alleged suffering.

What could she expect at Scuffold?

Minerva straightened her bonnet. She longed for someone to talk to, but despite the jostling motion inside the carriage, her mother had managed to fall asleep. The further away from London they drove, the more the roads worsened, and even the extremely good suspension of the carriage seemed to not be able to handle such rough jarring. At her mother's continued urging, her father had agreed to allow them to travel in the comfort of their family-owned carriage. Only a clear hint from her mother about the dangers which a young woman in the postal carriage would have to face had led him to change his mind.

Minerva had begged her father to let her maid come with her, but that request had been denied flatly. "Your aunt and uncle have everything you will need," he replied, and his voice had thundered like that of Zeus, the Greek father of all the gods. "You will need to learn to live with what you have got. A bit of simplicity and humility is exactly what you need." For a moment, Minerva had wondered if her father was right. The fact that other people saw her as a spoiled young woman was not exactly pleasant. She blushed and decided to talk about this problem with her friend the next time she saw her.

It was absolutely possible that her mama would send for Antoinette once her father's nerves had calmed a little. After all, even from a young age, she had always had someone to help her get dressed and style her hair. She was sure that her mother would not allow her to walk around with wild hair or to visit people with a loosely-tied bodice. A smile twitched around her lips when she imagined not wearing that much-hated thing at all.

She wondered what her aunt and uncle did all day. What was there to do out in the country? What if you wanted to have a conversation? Apparently, her Aunt Catherine was a passionate whist player and a good one at that. Minerva remembered one evening when she and her aunt had beat her parents together, as partners, with an incredibly high score. It had been a very pleasurable party, especially since Minerva had won. However, playing whist every single day was not really something she was looking forward to. In addition, there would be only four of them. Minerva groaned quietly, as she imagined her aunt and uncle might invite some of the marriageable gentlemen of the area and force her to sit down at the card table with them, every night.

On the other hand, Minerva could not really imagine her uncle following the activities that gentlemen who lived in the countryside usually followed. He did not like to ride horses, as he himself had admitted, which also ruled out hunting as another pastime.

So, what did a gentleman do all day, if he did not work, as her father did, or like the noblemen who sat in government during the season? To her, it was an enigma – and not a very interesting one.

However, there was one thing that lifted her desperation slightly. She had packed a new blank notebook, and she very much intended on using it. Perhaps being away from everything, out in the countryside, would have some advantages after all. Minerva wanted to start a new novel, and she hoped to find some peace and quiet down in Kent for a book that she was planning to offer to a publisher under a false name. So far, her stories had found no mercy before her own eyes.

However, she was determined to change that and write a novel that would be the equal of those written by the female authors whom she very much admired.

She and her mother had already been travelling in the carriage for a full day and a half. Until now, Minerva had only experienced the tiny village in Kent through her aunt's eyes. Her aunt was a passionate letter writer and would fill long pages, where she wrote all about her latest acquaintances and the incredibly beautiful landscape of the shire in which she lived. Minerva had only listened half-heartedly as her mother read the letters, which was something she now regretted.

The journey had been extremely exhausting, despite an overnight stop at an inn last evening. The "Graveyard Inn" had been loud, dirty, and overcrowded. Minerva had observed it all with wide eyes, memorising every single detail, before her mother had dragged her into the tiny bedroom upstairs, for which she had paid the host a handsome amount of money. The bed was worth its weight in gold – those had been her words – but Minerva did not even notice, as she was very much occupied with finding out where all the nasty smells that tickled her nose were coming from. The aroma of the establishment, with its untrustworthy name, was a mixture of fire, rancid bacon, and the bodily odours of the visitors. As concerned the latter, she was not entirely sure what it was, as she had never been confronted with such a stench before. In London, everything was overpowered by the smog that regularly engulfed most of the streets of the entire city during the night, regardless of the time of year.

Her mother took bedsheets from her overnight bag and instructed the maid, who had accompanied them upstairs, to exchange the inn's sheets for their own fresh ones. This cautious measure turned out to be very wise indeed, for Minerva saw bed bugs running away in fear as the young woman began the task.

THEY WOKE EARLY the following morning in order to cross the border to the shire before noon; Minerva was tired, but oddly happy. She had not slept much (the tiny creatures had come back to tease her), but so far, her objection to marrying Mr Meade had not caused her too much discomfort. Quite the opposite – she enjoyed the adventure of their long journey, and she could not get enough of all the faces of the new people she saw as the carriage passed by.

All the praising stories about living in the country, which she had read about in her novels (but which had always seemed strange to her), started to make sense. The people seemed so content, Minerva thought. They smiled and waved, and Minerva waved back happily, despite her mother's stern admonishment. As soon as the wheels of the carriage had carried them past, the waving workers would turn back to what they were doing. Sure, they were poor and had to live off what the land provided, but Minerva envied them for the poignant simplicity of their lives.

She leaned back into the plush cushions of the coach bench and imagined how she would kiss her husband goodbye in the mornings and busy herself preparing a delicious meal for when he returned, using all the goodies she would harvest from their garden. She saw her children running happily around the house, and she saw love shining in her husband's eyes when he thanked her at night for the thoughtful way she managed the household.

"We have everything we need," he would say.

She would hand him his slippers and his pipe, and they would settle in to read the latest accomplishments from Thomas Love Peacock or Miss Austen, together. A man such as her husband would not shun such works as Lord Byron, and he would also never prohibit his wife from reading them. Quite the opposite, he would encourage her to follow her most secret and greatest dream, and to make it a reality. She would follow straight in the footsteps of the mysterious and anonymous woman who had written those wonderfully entertaining novels.

Minerva barely noticed the glorious English countryside that her mother continually pointed out to her, she was too preoccupied with her dream of a simpler life. It was only when she could hear nothing but the noise of the turning carriage wheels that she realised how quiet it had become around her. It was completely different to the overcrowded streets they had experienced when they left London. Even Hoskins, their driver, had fallen silent, instead of hurling his usual threats at those who would not let him pass.

There simply was no one to shout at, nor indeed any other traffic on the empty country road.

"I hope we will arrive at Scuffold soon," her mother

said and dabbed her forehead. The air in the carriage was stuffy and the midsummer temperatures did not help to make the journey any more comfortable. "I would prefer it if we did not have to spend another night without the comforts of a proper bed." The fact that her mother had mentioned this, meant that she really did not feel well.

"I am sure that we will be there soon," Minerva returned and felt more of a grown-up. "Aunt Catherine and Uncle James will have prepared everything for our arrival. I am already looking forward to a nice, hot cup of tea." The tempting thought of the reviving brew did what she had intended it to do. Her mother's face brightened up, and she even started to smile.

"You are a good child, Minerva," she said and took her daughter's hand. "If only you were not so stubborn and outspoken. However, I suppose that your father and I are entirely responsible for that. We should never have allowed you to read so many books."

"Oh Mama, do not blame yourself." Minerva pondered how she could best comfort her mother and squeezed her hand. A moment such as this was valuable to Minerva, since it did not occur often. Her father's presence created an invisible barrier between her and her mother that Mrs Honeyfield never dared to cross. Then again, was this invisible barrier just another one of Minerva's wild imaginations? "Maybe, in Scuffold, there will be a gentleman I might actually like."

"Your uncle might be retired, but I am certain that he knows a few gentlemen who would be suitable. He is still highly regarded in society. As I have heard, even the Duke of Scuffold consults him for his advice, now and again."

Minerva sighed silently and tried to suppress her rising impatience. There were so many other, more exciting things she could think of, rather than having to converse with her uncle's former colleagues. She imagined they were all old, musty, and boring. Uncle James was very much like her father. These men always talked about the things they had done in the past. What on earth was so fascinating about the things that had long since passed into history? At almost twenty-one years old, she lived completely in the present. What was important to her was what happened here and now! But she was sure that, even when she was forty years of age and happily married, she would never wallow in the past.

Minerva vaguely remembered the last letter they had

received from her aunt, where she had mentioned a minister who was young and seemingly quite modern in his ways. Presumably, what Aunt Catherine and Uncle James called "quite modern" was in fact an advance of progress that was just to Minerva's taste. In her heart, she nurtured the faint hope that she might find a like-minded companion in the wife of the priest, or maybe even a friend?

They reached their destination just as the sun began to sink slowly beneath the horizon. Her relatives' house sat right on the main road – or what they would call a main road here in this corner of England – and from the outside it looked rather neat and surprisingly large. The main doorway was framed by two large pots that held tidily trimmed little bushes, which at closer inspection resembled a dog and a cat staring vigilantly at each other. It was such a delightful and surprising element that Minerva felt some of the weight of worry fall off her shoulders, which had appeared when she noticed that the road was completely empty. Someone resided – well, lived – here who had a real sense of humour.

At least, that was what she was hoping for.

* * *

A SMALL SLIVER *of light appeared on the horizon. For Lady Marianne, it was the epitome of hope after the longest night of her life.*

"GOODBYE, MAMA." Minerva waved after the carriage, which quickly disappeared into a veritable cloud of dust. Her mother had recovered for three days from their long journey here, before she had grown restless and wanted to return to London. Her husband needed her now more than her daughter did, she had said, since she knew that her child was going to be very well taken care of.

The first few days in Scuffold were wonderful. Minerva received her elders' approval to explore the little village, accompanied by Anna, one of her aunt's servants. Before Minerva's arrival, Anna had been responsible for many different chores in the Buckley household, and now she was also serving as Minerva's maid, looking after her wardrobe and doing her hair. Anna did her best, but between all the tasks she had to do inside the house, she had very little time to attend to Minerva's needs.

Minerva decided to try to convince her aunt to employ a girl from the village to tend to her needs. Even if the girl did not have the slightest idea about fashion, as Minerva fully expected, Minerva could at least try to teach her the basics.

Her aunt and uncle had allowed her to look around everywhere (except the tavern), as long as she was not unaccompanied, and if she did not go further away from the village than an hour's walking would take her. Much to Minerva's misery and, she supposed, much to Anna's relief, the maid's household responsibilities often kept her from accompanying Minerva on excursions through the small hamlet. The only other distraction was a weekly dinner that her aunt organised, and to which the 'modern priest', whom Minerva had heard of, was also invited. Unfortunately, the man did not seem half as daring as the letters from her aunt had led her to believe. He also did not come with an adventurous young wife.

Minerva had had great hopes for the first dinner. Beforehand, she had imagined how she would dazzle all the guests with her wit and spirited conversation. However, the conversation had mainly been about legal quarrels in court, such as was to be expected from a former lawyer and his male friends, and none of it satisfied Minerva's lust for adventure. Who cared about a squabble about property lines or a cow that had mysteriously switched its branding? Definitely not Minerva. She had thought herself lucky when one of the gentlemen had suggested a round of whist, and they had played cards for the remainder of the night. But even the game had not excited her for long as all the surprises had vanished after the second round, when she remarked that the lawyers and judges played the game exactly as their characters would have them play – extremely cautiously and with no one being inclined to take any risk.

At least there was a pianoforte in the household of Mr and Mrs James Buckley – not that Minerva felt a sudden urge to play it. Much to the disappointment of her parents, she was so musically untalented that even Minerva's governess had implored her mother to forego any musical presentations from her daughter, particularly if she wanted to find her a suitable husband in the near future. As Minerva let her fingers glide across the beautifully made instrument, she wondered if this wouldn't be a suitable method of scaring away all the unwelcome suitors.

She sat down on the cushioned seat, placed her fingers onto the piano keys and played a small melody. If she were to start singing right now, to accentuate her rendering of the broken note sequence with her voice, she would surely scare every man into fleeing – unless they truly loved her.

"Oh, how lovely," she heard a voice behind her. It was her Aunt Catherine, who had followed her into the salon, unnoticed. "Would you like me to turn the pages for you?"

"No, thank you," Minerva replied, attempting to rise from the chair. "Unfortunately, this instrument exceeds my capabilities... however, I wonder if we could not organise a small dance event? Whenever it is suitable, of course," she quickly added, since she anticipated her Aunt Catherine's reaction. If they were to roll up the carpets and move the furniture to the walls, then the salon of the Buckleys' house would offer enough space for three or maybe even four dancing couples.

Her aunt stepped aside so that Minerva could stand up. "Maybe that would not be a bad idea," she admitted slowly, and for a moment her eyes glittered with mischievous excitement. Or were they memories of her own youth?

When Minerva realised that her aunt was not opposed to her idea, she clapped her hands. "Oh please, Aunt Catherine! It would make me happy to have the opportunity to make the acquaintances of some of the younger ladies nearby and maybe even find some friends amongst them. I am sure that Uncle James would not mind." The statement was entirely made up, but Minerva had the feeling that she had to take advantage of the moment.

"That may be true," her aunt confirmed. "Back in the day, your uncle was a formidable dancer, and he has never objected to young people having fun in his house, as long as it is in a befitting manner." Minerva resisted the impulse to throw her arms around her aunt's neck, so she stood on her tippy toes instead and kissed her cheek. "Regrettably, all the young women, who seem suitable for you, are currently spending their time in London for the season."

"But..." Minerva wanted to object, but her aunt lifted her hand firmly.

"No back talk, my child. I am responsible for you, and

therefore I am responsible for the people you come into contact with." Her face softened. "I understand that it must be hard for you having to leave London and being sent out into the country, but your father had good reasons for his decision."

Minerva sank down onto the sofa slowly and stared into her hands, which she had folded neatly in her lap, just so she could hide her tears.

"However, I am certain that your uncle and I are allowed to take you with us to the horse market in Crowell on Friday."

Minerva had no idea how to react to this new piece of information. She had no idea what to expect from a horse market. Horses, of course, and presumably plenty of other animals. It really was not easy for Minerva to imagine the excursion as something positive, but she was willing to try. After all, it was not her uncle or aunt's fault that there were not the same pleasurable and exciting things to do here in Kent as Minerva was used to doing in London.

And... what on earth was she supposed to wear?

MINERVA HAD WORRIED FAR TOO much about her appearance than was suitable for such a small country event, but in the end, she was pleased with her decision. Although she had spent entirely too much time choosing her dress and had had to wait even longer for clumsy Anna to close all of the buttons in the back, she was glad she would not have to hide behind all the other beauties as in London. She secretly wished that her dress was of a livelier colour, but she had to admit that the slightly creamy tone of the white dress accentuated her beautiful complexion. The light blue violets on the upper skirt matched her eyes, as did the colour of her spencer. She had thought long and hard about what kind of jewellery a young woman would wear to a horse market and had decided that the least valuable necklace and earrings with semi-precious stones would do. It was a set her parents had given her for her twelfth birthday. A bonnet in dark blue with only one artificial flower and a little back bag completed her look.

The only thing she was still worried about were her shoes. She had immediately known that her delicate silk slippers would be unsuitable for such an outing, so she had chosen the roughest pair she owned, which, while made of leather, were by no means sturdy enough for a walk in the countryside.

Sometimes, when the weather demanded it, her mother wore metal shoe protectors, which were equipped with a small stilted heel in the middle. Minerva had laughed those ugly devices off as absolutely atrocious, but now she knew that they would have served her very well for her day at the market. She wrinkled her nose when she realised that all the animals there would undoubtedly contribute to the state of the walkways – and not in small amounts either. Well, she would just have to watch where she put her feet, and if her petite little ankle boots were ruined afterwards, her aunt and uncle would have to order a new pair for her.

If Minerva was honest, riding in the open carriage to the Buckleys' acquaintances was the first highlight of her trip, and it lit up her – so far – tedious stay. The heat of the late morning was somewhat oppressive, but the soft breeze from driving made it all the more bearable. Her Aunt Catherine had to remind her, twice, to pull the brim of her bonnet down lower over her face, so that the sun wouldn't create unsightly freckles around her nose, but Minerva sneakily pushed it up again, twice, when her aunt was not looking. Uncle James, who was in an excellent mood today, winked at her and looked in the other direction when her hand pushed the brim of her hat back up again.

Minerva had to admit that she was actually growing fond of her relatives. Her aunt's small peculiarities, and the slightly strange combination of independence and agreeability that her uncle cultivated, were quaint and quirky, but she could live with that. They really made an effort not to make Minerva's life harder, despite her father's explicit, written instructions to continually remind Minerva of her duties as an obedient daughter. She could very well imagine her father's words and what he had written. She wondered whether he missed his daughter even a little bit.

"We are almost there," Aunt Catherine said, which brought Minerva back into the present. "Do you see the colourful tents over there?" She pointed discreetly with her gloved hand towards a spot ahead of them. A true lady would never point her finger towards anything that drew her interest, but the excitement that seemed to engulf her aunt was palpable. "The horse market takes place on a meadow just outside of the village," she explained. "We will leave our carriage at the

Inchmans' residence. From there we can walk to the horse market on foot." She glanced at Minerva's boots and nodded appreciatively. She recognised Minerva's obvious decision to wear a "suitable" pair of boots, even though they did not match the rest of her wardrobe, which was the first step in showing that she was ready to adapt herself to her changed circumstances.

Maybe, her aunt thought, Minerva might be becoming more amenable to other ideas as well – including marriage.

* * *

A LIGHTNING BOLT darted across the night sky and thunder rolled across the land. Was this an indication that fate would change her life forever?

AT FIRST GLANCE, the Inchmans were somewhat of a disappointment. Just as old as her aunt and uncle, they very much seemed the epitome of respectability. Mrs Inchman immediately regarded the thin fabric of Minerva's dress with an utterly disapproving glance, even though it had stood up to Aunt Catherine's eagle-eyed scrutiny. Well, if Mrs Inchman preferred to die of excessive heat in her very thick dress (which was entirely too heavy for such a summery day), then she should do just that. On the other hand, her disapproval could very well stem from the way Mr Inchman had looked at Minerva with obvious appreciation. She stayed close to her aunt's side, in case Mr Inchman overstepped the bearable limits of enthusiastic familiarity. Aunt Catherine gave her friend a serious look, which pleased Minerva's heart. Her aunt was a conventional woman and her facial expressions alone were the equivalent of a public rebuke. Even the reprimanded Mr Inchman seemed to understand that he had taken too much of a liberty, because he excused himself and turned towards the tavern, where he would most likely find more appreciation for his advances than from the ladies he had planned to accompany to the market.

Now it was up to her uncle to make sure that the ladies were well taken care of. He did this in style and invited them to partake of a light ale, which immediately went to Minerva's head, so that her aunt had to take it from her after just a few sips. Perhaps it had not been the ale that had gone to her head and made her giggle uncontrollably, but rather the sheer excitement that had overcome her as soon as they reached the market. Her uncle had assured her that, by the time they arrived, most of the business would have been taken care of and that most of the animals would be on their way to their new homes, but it was still a rather breathtaking experience. With his friendly yet firm personality, Uncle James led the ladies through the large crowd, which made Minerva feel safe amongst all the animals and people. The many odours of furry and feathered creatures, alcoholic beverages, sweet treats, and rubbish blended into an almost unbearable aroma, which Minerva was certain would cling to their clothes long after they left. Everywhere she looked, people were falling into each other's arms, laughing and calling out names whenever they recognised someone. Here, in this market, status did not seem to matter, or – at least – it did not matter as much. Minerva saw ordinary servants standing right next to well-situated ladies, all looking wistfully at the same goods and products. There was so much more to see here than just horses that she felt dizzy and asked her Aunt Catherine if she could be allowed to step away from the crowd for a moment.

Her relatives and Mrs Inchman, whose ruffled feathers had been soothed by her husband's departure, led her towards the outer edge of the market. "I am surprised that the crowd is troubling you so much," Mrs Inchman remarked. "Are you not used to much worse in London, Miss Honeyfield?" Her voice actually sounded quite worried, and Minerva smiled weakly. Apart from one colourful tent with lots of coloured ribbons, ropes and jingling ornaments near its entrance, there were no other market stands to be seen and it was beautifully quiet. Strangely enough, no one was to be seen in front of the tent, which offered different types of knick-knacks, although just the ornaments alone did not make it evident what was on sale there. Maybe it was a place to rest, where exhausted ladies like her could recuperate?

"... not be honouring us this year with his attendance either," Mrs Inchman was saying at the same moment that Minerva noticed something moving behind the stall's glittery curtain.

Her aunt fell silent for a moment, before she answered with a mere whisper, even though nobody, apart from the four of them, were within earshot. "Well, good... it's much better this way. No one knows whether he would be able to comport himself in an appropriate manner, amongst all of the young, innocent women.

The young things do not yet know that something dangerous can hide behind an attractive face." Minerva started to listen more closely, while still pretending that she did not feel quite well.

Her uncle had distanced himself and sat on a tree stump away from them, maltreating the grass beneath him by stamping it down with his elegant walking cane.

"He *is* extremely attractive," Mrs Inchman remarked with a slightly dreamy voice, before she cleared her throat and quickly added, "... but he is a deeply immoral person and the very fact that he doesn't even bother to stand up against all those rumours, speaks for itself."

Who were the two women talking about? Minerva opened her mouth to ask them, but at that moment, a woman stepped out from behind the pearl-beaded curtain. She did not look like anybody Minerva had ever seen before in her entire life. The first thing that struck her was the royal posture with which the woman stepped through the fluttering ribbons. She held herself straight, but she had a certain swing in her hips, and the way she walked had something seductive about it. The woman was not even wearing a bodice, and she was not afraid for that to be noticed! Her black hair fell untamed over her shoulders and her wide, red mouth with its lush lips smiled half threatening, half friendly.

"Which one of you ladies would like to look into her future?" the woman asked, and it seemed as if her question was particularly aimed at Minerva. It felt as if she was tempting Minerva to step into her mysterious world. "No lies, no excuses. Marie-Rose will tell you only the truth and nothing but the truth." The woman's heavy-looking golden earrings seemed to nod enticingly towards her, so Minerva took a step, wanting to follow that alluring smile.

"Minerva!" Her aunt's sharp voice snapped her out of her daze. "Get out of there immediately."

"But my Lady, please," Marie-Rose said soothingly and waved to Minerva to step into her tent. She quickly passed behind the strange-looking curtain with all its ribbons and pearls, and felt a feather tickling her neck.

"I swear on all the saints that nothing will harm this child." The woman's voice moved away, as she left Minerva alone in the tent to speak to Aunt Catherine. A short moment later, Minerva heard Uncle James's voice, muted and deep above all the high-pitched female murmuring.

Minerva sat down on one of the cushioned seats and looked at the table in front of her. A cheap and colourful cloth covered it, and nothing was laid upon it but a stack of cards. Her heart was pounding, and she lifted the first card from its deck – and immediately dropped it again. It showed a red-horned creature, naked to its hips and surrounded by other, equally undressed and seemingly dancing creatures of both sexes. Despite the repugnance she felt for the horrible image, Minerva lifted the card that had fallen face down onto the table, once more. Looking at it more closely, she could see that the card was not actually as horrible as she had first thought. Of course, the devil still seemed rather disconcerting, but he had a mischievous look, which reminded her a little bit of Uncle James, who was by no means an evil person. The other naked people, well... there was not really anything that made it particularly scandalous. The figures had been detailed so little – they could have just as well been wearing skin-coloured suits.

"I see that you have already chosen your first card." Marie-Rose sat down across from her and smiled at

Minerva mysteriously. Then she pushed the deck of cards closer to Minerva, who suddenly became very nervous. "Take two more cards, and I will tell you what your future holds, Miss."

"How am I supposed to pay you?" Minerva enquired and once again regretted that she did not have any money of her own. "I do not have anything I could give you."

"That is not entirely true," the Roma woman replied and nodded towards Minerva's earrings.

When Minerva gave her a startled look, she laughed softly. "It's all right. I was only making a joke. How about we say that you'll pay me handsomely when our paths cross again, and by then you'll have become a duchess or a marquise."

"Really? I will marry a duke or a marquis? You are able to tell from this one card?"

Marie-Rose laughed freely. "Oh no, that I can tell you purely out of common sense, Miss. You're young, very beautiful, and obviously you have been blessed with wealthy parents. It would be some kind of miracle if someone like you did *not* marry into the nobility. Even if he doesn't have a noble title, he will still be one of the rich men who can afford to maintain a duke's lifestyle." Minerva realised that she was being manipulated with this disarming combination of honesty and charm, and yet she was unable to prevent herself from becoming excited by the Roma woman's words.

"All right then," she said with a slightly challenging undertone. She took the deck of cards into her hand. and for a moment she wondered why her hands felt so warm. Marie-Rose's eyes rested upon her knowingly, whilst she pulled out two more cards and placed them onto the table without looking at them. "Now, apart from a duke, what else is waiting for me in my future?" she asked nonchalantly.

"We have the Devil, the Tower, and the Ace of Cups," the Roma woman said, and she pushed the cards on the table around until they lay directly next to each other. "First, you'll have to face tremendous seduction... from a man in whose shadow destruction awaits. However, since you're strong enough to withstand any sinful temptations, great happiness will be waiting for you in the end... and it will follow you until the end of your days. But you will need to decide very quickly, and maybe you'll have to choose someone, who at first doesn't comply with your romantic notions and expectations."

"Ah," Minerva said. "What else has my aunt given you to make me understand that I should better marry the next best candidate?" She got up. "You are a charlatan. I may be able to forgive my aunt, because I know that she only has my best interests at heart, but you – you have knowingly lied to me for gain."

Marie-Rose was still smiling, even though it looked a little strained. "Not everything was a lie," she said, but Minerva had already left and only heard those words faintly. It really seemed as if everyone was working against her.

In the end, she probably had no choice but to marry someone, just so that she finally may have her peace.

CHAPTER 2

The deep dark moor stretched out in front of her, as far as her eyes could see.

THREE WEEKS after her visit to the horse market, Minerva understood what her father had meant with his threats of teaching her about boredom. As of this moment, she had been in Scuffold for exactly twenty-four days and sixteen hours and was starting to feel at her wit's end. So far, she had not been able to come up with a suitable beginning for her novel, which meant that dealing with written adventures as a distraction from the daily monotony was out of the question.

Uncle James did not own a library that was worth a second look. All of his books were either dusty old manuals and reference books, or religious and moral tract, which would not even have interested her father, let alone herself. Her only escape was to write, either letters or in her diary. However, even her best friend Georgiana had her limits, and Minerva did not want to continuously repeat over and over again how incredibly bored she was. What was the point in keeping a diary when the most exciting thing in her rural life was the fact that Anna had broken a teacup this morning? No, that accident was not worth recording anywhere. If only she had experienced a real adventure at the horse market and not just the shameful attempt to make her a wife as soon as possible. She had a beautiful notebook that was just waiting to be filled with adventures. But other than the notebook, she had nothing – no books and no life worthy of being called that. She had nothing but her imagination. She could pretend to be indisposed, close her eyes and dream herself away into a different world – one where she was brave and strong, and where she would meet the one true love, who would not just marry her for her dowry.

She sat down. She had a lot of imagination and she

knew how to bring words to paper eloquently. What was she waiting for? She would start right now. If she did not like her beginning, she could always go back and change it later. She found ink and a quill in her Uncle James's study and ran up the stairs clinging to her valuable spoils, her heart pounding with anticipation.

Entry of September 10th:

Her hands were still trembling from the exciting encounter that had happened to her ten days after she had arrived in Blackmoore. Oh, what wonderful coincidence, or what divine providence would Lady Marianne de Lacey have to thank, for the tediousness of this place had been mitigated with the arrival of...

She paused. After a slight hesitation, Minerva crossed out the word tediousness and replaced it with monotony. She dipped the quill once more into the inkwell that she had stolen from her uncle's study, and she wondered what her future readers would like to hear more about. About a horse market and the Roma woman who pretended to tell someone's future – or about the unfortunate barmaid who had promptly fallen in love with the duke, after he had appeared in the tavern where she worked? In truth, said barmaid was not really a barmaid – she was the daughter of a duke, who had been kidnapped straight from her crib at the tender age of two years old, and who now lived with the travelling didicoys... Satisfied, Minerva smiled and continued her work, only stopping when her wrist started to hurt. Her unfavourable posture in which she was leaning over the small desk did not really help.

She got up, stretched her limbs in the most unladylike manner and looked outside. There she saw Sally, the barmaid from "Dog & Bones", the local tavern.

A thought shot through Minerva's mind. Her relatives had prohibited her from entering the drinking hole, but they had not forbidden her from talking to Sally. As quick as lightning, she grabbed her shawl and ran downstairs, coming to a sudden halt right before the front door. She could hear the muted voices of her Aunt Catherine and Uncle James from inside the salon, and Anna was nowhere to be seen or heard. Quickly and silently as a cat, Minerva snuck out of the house. She assuaged her guilty conscience by telling herself that she would honour her uncle and aunt with the first edition of her book, including an impressive inscription dedicated to them. After all, she wanted to write a novel that would captivate her readers from the first page – and what would be better at attracting people's attention than by writing a story that captured real life and turned it into suspenseful literature? However, that was also the tricky part. Minerva had not the slightest idea what a barmaid did all day, even if she was in truth of noble blood.

"Sally! Please wait for a moment!" She muted her last words once she noticed just how unladylike and unworthy of an upcoming author she was behaving. The young woman, who she guessed was just a little younger than she herself, stopped in her tracks.

"Yes... Miss? What can I do for you?"

Minerva was trying to think of the right words. Now that she had to formulate her intentions aloud, she did not know what to say.

"I..."

Impatiently, Sally put down the basket of eggs that she had been carrying across her arm. "Go on then. Tell me what's bothering you, Miss." Her hazelnut-brown eyes glinted mischievously. She had pretty and yet bold features, Minerva thought. Tiny little curls of her bright red hair peeked out from under her mutch, which had been embroidered with (now faded) violets, and in places it had been patched with a thorough hand. The sight struck Minerva strangely and she realised she was staring at Sally as the girl bent down and reached for the basket. "If you want to ask me to retrieve a letter for you... then I wouldn't say no." She winked at her. At first, Minerva did not really understand what Sally was referring to. When she finally understood, she blushed, half due to embarrassment and half out of pride. Sally honestly believed that she was worldly-wise enough to have a secret admirer with whom she corresponded behind her aunt's back!

Truth was that, despite her heritage of life in a world city like London, she was much more naïve than she wanted to admit.

"No, no," she denied anxiously. "I actually just wanted to ask you why you are working in the Dog & Bones, of all places... and not somewhere else? Why don't you work as a maid with a family, for example? I would like to accompany you for a while, if you do not mind."

The way to the tavern was not far; however, Minerva had forgotten to put on a bonnet and a shawl when she had run out of the house so hastily. She hoped that nobody would see her and report her scandalous appearance to Aunt Catherine. At least her skirts and the seam of her white muslin dress were clean. The question was how long her clothes would stay in this desirable state. She carefully stepped around the evidence that a horse had come down this road just recently, before she fell into a cautious stroll beside Sally. The barmaid looked at her with an unexplainable look and cleared her throat. "Well, Miss, I 'ad no other choice. Where else should I work?"

Minerva felt embarrassed for her inconsiderate question. Someone like Sally, who probably came from a large family and had to contribute in putting food on the table, did not have much choice in where she could work or not.

"Would you like to work somewhere else?"

Something flashed across Sally's eyes that could only be described as calculating. "Of course, I would." She put her basket down again and showed Minerva both of her hands. They were reddened and calloused, despite Sally's young age. Minerva quickly hid her own hands behind her back. "Unfortunately, in a small town like Scuffold, there aren't many jobs to be 'ad and 'onest work 'as not 'armed anyone, as my pa would say.

I would 'ave liked to 'ave worked as a chambermaid somewhere. You don't have to get your 'ands as dirty, not like when I 'ave to do the dishes." She paused for a moment and an almost dreamy look flashed across her pretty face. She shook her head, as if she wanted to shake off all the high-flying dreams once and for all, and she squinted slightly. "Then again, I'm starting to wonder why you want to know all this... and if that's something that your noble relatives shouldn't really know about... in that case, I'm thinking that a small token of gratitude would be appropriate, don't you think, Miss? I do work so very 'ard and I 'ave already answered more than one little question."

Minerva blushed for a second time in Sally's presence. "I do not have anything on me that I could give you," she said and frantically calculated how much money the barmaid could possibly be expecting. Not much – that she was sure of. Unfortunately, her parents did not have any reason to give Minerva any money. Everything she needed, she got from the Buckleys. Was there anything else she could give her instead?

Sally shrugged her shoulders. She seemed to have practised this movement rather well, since none of the fragile goods inside her basket moved. However, Minerva's disappointed face did not leave her untouched. "I shall tell you one more thing, because it's you. One last question, but then it's enough. You ask, I'll answer. After all, I still 'ave got work to do." Her eyes seemed to dance, and it was rather obvious what she was thinking, which was that certain rich people could afford curiosity, unlike a hard-working barmaid.

Minerva thought about what she wanted to know the most. "What is the strangest thing that has ever happened to you at work?"

For a short moment, Sally's eyes lit up, before they went dark. "You mean, apart from the fact that Sid Green constantly wants me to... oh well, it doesn't matter." She frowned. "All right. Once, there was a gentleman who was searching for butterflies. Or some bugs – I don't remember exactly."

Minerva listened intently, because she did not want to miss any details.

"On the third day, 'e didn't return for dinner." Sally lowered her voice to an ominous whisper. "We wanted to send Davy out to look for him, but shortly after midnight..." Minerva leaned closer to her, so as not to miss one word. "... shortly after midnight 'e finally returned. 'is 'air 'ad turned white and 'e was very pale, as if no more blood was running through 'is veins. 'e 'ad seen a ghost."

After that, she turned away from Minerva and disappeared with swinging hips inside the tavern. What kind of a story was this? It did not even have a proper ending! What kind of ghost had the man encountered and what had happened to him?

Minerva sighed and started to walk back home. She needed to find a way to extract more information from Sally, so that she could learn how this ghost story ended – either that or she needed to focus on a different subject. Which, considering the fact that she wanted to write a novel that would be taken seriously, was perhaps the better idea.

Determined, she marched back home. Surely Aunt Catherine knew some anecdotes she could tell her. Or Uncle James! He had been a lawyer, after all, and perhaps she could persuade him to tell her about a dramatic case from his work. It was not surprising that usually thrilling novels were extremely successful with the public. Had it not been a *woman* in Mrs Radcliffe's book, "The Mysteries of Udolpho", that had caused a sensation in London's parlours? Satisfied and smiling,

Minerva snuck back into the Buckleys' house. Perhaps her fate was not to return home from Kent with a husband, but with a finished novel.

It was such a shame that a manuscript wouldn't impress her parents half as much as a husband would.

CHAPTER 3

His betrayal was all the more gruesome, since she herself had revealed her secret to him, purely through her own negligence.

MINERVA HAD WRITTEN EAGERLY over the following two weeks and felt that her story was making good progress. She wrote every day, apart from Sundays, whenever she could escape to the silence and peace in her room. It was her ink-tainted fingers that gave Minerva's secret away.

"Where did you get this absurd idea from?" Her aunt sounded outraged, downright shocked. "A young woman is supposed to spend her time with appropriate things such as sewing, music, and learning how to run a household, not with... something like *this*. This is absolutely scandalous! Do your parents know about it? Of course not," Catherine answered her own question. "I cannot imagine that my brother would allow such a thing. By contrast, your mother has always been too much of a dreamer. You must have got that from her. I have always said that too much education isn't good for the female gender."

This went on for an entire hour. At some point, they heard Uncle James clear his throat from the corner where he was sitting. "I think that Minerva could have chosen many other, much worse, occupations, than spending her time writing, Catherine." As they were in the intimate setting of the home, her uncle used the informal way of addressing his wife. "I seem to remember a time when you yourself had a particular liking for the works of Mr Walpole, my dear."

Minerva thought that she had heard that wrong. Her aunt had read gothic novels? And more importantly, was her uncle actually taking her side?

"Just let her write, if that is something she likes to do. This will not ruin her for the marriage market any more than she is already." Minerva was not sure if she liked that sentence, but her Uncle James mellowed the harshness of his words by winking at her. "At least, now I know where my inkwell went."

"You cannot be serious," Aunt Catherine finally found her voice. "What are we supposed to tell her parents if they find out? The whole world will point their fingers at Minerva. She is dishonouring the family name."

"Enough," Uncle James exclaimed, as he rose from his chair. "I say that the child can keep her rather harmless enjoyment. As long as you do not tell anyone about it, nobody will know." His bushy eyebrows rose when he looked at his niece. "Or have you already told someone about his?"

"No, Uncle," she replied honestly and tried to infuse her voice with as much gratitude as she could. Aunt Catherine looked at her angrily and announced that she needed to excuse herself with a headache. Minerva also wanted to return to her room, but her uncle called her back once more.

"If you ever need any advice or help regarding your writing abilities, please feel free to ask me."

"Have you written something yourself, Uncle? Maybe

you have already published something?" Her heart beat loudly with excitement. She had found an ally, and in a place she would never have imagined.

"We will talk about this another time," he evaded her questions. "I do want to remind you that my agreeing with you in this particular matter does not mean that you can ignore any of the other rules in this household. If I ever see you sneak out of the house without a suitable companion, it will have serious consequences for you, young lady."

So... did he know that she sporadically left the house on her own to speak with Sally?

"I promise, Uncle. Thank you," she quickly added and ran up the stairs to her room.

Her hands were trembling, and she managed to ruin one valuable white page with two ugly ink blots, before she regained her composure.

Although in the light of the setting sun his shadow towered over her like some sinister fortress, Marianne de Lacey mustered up all her courage and...

Two hours later, Minerva sank back into the soft cushions of the chaise longue with a satisfied sigh and read back what she had written. Not only did her wrist hurt, but all of her limbs had been overcome by unforeseen stiffness, which not even unladylike stretching could ease. Most likely, Aunt Catherine would have reprimanded her, but her aunt and uncle had left the house for the afternoon. They had gone to pay a visit to an acquaintance, whose name Minerva had already forgotten.

Her aunt's sour face and the fact that they had not invited Minerva to join them could only mean... something bad. Her head felt empty and sluggish from all the thinking she had done.

And yet, something was still missing from her work. Something that gave her words a touch of truthfulness. Something that sounded real instead of made up. Minerva wanted to write a book that would captivate her readers with her incredibly realistic account of events from the very first page all the way to the last, and for that she needed to get out of this... prison.

For a second, she contemplated going to find Sally, but so far, she had not been able to think of anything she could give the young woman in exchange for her life story. Minerva did not want to beg her to help her, and she wanted even less to take up too much of her time, which the young woman needed for her work. She would have to find inspiration elsewhere. Surely the beautiful nature surrounding her would be a wonderful location for some of the revelations in her story. Full of new-found vigour, she jumped up, pulled on her leather boots, which had not been ruined at the horse market after all, and looked outside.

It was early afternoon. The sun was shining onto Scuffold from a blue sky, and suddenly she knew what she wanted to do. She quickly grabbed her favourite shawl that was knitted from very soft wool, put on the first hat she could find (which actually harmonised perfectly with the blue shawl) and stepped out onto the main road. She knew every single house in Scuffold, with its almost two hundred residents and twenty-three houses (she had actually spent one long afternoon counting them all), and she felt she knew it down to the very last rock. Now, Minerva wanted to venture a little further afield. She soothed her uncle's warning voice ringing in her ears by the assurance that she would be back home long before her relatives returned from their visit.

The fields around the village had already been harvested. Minerva enjoyed the soft breeze and the vista of lush green that greeted her from the meadows along the way. Somewhere in the distance, she could hear the happy sounding gurgling of a small river as it found its way across the landscape. Birds were singing, and even a butterfly came to dance right next to her for a while. Life in the countryside was simply wonderful! If her father knew that she had not once looked at Fordyce's *Sermon to Young Women,* or how much she actually appreciated the peace and quiet out in the country, he probably would have immediately ordered her back to London. *Pah!* she thought and maybe she had even said it out loud. *Who needs balls, rides in carriages, and Hyde Park, when there are such beautiful forests in Scuffold?* The last thought was brought to mind when the small road that had initially taken her alongside open fields and meadows, now became a narrow pathway through the forest.

The shady coolness embraced her and sent a shiver down her spine. Was there a ghost hiding behind those majestic old trees that was watching her from cold, lifeless eyes? She laughed aloud at herself, because she was already beginning to think like Marianne de Lacey and winced at the loud sound of her laugh echoing back from the trees. *Nonsense,* she chided herself and followed the path deeper into the woods. There were no ghosts here. If at all true, ghosts haunted places like cemeteries, or a desolate ruin – much like the one ahead of her, which had just come into her view. Had Sally not spoken of a ghost in the woods?

Her curiosity was fighting a battle against her fear of the unknown. Her curiosity won and so, despite her racing heart, Minerva moved closer. A pavilion... that was what it was... but right in the middle of a forest? It stood in a clearing and must have been (once, a very long time ago) a wonderful place for contemplation. The brick that the pavilion had been built with was porous in places. Moss covered the bases of most of the pillars, and vines had woven their way into the nooks and crannies of the once majestic building. Its proportions were harmonious and balanced, and it was such an unexpected find, that Minerva thought she had travelled into a different time. Or had she gone through an invisible door and entered the world of fairies? The pavilion appeared like a mystical place, where everything was possible – if she was only brave enough to enter it.

Was she brave enough for this adventure? All of a sudden, Minerva realised how quiet it was around her.

Even the birds had stopped singing. No cracking branches, no rustling leaves. What could she be scared of out here, in nature? There was nobody here who would harm her.

Just a short while ago, had not *she* longed for a real adventure?

"This is not an adventure," she murmured reassuringly, "... because where there is no danger, there is no risk. And where there is no risk, there is nothing to gain." That's something her father always said when he bored his wife and daughter with his businesses. The thought of her overly cautious father felt comforting. Her anxiety vanished and with it her imagination of a ghost that was stalking her in the shadows. Minerva stepped closer until she could peek over the low balustrade.

The wind had blown fallen leaves through the wide, open arches. The place smelled musty, but not un-pleasantly so – just enough to make it feel somewhat cosy, like on a cool autumn day in Hyde Park. A low stone bench was built inside, and if she were to bring a blanket, she could very well sit here and dream. Her imagination ignited at the thought of her sitting here in this enchanted place, whilst writing her novel. Yes, this was the perfect place to phrase one spooky event after another. If she was only allowed to sit here and ponder the right words that so often escaped her in the dullness of her room!

Who had built this pavilion and then forgotten about it?

Minerva decided to unobtrusively sound out her Aunt Catherine at the next available opportunity.

THICK FOG SURROUNDED *the castle like a burial shroud spun from the finest silk and just as cold as the breath of a ghost.*

"PLEASE TELL me that you did not leave the safety of the village, Minerva?" Aunt Catherine eyed her niece suspiciously. Whilst she was still searching for the right answer that was not a direct lie, her aunt continued. "I warn you explicitly, do you hear me? I *ex-pli-cit-ly* forbid you to enter the duke's property. He is unpredictable. On top of that, the pavilion is haunted."

A ghost! So, her feeling had been right about that after

all, and it had not just been a product of her exuberant imagination that had been fired up by Sally's short story about the guest in her tavern.

"I cannot believe that," Minerva said, knowing full well that this soft objection would entice her aunt to keep talking, and if Minerva had any luck, it would also distract her from her earlier question.

"Oh yes, it is true. I have heard it from Mrs Dalrymple, and she heard it from her cook."

"Oh, really? And in what manner does this alleged ghost manifest itself?"

"Apparently you hear a woman cry," Aunt Catherine said, and then looked vacantly at her hands which were resting in her lap. "Especially around midnight – the place is quite scary. The cousin of the cook, a frivolous young thing, was there to... she was there for a walk." Minerva wondered what business a young girl had in the forest at midnight, no less. It could only have been an adventurous, romantic encounter, she was certain. In her mind, she could already imagine where she would send Marianne de Lacey next:

The dark and gloomy night sky was lit up by a full and round moon. Branches brushed brutally against her face, as Marianne tried to escape through the woods. Behind her sounded the terrifying howling of wolves, the duke's emissaries...

"Well, regardless. She swears that she saw the shape of a woman, who was tearing her hair out in misery, and was crying and calling out for her love." Did Aunt Catherine's hands tremble?

"You do not need to worry, Aunt. I will not be as irresponsible as the cook's cousin." Minerva was not planning on leaving the house in the middle of the night to go and look for a ghost. She was a sophisticated young woman and she knew that ghost stories had one purpose: to scare women and children and to discourage them from doing anything stupid. However, she could go there during the day, when her relatives left for another visit, and immerse herself in the mystical atmosphere. If she could not question Sally without having to pay her, then this was the only other possibility for inspiration.

"Well, regardless," the older woman sighed and eyed Minerva suspiciously. "You might be right. The ghost is the least worrisome and poses the least danger. It is the *duke* who you should never meet, under no circumstances."

"Why?" Curiosity was written all over Minerva's face, which resulted in a very rigid and straight hard line forming in her aunt's otherwise rather soft and round face.

"He is a corrupt man," she said curtly. "They say that he murdered his own wife, because she... had gone astray." Minerva tried to hide the interested gleam in her eyes by staring earnestly at the neglected embroidery in her lap.

That was probably the man Aunt Catherine and Mrs Inchman had spoken about at the horse market. With that, the memory of the well-intentioned, but terribly hurtful deception of her aunt came to mind. Minerva decided to question her Aunt Catherine a little more – even if it made her nerves jittery. "So, it is *her* ghost? The dead woman, I mean?"

"Child, if such horror stories delight you so very much, at least do me the favour and speak in full sentences."

"I apologise, Aunt. So, is it the spirit of the dead woman that haunts the pavilion?"

She had sounded flippant and now her aunt looked at her with a disapproving look on her face. "You will most certainly not find that out. No, Minerva. What I am trying to tell you is that you cannot ever set one foot on the land of the Duke of Scuffold. It could be dangerous. His Grace Robert Beaufort might be handsome, but he is unscrupulous and brutal. His young brother is Lord Thomas Beaufort – you might have heard of him. He married an actress – it is just inconceivable!" She narrowed her eyes to slits and the disapproving tone in her voice made it clear, beyond any doubt, that she did not agree with any of it, as she continued. "Since the night the duchess passed away, Lord Beaufort has never been seen again. It is rumoured that even he had failed to reason with his brother."

This story was getting better and better! It was such a shame that Minerva did not have her notebook with her.

"Up there in the manor, the duke has not one female servant – at least, that is what they say. I cannot really imagine how he could manage without any female help. He must be entirely immoral by now. Not that I would wish this fate on any maid or wench, but one would assume that a man as wealthy as he is, would marry a second time. But no, he lives up there alone and receives no visitors. It truly is just incredible! Not even the dignitaries of the village or the surrounding areas visit him." She shook her head in utter bewilderment. "Of course, everyone wonders what happened back then, but Doctor Springfield has never said one word about it and will probably take the truth to his grave."

Every time she paused, it was expressive enough that Minerva was fired with anticipation every time. "But... Do the authorities not get involved when someone dies under suspicious circumstances?"

Her aunt nodded in agreement. "That is the strangest thing. The duke either covered up his own atrocity, or his wife committed the biggest sin and took her own life. Although they gave her a proper burial, I am still wondering if all of it was done in the right way. After all, his family belongs to one of the oldest families in the country, and apparently, they can trace their ancestry all the way back to John Lackland – which is absolutely plausible, since the Plantagenets have always been a thoroughly corrupt bunch, if you ask me."

"And nobody has seen him since then? Maybe on the same night when his wife died, he had a terrible accident and his face was so badly distorted that he will not show it to anyone, apart from his most loyal servants, of course. Or to his doctor," she added, pondering how she would incorporate every single detail of this extraordinary story into her novel. She would surely find a way. Even though the duke in her book was not actually disfigured, that shouldn't be a problem. Lady Marianne could set something on fire – unintentionally, of course – and he would escape those flames, only to show the world his true face. He was a monster; everyone would know immediately when they looked at him. Ha! That was a worthy ending to her novel, Minerva thought. His wife... how could Minerva include her into her story? She held her breath when she had a wonderful idea. The duke wanted to force Lady Marianne to marry him in order to get hold of her wealth, which she had somehow got back in the meantime. However, the duke was still married to his first wife, who had gone insane and who he had to hide upstairs in the attic!

"Are you even listening, child?" Aunt Catherine had grabbed her by the hand and was staring at her with a chiding look. "This man is by no means a worthy object for the romantic fantasies and hopes of a young lady. Even an imagination such as yours will not change the facts. He is through and through corrupt, immoral, and the rudest person in the whole county. On top of that, it is unsafe to get anywhere near him."

"Why is that, Aunt? His wife's death occurred a few years ago now, did it not?"

"That is true, but the strange happenings people talk about seem to have increased since he has returned. One of his servants died mysteriously during a hunting excursion... and he himself has called upon Dr Spring-field twice already, since he has been back, to get treatment. I do not even want to know what diseases he has caught during his travels across Europe. Apparently, he is also a friend of Lord Byron and stayed with him and his unspeakable entourage at his residence by the Lake Geneva for some time. I also do not want to know what gruesome things they were thinking about *there*, just to amuse themselves."

Then, as if she suddenly realised who she was en-trusting all these indiscretions with, her aunt's eyes became alert. "Should you ever be seen with him, or even just talk to him, I can promise you this. No man of honour and morals would ever consider taking you to be his wife, regardless of how big your dowry might be. Stay away from the duke and Beaufort, then you will not have any difficulty finding a decent husband – even at your age."

Minerva opened her mouth to disagree resentfully, but

she decided against it. Her aunt had finished talking, and there was nothing she could do to coax her into continuing. Dutifully, she turned back towards her embroidery, but her Aunt Catherine took it from her hands and looked at it with eagle eyes.

"I fear that you will never be a good wife," she determined. "Your rose buds look withered and the violets up here do not help with the overall appearance." She handed her the tiny needlework scissors. "You will have to unravel all of it and start again. However, this will guide your mind towards more suitable thoughts, which will be much better for you than those absurd ghost stories, my dear. Just remember always – you have a reputation to uphold." The switch from her embroidery back to the Duke of Scuffold was a daring one, but Minerva understood what her aunt was trying to tell her. For someone such as her, a prospective author, it was of even more importance to live an untainted life without any scandal. However, her breath quickened – her secret activity offered her an escape.

For if she was a woman of questionable morals already, well then – what harm would yet another small escapade do?

CHAPTER 4

*L*ady Marianne de Lacey looked at the duke's face and immediately shuddered.

AFTER A WHILE, which had seemed endlessly long to the impatient Minerva, her aunt and uncle left home to visit some other acquaintances. She had had to wait a full eight days for that long-awaited opportunity to explore her discovery in the forest. This time, they invited Minerva to join them, but she turned them down, pretending to have a headache, and she even skipped lunch to emphasise her situation. The time had come.

She waited for a while until a hasty return could be ruled out, in case her aunt had forgotten something, and sneaked out of the house. Across her arm she carried a basket, similar to the one Sally had brought along at their first encounter.

Hidden underneath a cloth, she had brought her notebook, the carefully closed inkwell, and her favourite quill – the one that lay in her hand ever so perfectly. The cloth not only hid the contents of her basket, but it would later also serve to cover the dirty seat inside the pavilion. Minerva was prepared for everything.

If someone were to ask her what she was up to, she had already thought of an excellent excuse. She was picking mushrooms.

Only when she was already halfway out of the village, she thought of something. Was there not some kind of season for mushrooms? She thought that she remembered her aunt and Anna had said something like that when they were planning a dinner. Regardless, Minerva walked onwards with her head held high, relieved that all residents greeted her, but nobody asked about the basket or her destination.

As soon as she reached the forest, she knew that she

had made the right decision to allow herself some freedom and this little pleasure behind her relatives' backs. She was no longer just a child who needed constant supervision, even if the rest of the world seemed to think that she still did. Her father had sent her away, without asking about her wishes or listening to her reasons for why she had denied Mr Meade's proposal. She was ready to get married – however, she did not want to marry somebody who was after her significant dowry or taken by her pleasant appearance. Was it really too much to ask that she should retain some hope for happiness and true love?

She laughed quietly when a rabbit hopped in front of her across the path, before disappearing beneath the bushes. It was so cute, the way it had looked at her with its big round eyes, and it seemed to have nodded towards her, as if it were agreeing with her less than prudent behaviour. Even this creature had more freedom than her! Was it really that inconceivable for a woman to do something entirely by herself? Minerva had heard that Mary Godwin, who was surrounded by scandal, had not only fought for an educational system for young girls, but she also demanded equality for women. Minerva shook her head. She did not even want to sit in the parliament and vote on political decisions, nor, God forbid, take a lover, as some women of the Beau Monde allegedly did. No, all she wanted was a husband who would love her for who she was, and who would grant her the freedom to be herself.

Without realising it, she had quickened her steps and stepped out rather vigorously. She was hot, and when Minerva held her hand up to her cheeks, she felt the heat radiate from her skin. She assumed that her hair was now in complete disorder as well. The curls she had styled so carefully this morning, and all without Anna's help, stuck to her forehead. The hem of her light-coloured muslin dress was dirty, just like her shoes and probably her underskirts. She hoped that she would make it back to the house before her aunt returned, and convince Anna to clean her clothes, at least provisionally.

With a touch of defiance, Minerva thought that now that she might have given her secret away, she should just do what she had come here to do – continue writing on her story.

She sighed with relief when she stepped into the abandoned building. The pale English sunlight shone through the tree cover, providing just enough light for her to be able to see her words. She looked around to find the perfect spot to sit down where she could safely set down the inkwell, but that proved to be difficult. Well, then the narrow ledge of the balustrade would have to serve as her inkstand. It was a little inconvenient that she had to turn around every time she needed to dip the quill into the ink, but there was nothing she could do about that, now.

She frowned and reread the last paragraph she had written. Marianne de Lacey had been able to escape the sinister duke at the very last minute, thanks to her ability for making witty conversation. Only because of her skilled tongue, had she managed to distract the brutal villain long enough to be able to sneak out of his castle. She had fled through the surrounding woods, had steered the trained wolves in the wrong direction, and now she stood at the edge of a cliff. Behind her, she heard the thundering hoofs of the duke's stallion as he rode after her, and below her she saw the steep rocks and the roaring sea.

How was Marianne supposed to get out of this situation? She should have thought of some alternative for her heroine. Now, she sat here in the Duke of Scuffold's forest, chewing on her quill, and she had no idea how to continue her story. For a moment, she considered having Marianne jump courageously into the rushing sea, but could Marianne even swim? She thought about Lord Byron, who was supposedly one of the bravest and best swimmers in all of Europe – had he not swum across the Turkish Hellespont and almost died when he did that? Also, why shouldn't she create a woman who was just as physically capable as a man? Jumping off a cliff was a daring move, but the biggest obstacle would not be her heroine's lack of courage. It was Lady Marianne's clothing that troubled Minerva. How quickly would a dress and coat soak up all the water and then undoubtedly drag the lady all the way down to the bottom of the deep sea? Or maybe she could let Marianne flee in just a night-gown? No, that was equally impossible.

Minerva sighed. Marianne de Lacey had no other choice. She had to surrender herself into the duke's hands and hope for his mercy, or to perish. She wouldn't be able to distract him a second time, since he was not only an attractive and evil man, but he also possessed an almost devilish intelligence. Minerva wondered what he would do to Marianne as soon as he had her back in his claws. Did his castle have a dungeon, where he would chain her to a wall and gloat every day anew over her sheer helplessness? Marianne would no longer be able to escape on her own, so she needed help. But unfortunately, all of the duke's servants had sworn their loyalty to him until their death.

Minerva looked up as she heard a soft cracking sound.

Was someone watching her? No, she was alone. Something rustled behind her, but no matter how fast she turned around, there was nobody there. She assumed that it had been an animal – maybe just another curious rabbit. Or… could it have been the ghost?

She shuddered and instantly chided herself. "Ghosts do not exist," she said loudly, immediately wishing that she had not done that. In the seclusion of the forest, her voice sounded strange and anxious. Her heart was beating so loudly that she was unable to hear anything other than its wild thudding. Her throat felt parched and tight. For a moment, she considered staying in spite of her discomfort, but in that second, a rustling sounded immediately behind her, much louder and closer than before. She startled and jumped up from her seat.

Hastily, she scrambled to gather her scattered belongings together, threw the blanket into the basket and wrapped her shawl around her shoulders. Maybe it had not been such a good idea after all, to come here by herself. Nobody knew where she was, and if something was to happen to her... she carefully placed one foot in front of the other, avoiding the slippery areas on the ground, which were covered with fallen leaves.

She had almost managed to leave the pavilion behind, when her gaze fell on something that did not belong here. Feet – male feet, clothed in heavy leather boots, which ended at the knees and turned into legs that were clothed in breeches... Minerva jumped backwards and released a most unladylike squeal, before she fell, landing on her back like a helpless beetle.

"What are you doing on my land?"

The voice sounded dark and coarse, as if it belonged to someone who wasn't used to speaking anymore.

Minerva looked up and stared into a face that was sinister, masculine, and beautiful, all at the same time. Tan-coloured hair, which was slightly too long for the current fashion, formed a bright halo surrounding his face. Eyes that changed from gold to hazelnut-brown, stared at her from underneath angrily frowning eyebrows. His mouth was wide... however, she could not see his lips, since they were pressed together into a thin, hard line. He leaned down nearer to her, and Minerva could do nothing else other than make herself stiff and small, while praying that he wouldn't harm her. She opened her mouth to reprimand him, but she only managed to emit a weak croaking.

"Can't you talk, or are you refusing to?" He pulled up one of his perfectly shaped eyebrows, whilst he looked at her with utter contempt.

This was the first time she noticed that he was wearing exquisite clothes. They had a practical cut, but they were made from the finest material.

So, this was the Duke of Scuffold, the man Aunt Catherine had so strongly warned her about! Why had Minerva thrown all caution to the wind and ignored her aunt's warnings? Now it was too late. She would consider herself lucky if she – similar to Marianne – did not end up in his dungeon.

"Come, let me help you up," he stretched out his hand impatiently, and when Minerva didn't react, he simply grabbed her hands. He pulled her back up onto her feet, and the unexpected momentum not only catapulted her upright but also pulled her much closer to him than what would be considered decent. For a second, her head leant against his chest. Marianne – no, Minerva, she was not her own novel's heroine! – thought that she could hear his heart beating, strongly and steadily. It was a masculine sound, just like his scent, which was clean and fresh, and yet somehow... manly. She lifted her head and looked up into his surprised eyes. She had never seen anyone whose hair and eye colour were so alike. It was fascinating and enchanting to behold. He was by no means disfigured, as she had imagined, but instead he had an... attractive face. She swallowed, embarrassed for her inappropriate thoughts.

"I will ask you one more time. What are you doing here? Are you even aware that you could have easily injured yourself inside this crumbling old building?"

Hastily, she stepped further away from him. To win some time and hide the trembling of her hands, Minerva started to knock the dirt off her dress. "I was looking for a place where I would be able to... think in peace," she answered, with as much dignity as she could muster. "I am sincerely sorry that I ended up on your land, but I did not think that you would care about it. You are the Duke of Scuffold, are you not?"

"Yes. I am. At your service, Miss." He quickly bowed in

front of her, which seemed more ironic than she would have liked. "And you are?"

"Miss Minerva Honeyfield. I am living in Scuffold with my aunt and uncle – Mr and Mrs Buckley." Why was her heart beating so quickly?

"You are the niece of the lawyer – the one who was sent away into the country by her parents," he determined. "What was it you did that was so terrible that your own parents sent you away? A secret dalliance with a young boy?"

That was unacceptably cheeky, and she did not acknowledge his impertinence with a direct answer. "Sir, please accept my sincerest apologies for having crossed your boundary. I would like to go now." She bent down and began to pack her scattered things into the basket. The inkwell was still intact, and her notebook only had a few stains on the outside but was otherwise fine. God only knew what she herself looked like in this very moment, but Minerva would worry about that later. Right now, she had to concentrate on getting out of there.

"If you would be so kind as to let me pass," she asked,

hoping that he would at least have the decency to step out of her way.

He did not. Instead, he grabbed her basket and looked at its contents.

"How dare you!" Her protest sounded less appalled than she had intended it to. "Not only are you impolite, but your behaviour is downright rude. Please let me go."

"Tell me the truth about why you came here, and I will let you go," he replied and let his fingers glide across the binding of her notebook. This was a surprisingly gentle gesture, almost as if he were stroking an animal.

When he lifted his gaze, Minerva noticed that his eyes had changed too. Instead of their earlier austerity and coldness, they now seemed almost warm.

"I write," she admitted with a quiet voice, and immediately regretted her words. During those last few minutes, she had broken every promise she had ever made, although involuntarily, to her Aunt Catherine. Here she stood, with the notorious Duke of Scuffold, and on top of that, she had admitted that she was writing a novel!

"Why? Do you want to become famous? Or do you miss London's conversation and write purely out of boredom?"

"Neither one of your suggestions is true. I write because it is a need." Getting braver by the minute, she pushed out her chin, a gesture he acknowledged with a slight twitch in the corners of his mouth.

"And for that you need to come to this forsaken place?" The irony had almost completely disappeared from his voice. He sounded curious and maybe even a little nostalgic. This was very strange indeed, but Minerva was determined to use his softness to her advantage.

"Yes, it is beautiful here. I love the clearing in the trees and the pavilion, even though it is in such disrepair and so very lonely."

"Well, well, look at what we have here, a hopeless romantic." He frowned. "What do your relatives think about the fact that you are not only an eager writer, but also that you are walking around in the grounds of a stranger, without company?"

"They *do* know where I am," she lied and hoped that he wouldn't notice the redness rising into her cheeks. "If I do not return shortly, they will come to look for me." She hoped that this was clear enough, even if she didn't say aloud what she really wanted to say.

"I will make sure that you arrive home safely," he said. "Would you allow me?" He stretched out his hand towards the basket, but Minerva hastily pulled it away and out of his reach. Everything was allowed to happen, just not that! If anyone were to see her together with the duke and told her aunt, then it would all be over! Her aunt would not only prohibit her from leaving the house for good, but she would also take away her writing!

"No," she said quickly. "Thank you, but that will not be necessary. I shall find my own way back." Since he did not budge, she pushed herself past him, trying to keep as much distance as she possibly could.

"I think it *is* necessary," he insisted. His eyes gleamed mockingly. "After all, I need to make sure that you do not get lost in these woods. Or, that you are frightened... by a *ghost.*"

The heat in her cheeks deepened. How long had he been there, before she saw him? Had he listened and heard her talking to herself?

"Please," she said one more time, and this time she

didn't try to hide her desperation. "If you accompany me back home, my aunt will most certainly hear of it, and I will never be allowed to come back here again." She bit her lip and suppressed a moan of frustration. Now she had given everything away! "I mean, of course, that I do not intend to set foot on your land again. I promise. But my aunt will lock me up, if she hears about this."

"Well, that would be catastrophic," he agreed with her in earnest.

For a second, Minerva was convinced that she had won. Just like Marianne de Lacey, she had managed to distract the unscrupulous duke with her wit and her words, and had manoeuvred herself out of an impossible situation! But her feeling of triumph died quickly when she saw his smile. His eyes gleamed provocatively. Before he said anything, Minerva already knew that she wouldn't be able to escape as easily as she had hoped.

The duke took her hand and leaned over it, as if he wanted to kiss her fingertips. A tiny ball of fire appeared inside Minerva's chest as she felt his warm breath caressing her skin. "I want to propose a deal," he said thoughtfully. Minerva felt ice-cold. What would a man like him demand from a woman, whom he had completely in his hands?

"You will return here, in one week, at the same time, and you will allow me to read your work. In turn, I will not tell your relatives about your secret."

Minerva made a noise that was a cross between a complaint and surprise. "I will not be able to do that," she objected. "I can only ever come here when my aunt and uncle are away visiting their friends. I do not think that they will leave the house again, so soon."

In fact, it was actually *highly* unlikely that her Uncle James would leave the comforts of his study any time soon. For him, a certain amount of time had to pass between excursions, so that he was able to recuperate from the strain of the last visit. Knowing him, one week would hardly be enough to prepare for the challenges of talking to other people, which he considered mere gibberish. The duke tilted his head sideways. In his eyes, she saw a dare which scared Minerva, and at the same time she felt a growing need to laugh hysterically.

"You can leave that to me, Miss Honeyfield." He almost purred with satisfaction and let go of her hand, which he had held indecently long in his own. "I will await you here in exactly one week."

Minerva watched as his tall figure disappeared into the woods – carefree and with a small melody on his lips – without looking back at her one more time.

She was caught in a trap.

CHAPTER 5

It was of such infamy, it had no equal.

WITH DEEPLY REDDENED CHEEKS, a hem crusted in dried mud, and in a state of mind that bordered on panic, Minerva returned to her relatives' house. At least Aunt Catherine and Uncle James had not yet arrived back from their visit. As quietly as possible, she snuck into the home and released a sigh of relief when she overheard Anna talking to the cook in the back of the house. It sounded as if the two women were involved in a heated debate, but Minerva did not take the time to listen in. She hurried up the stairs, climbed clumsily out of her dirty dress, and hid it quickly inside the travel trunk. In her haste and awkwardness, Minerva had not only stained the light-coloured muslin even more, but she had forgotten to take off her mud-covered boots first, which resulted in a deep tear in the fine fabric. How should she dispose of it? She was almost certain that Aunt Catherine would notice if she burned the unsalvageable dress. As she slipped into her bright green muslin, thoughts were racing through her mind. No, although Lady Marianne would have burned the dress – it would make a wonderfully dramatic scene – how could she have succeeded in the endeavour, without the smell of burning betraying her?

She would throw the dress away at the next available opportunity. Or, she could ask Anna to wash it for her, secretly.

She would have to think of some excuse for why she had changed her clothing. That was not the most pressing problem. No, that honour went to the Duke of Scuffold, whose threat gave her a headache. What would he do if she decided to ignore his demands? So far, her uncle and aunt had been rather lenient with her, when it came to reprimands. Much more lenient than she deserved, given her continuous disobedience, she thought, slightly embarrassed at her behaviour. She strained to reach the buttons at the back of her dress, closed her eyes and took a deep breath. What kind of human being had decided that women should wear corsets? This uncomfortable thing made any of her movements simply impossible! Once she was married, she would never wear one of these fashion-items again, she promised herself silently. After all, her waistline was slender, even without the restricting concoction with its stiffening bones. Angry at herself, at the duke, at her parents, and even at Mr Meade, who had started this whole chain of events in the first place – she threw her stockings into one corner of her room, before she fell onto her bed exhausted.

No, she would not cry right now.

Nor would she admit to her relatives what she had done this day.

There had to be a way to escape the duke's clutches without her relatives finding out. If only she had an ally, someone she could talk to and confide in! But here in this God-forsaken village, she did not even have her own maid. What was her family thinking?

How was she supposed to find a suitable husband when she was forced to run around like a rantipole?

Minerva held her breath as a thought started to form inside her head. Maybe there was a way she could solve at least one of her difficulties. She got up from the bed and studied her ruffled appearance, despite her careful attempts this morning. Her finger wiped away a speck of dirt that stretched across her forehead like an accusing mark. How on earth had she managed to get mud even on her face? Her first impulse was to rub her fingers across it, but then she lowered her hand. No.

The less presentable she looked the better.

It WAS MUCH EASIER than Minerva had anticipated.

"Child, you look terrible," her aunt had commented, when Minerva ran down the stairs to greet them. "What happened? Where have you been?"

"I am so sorry, Aunt," Minerva replied after deciding to simply ignore the last question. "I was outside and fell, and when I saw how much work Anna was having, I did not want to keep her from her chores. I tried to fix my hair myself, just in case you are bringing back company, but..." She lowered her gaze.

Her uncle stepped closer and examined her carefully, as Minerva noticed from the corner of her eye. It was quite possible that he was scrutinizing the colour of the dirt to divine where she had been according to the consistency of the streak of mud. So, she kept her eyes averted and prayed that her aunt would come up with the desired solution for this problem all by herself.

"In the future, you will have to pay more attention to where you step," she said. This was not how Minerva had hoped the conversation would go. Feverishly, she searched for a riposte that would steer her aunt in the right direction, but without revealing her little intrigue.

"I will be more vigilant, Aunt," she answered obediently. "It was not really my fault – however, I am glad that none of your acquaintances saw me in such a state." She shuddered dramatically. "What if a gentleman who happened to come by had seen me like this? It is inconceivable what opinion he might have had of *me*," she emphasised the word inconspicuously. She held her breath. In the silence that followed, the noise that escaped her uncle's lips was clearly identifiable as a disgruntled snort. She peeked up at his face. His expression was serious, and he carefully watched her face, but his lips were twitching.

Encouraged by his reaction, she now said openly: "Is it really impossible for me to have my own maid while I am staying here?"

"Hmm," her uncle grunted, settling in a chair by the fireplace. "What do you say, Catherine?"

"Well," her aunt started but fell silent again. Minerva looked at her pleadingly and, as she hoped, innocently. "Her father has explicitly written to us that she is supposed to learn to live with what we can provide her."

"That is what he said?" Minerva had a very good idea what her father had intended by that. He wanted to drive her into Mr Meade's arms and teach her humility. "Even my father can't possibly wish for me to walk around like a..." she was searching for the right word but could not think of one.

"The question is," her uncle interrupted, "... how do we interpret your father's words? Are we able to provide Minerva with a maid? The answer to that would be affirmative. Our financial resources allow it. The next question is whether we want it. Well, Minerva," he nodded towards her, "... do you have valid arguments for that?"

She looked at him irritated. *I do not need arguments,* she wanted to say, but realised at the last minute, how childish that would sound. "Would you like me to plead my case as if I were in court?"

"I want you to learn how to act like an adult, which you are claiming to be," her uncle retorted. Minerva's cheeks turned bright red. "Oh, that hurts, doesn't it?"

"Yes," she replied stubbornly. Her uncle wanted good reasons? Very well then. "I don't want to keep Anna from her chores in the house," she began. Neither her aunt, nor her uncle looked pleased with her answer. "My parents wish for me to find a husband. But how am I supposed to ever find a husband, if I do not... look clean and decently dressed?" Encouraged by her Aunt Catherine's approving nod, Minerva continued: "Any man who looks at me is supposed to see in me his ideal wife – but how could he do so if my appearance fails to match his honour or if he should be ashamed of me?"

"Isn't that mostly based on the way you behave, my

dearest niece?" Uncle James's question had been asked in a calm manner and without a hint of an accusation. "I would like to propose an exchange. We will agree that you will get your maid, a girl from the village, who will help you to get dressed and ready..."

"Thank you, Uncle. I appreciate it very much," Minerva said, and she put all of her gratitude into her voice.

From beneath his bushy eyebrows, he glanced at her with a sceptical look. "... however, in return, your aunt and I would like to see some goodwill from you," he continued and took a deep drag from his pipe. Minerva was not used to smoke, since the gentlemen at her parents' house smoked in a different room to the ladies, and she started to cough.

Her uncle waved the white smoke away with his hand and waited for her coughing to subside.

"We, which means, your parents, have found another candidate who is interested in your hand in marriage. He is visiting his relatives here in Kent and will most likely pay us a visit within the next few days. I expect you to do what is expected of you, do you agree?"

"Of course," she replied with a husky voice. Her chest

tightened. There had been hours, even days, when Minerva had completely forgotten why she was here. She had actually begun to see her time with her uncle and aunt as no longer a punishment! Minerva was just about to say something when her aunt rose from the chair.

"I think it is time for us to go to bed. Tomorrow morning, we will talk about who is the most suitable for you as a maid. Have a good night's rest."

IT TOOK Minerva rather a long time, before she finally fell asleep. She tossed her uncle and aunt's words back and forth in her mind. Today had been full of surprises, and unfortunately, most of them had been unpleasant. The infamous duke had her in his hands, her family wanted to force her into marriage by all available means – and she had nobody in whom she could confide her misery.

In her last letter, Georgiana had announced that it would take a little while longer for her to write a following letter, as her mother was also sending her to the countryside – to visit relatives in Yorkshire! Georgiana had sounded inconsolable. She considered Kent "more civilised" than the part of the country where she was banished to, and she said that she had no idea what to expect. Minerva had written back to her with encouraging words, and she had asked her to describe to her the wild, rugged landscape, so that she might use it in her book. Maybe that would distract Georgiana and perhaps even open her eyes to the beauty of her surroundings.

There *was* one good thing about the turmoil she had fallen into. Her decision to write a suspenseful novel was stronger than ever. She took a deep breath and clung onto the thought that burned inside of her like fire. If she were never to marry, then there would never be a man to prevent her from following her dreams and becoming a writer.

This in turn brought up yet another thought, which filled her with a strange restlessness. Now that she had lost all hope, she could meet the duke and his impertinent demands in a way she had not thought possible before. As it stood, she had nothing to lose. Not her good reputation, which would be ruined the moment her first novel was published; not her parent's favour, who only viewed her as someone they quickly needed to marry off; finally, not the goodwill of those who considered themselves leading the way in society.

However, before she turned her back on the Beau Monde entirely, she would make sure that she taught the Duke of Scuffold a lesson.

Like so many others, he believed that she was nothing more than a silly little girl. Minerva would convince him of the contrary.

She just didn't know how.

CHAPTER 6

As unexpected as a rain shower after a long sunny day, Marianne met the duke's sinister smile.

THE FOLLOWING week brought two surprises.

Aunt Catherine, who always got up early in the mornings to clear up her garden behind the house with an iron hand, was waiting in the breakfast room for Minerva, nervously crumbling up a slice of bread. "There you are, child," she greeted her niece. "I don't really know where to begin," she mumbled, partially turned towards Minerva, partially talking to herself. Minerva noticed two letters lying on a plate next to her aunt.

The seals had already been broken. One letter was in the very fine handwriting of her mother – the other one had been written by someone whose writing she was not familiar with. Bold, energetic strokes embellished the top of the paper.

Minerva sat down across from her aunt and took a slice of toast. "Have you found a girl from the village, who will be able to help me?"

"No, that is not as easy as you might think," her aunt replied, whilst absentmindedly taking both letters into her hand, then putting them back again and running them through her fingers once more.

"The trustworthy girls are already employed somewhere else. It is not easy to find good servants when you are living in the country."

"I think I know someone," Minerva mentioned casually. "There is this girl with red hair – her name is Sally, I think. She is very friendly, it seems to me."

"Sally is not someone you should be spending time

with," her aunt answered her suggestion. "She works in the tavern."

"Oh?" Minerva acted surprised. "So *that* is what she was referring to, when she asked me for new employment."

With that Minerva had gained her aunt's full attention. "When did you speak to her? What are you saying?"

"I met her on one of my walks through the village. Sally approached me. She said that she was looking for a better job, where she wouldn't be confronted by such immorality every day. I had the hope that I would be able to help her – she seemed very sincere, Aunt."

"Did she? That is very astonishing to me," her aunt replied drily. "Well, nobody can say that she is one of the dumb ones. She seems to be quick, too."

"Thank you, Aunt," Minerva squealed excitedly, taking advantage of the older woman's speechlessness. "That is so nice of you. I shall go and inform the girl immediately. I am sure Sally will not disappoint our trust in her. I will look for her and tell her!" She rose from the table, but this time, Aunt Catherine was not willing to let her niece get away so easily.

"If this matter was not so extremely pressing – if you didn't have to look presentable... very well. I will notify your uncle that we have found someone, for now. But," she repelled Minerva's friendly words, "... Sally will only stay in the house for as long as she behaves appropriately. Just one improper word, and you will have to do without a maid." She shook her head, as if she was surprised at herself. Minerva wondered for a moment if she should flatter her aunt for her generosity, but she decided against it – she did not want to arouse her suspicion.

"Your mother has written to me," Aunt Catherine continued. "She writes that the young gentleman she mentioned previously has approached your father for his approval to ask you for your hand in marriage. Your father has given his consent and advises you to receive Mr Nicholls in a friendly manner."

Minerva swallowed hard and waited, although she would have much preferred to storm out of the room and throw herself onto her bed. Her face must have revealed some of her inner turmoil, as her aunt sighed and looked at her almost piteously. "Said gentleman has also written to us, meaning your uncle and me. He has business to attend to with the Duke of Scuffold, which will bring him into our area within the next few days." Her mouth turned into a thin, disapproving line. "Since your parents have already met him and approve of his courting you, I cannot say much at this point, but," she paused for a short, meaningful moment, and it seemed as if she saw her niece clearly for the first time. "You know how I feel about the duke," she began quietly, almost mischievously. "And if you should decide that you do *not* want to accept the proposal of a man who associates with this corrupt creature, please rest assured that you will have my full support."

"But... Aunt... this is..." Minerva muttered – not knowing how to react to those unexpectedly understanding words. For a second, she even contemplated telling her aunt everything – her forbidden excursion and her encounter with the duke, as well as his scandalous behaviour and even her decision never to accept a man's proposal for marriage – but then sanity prevailed (or maybe it was her own lack of courage), and she stayed silent. The unusual moment of warmth between them vanished as the door opened and Uncle James entered the breakfast room.

"Something marvellous has happened just now," he

began, without noticing the silence between the two women. "The Duke of Scuffold has requested my assistance in a legal matter."

When she heard the news, Aunt Catherine inhaled sharply, but Uncle James didn't notice his wife's discomfort, or he was determined to ignore it. Minerva's heart, which had been rather calm before, now jumped painfully inside her chest that suddenly was much too tight for all the sensations that flowed through her. "He has invited us to his residence." He looked at his wife and seemed unaware that Minerva was also present. "I know that you will not approve, but it would be a gross discourtesy if we were to decline the request."

"But you are retired," Aunt Catherine objected weakly, knowing well enough that she could hardly object to her husband's painstakingly suppressed excitement.

"Yes, and I am bored to tears," Uncle James replied. "I long for a conversation that's about something other than the weather, or which young lady will soon marry which young gentleman." It was only then that he seemed to notice that he and his wife were not alone in the room. Aunt Catherine promptly intervened and asked her niece to go and inform Sally that she was being needed as a maid, immediately.

As much as she would have liked to stay and hear more about the duke's mysterious invitation, it wasn't really an option, since her aunt had asked her directly and Minerva could not think of anything to say to prolong her stay. Maybe she should listen into their conversation secretly? But even this plan was immediately foiled, because Anna appeared just at the very moment Minerva closed the door behind her. What would her heroine, Marianne de Lacey, have done? Minerva wondered. Well, most likely, Marianne would have done the obvious and made her way to Sally to inform her about her new fortune.

As it turned out, fortune was not really the right word, at least not if she read Sally's facial expression correctly, after she told her about the job proposition. It was almost impossible to interpret her reaction wrongly, since the barmaid matched her countenance with a flood of very clear words that were, thankfully, not obscene.

"And of course, you didn't even think once about actually asking *me* what I want, did ya?" Sally asked as she swung her brightly coloured red hair back over her shoulder.

Irritated, Minerva wondered why the young woman had not tied up her wild and curly mess, but her thoughts were promptly interrupted by a rather disgusting swear word. "Maybe I like what I'm doing," Sally said and placed her hands on her hips in an accusing manner. They were standing in front of the Dog & Bones and Minerva had the slightly uneasy feeling that she had bitten off more than she could chew.

"I bet there is something else behind all of this," the barmaid continued her ranting. Her facial expression could only be described as deceitful. "I'd be willing to 'elp you get dressed, but..."

"Yes?" Minerva had started to regret her initial idea.

"If I come to you and the Buckleys, Mr Charlie will not be too 'appy about it," Sally remarked. "One day, you'll be gone, and I won't 'ave a damned job anymore."

Minerva's brain was working hard. "I could always speak with my parents about keeping you on. Maybe...

you could come to London with me and help our cook," she suggested.

"Well, that would not be nice after I 'ad been your maid for a while," Sally returned and shrugged with her shoulders. "From a lady's maid to a cook's maid – naaa."

"All right then," snapped Minerva, who was slowly but surely starting to lose her patience. "I will make sure that you return with me as my maid. But if I do that, I expect two things from you." She did not leave Sally enough time to object. "Firstly, you will have to learn to speak in a more sophisticated manner." Had she hurt the young woman's feelings? It seemed as if she had. "Secondly, you must treat all my secrets in confidence." It was already too late. Minerva realised that she had actually admitted to Sally that she was doing things she shouldn't, behind her relatives' backs.

"Yeah sure, Miss. I mean..." Sally corrected herself with a slight smile, "... I agree with your terms. I'll just go and tell Mr Charlie and then I'll come to you directly." She turned towards the tavern, then turned back to face Minerva. "Oh, and I assume that the Buckleys will pay me?"

"That is correct," Minerva confirmed. She could hardly believe that she had actually managed to set a part of her plan into motion.

"That's what I was afraid of," Sally answered daintily and marched proudly into the Dog & Bones.

Minerva exhaled a big breath she had held. Only now did she realise how much her upcoming second encounter with the duke, scheduled for this afternoon, had actually unsettled her. Although she was now fortunate enough to have an accomplice, she wondered whether Sally's loyalty could withstand a full-blown interrogation by her uncle and aunt, or even her parents, which was also a possibility.

She had no other choice but to make the best of the tricky situation that the Duke of Scuffold had so skilfully forced her into.

She straightened her shoulders and hurried back to her relatives' house. The duke wanted to read something of hers? She shook her head and noticed that she had forgotten to put on a hat once again. What was the reason for this absurd imposition of his? She could not think of one rational reason why he should be interested in her and her unfinished novel. However, maybe this was the whole point, she thought, as she stepped into the house. He didn't need a rational reason for his behaviour. Most likely, the Duke of Scuffold simply marvelled in the thrill of manoeuvring young women, such as her, into compromising situations and enjoyed their discomfort. Minerva had two choices – she could confess her aunt everything, or she could go and teach this impertinent nobleman a lesson, in the stead of all the other young women whose lives he had already ruined.

The house was silent. Aunt Catherine had possibly gone to her room under the pretence of a headache, whilst her Uncle James sat in his study and prepared everything for his visit to his lordship's residence.

Taking two steps at once, Minerva rushed up to her room. She wondered how the duke planned to be in two places simultaneously. He not only expected her at the pavilion, but he had also invited her uncle and aunt to visit his home, at the same time. She was fully aware why this invitation had also included her Aunt Catherine, but how was it that her otherwise astute uncle had not noticed this strange breach of etiquette? Either the duke was looking for advice from her uncle, which would make it a business appointment, or he was trying to establish good neighbourly relations with them, so he invited them both.

Then again, this was not really a problem she had to resolve. It was her task to write something that would show the duke his very own arrogance.

Fortunately, Marianne de Lacey was already the captive of a brutal villain, who could easily be adapted to match the duke with just a few strokes of her quill.

Determined, she grabbed her valuable notebook and opened the first page. She wanted to have the duke read her story as if he were looking into a mirror, and she wanted to make sure that he did not like what he saw.

CHAPTER 7

There was only one possible escape for Marianne, if she wanted to avoid her own ruin.

THE FEW STROKES of her quill, which Minerva had initially anticipated, had grown into a rather large number of adjustments. The man, who threatened her heroine in her story, had at first appeared to her as the perfect villain. His hair was black and straggly and much too long, and his eyes gleamed in the darkness like smouldering coals. He had a thick black beard and a hooked nose, which stood out prominently on his pale face. He was also extremely tall and scrawny. When Minerva read her description of him, which she had so enthusiastically committed to paper, she realised that this had not been her smartest move. Even the least sophisticated reader could guess that the duke was not planning anything good for his victim, Marianne de Lacey. Maybe it would be more suspenseful for her readers, if she kept them in the dark about her villain's sinister character, at least for a while. With this in mind, Minerva saw her changes to the novel, which were initially meant for the duke, as improvements. She closed her eyes and tried to recall *her* encounter with the man. It was surprising, just how present the Duke of Scuffold still was inside her head.

Half an hour later, after numerous adjustments and crossings out, she had managed to amend the duke (in her novel), and she had given him a slightly less menacing appearance. *His golden-coloured eyes shimmered in the soft light,* she read. *Marianne shuddered when the fiery gaze of the man drank in her appearance. His tawny hair curled in a wild mane and fell all the way down to his shoulders. His imposing physique towered over her by more than a foot, and when he rushed towards her, she thought of an exotic animal, pouncing on her in an attack. His full lips curled into a cruel smile.*

Ah, this was wonderful! Had she exaggerated a little? Initially, it had been her goal to give him a rather inconspicuous exterior, but as she thought about it some more, she realised that the Duke of Scuffold was anything but unremarkable. Minerva read her words over and over again. This truly was the Duke of Scuffold, as he lived and breathed. Now, all she needed to do was to create a scenario with him and Marianne, which would mirror the despicable behaviour of the man. How much time did she have left? Not enough for her to be able to amend the encounter between Marianne and the duke to her own satisfaction. She sighed and put aside the quill. Today, his lordship would have to be content with what little she had been able to adjust.

She pulled on the rope to ring the bell. To her surprise, Sally appeared faster than Minerva had hoped, and she even tried a curtsey. "What can your subservient maid do for you, my Lady?"

"Do not overdo it," Minerva warned, but she could not help but smile. Ever the accomplice, Sally returned the smile mischievously, and for a moment, Minerva forgot about her uneasy feeling concerning the upcoming meeting with the duke. Not only did having Sally accompany her had the benefit of making her feel safer, but she could now justifiably claim that she had not disobeyed her uncle's instructions. He had allowed her to leave the village, as long as she was not alone. "We will be going for a little walk," she said and packed the notebook into her little bag. The small book, which was not particularly comfortable to write in due to its size, easily fitted inside the pouch.

"I will need sturdy shoes and a stout dress." She walked over to her trunk and opened it. Her hands found mountains of muslin and fine silk, but nothing that would be suitable for an extended walk in the woods. What she needed was... her eyes wandered across to Sally's brown cotton dress. It was truly an ugly colour, but one only saw dirt if one looked closely. Sally's shoes were also unsightly, but sturdy.

How very unfortunate that it was already too late for a charade. She imagined how she switched dresses with her new maid and how the Duke of Scuffold's interest would vanish in an instant. He certainly would not waste any of his time with an ordinary servant girl, would he? Was not this the way to escape from the trap she was caught up in? She looked at Sally. They had similar figures, which made a dress switch absolutely possible. Unfortunately, the young woman would not be able to deny her true heritage the minute she opened her mouth. With a decent hairdo and a pretty dress, Sally would look more than passable, Minerva noted. It was a peculiar realisation that it took nothing but a little fabric to turn a plain servant into a lady. Beneath all their clothes, they were similar, if not the same. Minerva had just been fortunate enough to be born into a wealthy family. Otherwise it would be her to scrub floors or make beds, not Sally.

What would it be like to slip into someone else's skin for only an hour?

With a deep sigh of regret, Minerva dismissed the plan as unfeasible (and not only because of the difference in their hair colours). It was an unrealistic figment of her fantasy, and this time even she had to admit that her vivid imagination had led her onto the wrong path. No, she had to face the duke in her own way, without bringing Sally into danger.

At last, the day arrived, when her relatives followed the duke's invitation. The noises in the house revealed that her uncle and her visibly reluctant aunt had left the house, on their way to Beaufort Castle. Minerva ran to the window and watched as her uncle and aunt got into the carriage. It was also time for her and Sally to begin their walk towards the forest, so that Minerva could face the duke. She had given her maid the strictest of instructions. Sally was to stay within calling distance, and she was to remain quiet and not give away that she was present. Minerva had left her believing that they were on their way to a secret rendezvous. How was she supposed to explain her situation, if she herself could not find the right words to express what she was trying to prove to the duke? Whenever she thought about him, the first things that came to mind were his mocking gaze from those unsettling eyes.

Her feet found the way almost by themselves. With rapid steps and a pounding heart, she made her way through the woods. As they neared the pavilion, she instructed Sally to hide behind a bush and she explicitly told her not to come closer, unless she heard Minerva call for help.

"And what if you don't even get to call for 'elp?"

With a wave of her hand, Minerva dismissed the argument, but Sally was not so easily deterred.

"What if the ghost of the crying woman comes, and it scares you so much that your tongue freezes?" Even Sally had heard about the mystical pavilion and the ghost of the crying woman. Her imagination concerning what might happen if one were to encounter the ghost was colourful, and Minerva's fingers started to tingle with excitement, knowing she could use it somewhere in her book. "There are no such things as ghosts," she replied firmly, even though she didn't feel all that secure about it.

"As you wish," the maid returned and pushed out her lower lip. She let herself fall onto the soft moss behind the bush.

"Remember, I do not want to hear a peep," Minerva warned her again. "You'd better not eavesdrop either!"

Sally looked as if she wanted to say something, but Minerva turned her back on her and marched straight towards the pavilion. She couldn't hide a quiet gasp of surprise, when she saw that someone had covered the holes in the floor with wooden planks. Only the duke could have ordered that – but why? He had entered into a deal with her, instead of simply chasing her off his land. Did that mean that the Duke of Scuffold had a certain interest in her? Maybe he liked her – or was that just an absurd thought?

She wasn't exactly a wallflower, but she was realistic enough to know what enticed a gentleman to ask her for a dance. However, the thought of herself as a potential partner for the Duke of Scuffold was almost ridiculous. He was rich; he did not need to marry a wealthy woman. And, he was so very different from the other gentlemen in her circle that Minerva was unable to figure out his reasoning. He truly was a strange man.

Minerva sat down on the stone bench and could not avoid noticing that someone had cleaned off most of the dirt. Had *he* ordered this?

She could almost imagine what the pavilion must have looked like in its glory days. It was a beautifully secluded and romantic place – ideal for a rendezvous between two lovers. The crying woman had, when she was still amongst the living, waited here for her love, Minerva was certain of that. Maybe her husband had caught her as she kissed someone else, and he had killed her in a rage of jealousy. She would only find eternal rest when justice had been served on her murderer.

A soft rustling caught Minerva's attention, and she had to reassure herself that ghosts did not exist. The noise was nothing but the wind moving some of the fallen leaves along. Or it was the duke, sneaking up on her. She peeked out, but she could see nothing but the trees, the grass, and the scattered rays of the afternoon sun. Unfortunately, today it was too dark to write. Minerva could do nothing but wait for his lordship to pay his respects. She wondered how he planned to simultaneously keep his appointment with the Buckleys *and* meet her in the woods. She imagined how he would be subjected to Aunt Catherine's disapproving looks, which made her laugh out loud. Her aunt had only agreed to go with her husband under great objection, which had been evident in the stiff way she had climbed into the carriage.

"I am happy to see that you are perfectly content in entertaining yourself without me," a voice said directly behind her.

Minerva suppressed a small yelp. She didn't want to give him the satisfaction of having startled her a second time. She straightened her back and turned around towards him. The Duke of Scuffold stood outside, in front of the pavilion, and stared at her with sinister eyes. "What were you laughing about?"

Minerva got up and walked outside. She only had to take a few steps around the small building, before she reached him. He looked to her like a gamekeeper, she thought, with his dirty boots and coat, which had started to show signs of wear and tear. *Breathe*, she ordered herself and remembered that Sally was nearby. He leaned his shoulder against the stone wall and seemed calm. The initially harsh expression on his face had been replaced by a rather amused superiority, which enraged Minerva beyond all measure. Before she could think of a fitting answer, she said the first thing that was going through her mind.

"I was laughing at you," came over her lips.

Shocked, she slapped her hand over her mouth, then lowered it again. It was the duke who prompted contradictory emotions within her. She felt fear for this man, who rumour had was responsible for his wife's... oh no. How could she have been so stupid!

For the very first time since yesterday, she actually saw

a connection between the man standing in front of her and the allegations she had heard, straight from her aunt's mouth. "It was... I apologise," she stammered and avoided his direct gaze. For a short moment, something flashed across the duke's eyes, which looked strange on his face, and it was something Minerva could not put her finger on. But the unexpected look vanished again as quickly as it had appeared.

"If you are incapable of speaking in whole sentences, how are you going to write a full novel?" His deep voice sounded gentle, and it stood in contrast to his harsh words.

"That is entirely different," she said, mustering up all of her courage. She needed to think about how to get out of the forest, unharmed. Calling for Sally was pointless, as she now had to admit. There was no chance that she would put her new maid in danger.

She had to take full responsibility for this dangerous situation.

"How so?" He did not leave her time to think, so quickly did his impertinent questions come. "Explain it to me."

"When I write, I can slip into someone else's skin," she

admitted. She had often thought about what it meant to her, to imagine things and to write them down. "I can live through their adventures, and I alone decide how my story will end."

During the time it took her to answer, the duke had not moved, and he stood still like an animal, even as he spoke.

"You are yearning for adventure," he repeated, "... and you would like to be someone else. Is this the reason why you are secretly meeting a man, whom they say killed his own wife out of jealousy?"

"May I remind you that it was you who forced me to come back here today?"

"Miss Honeyfield, you are a liar," the duke said peremptorily. There it was again, that shimmering in his eyes, like a lightning strike flickering across the black night sky. "I am certain that your relatives wouldn't have punished you too strictly, had you told them the truth about everything that happened here, earlier. Instead you prefer to come back into these woods, accompanied by a servant, who is currently sleeping blissfully. Have your parents never told you the story of Red Riding Hood, who encounters the big bad wolf in the forest?"

"You are no wolf," Minerva said, but for reasons of safety she took a step away from him. "You are just a man."

So, Sally had fallen asleep, instead of listening out for her call. What a wonderful accomplice she had chosen to bring with her.

"Just – a – man," the duke repeated her words and said each one of them individually. It seemed as if he was savouring every syllable on his tongue. Then it came back with a force – the fear she had managed to keep subdued with her chitchat. She opened her mouth to call for Sally, but it was already too late. The duke had pushed himself off the wall and closed the distance between them in two long strides. Now, he stood in front of her, much too close in fact, which took her breath away. With a possessive gesture, he grabbed her hand and brought it up to his lips. The blood was rushing through her veins and all Minerva could hear was the hollow sound of her own beating heart.

For too long, his cool lips rested on her hand. His unruly, tawny hair tickled the back of her hand. But the worst was that he was still looking at her from his half-bowed position. She forgot the danger she had thought she was in. At that moment, nothing else existed apart from him and her.

"Was this an adventure to your liking, Miss Honeyfield?" Even her name sounded different when he said it and was transformed into something new, and she was not sure whether she liked it or not.

However, his words had broken the magic of the moment.

Abruptly, Minerva pulled her hand back, and for a second, she stared at the part of her body, which seemed no longer to belong to her – and realised what had just happened.

As if that was not bad enough, her legs now started to shake terribly, and there was nothing she could do to make them stop.

"You are playing a game with me, which is not appropriate for a man of your standing. It is not very difficult for the notorious Duke of Scuffold to scare a young woman, as you are doing now. Are you not ashamed of yourself?" The more words poured out of her mouth, the safer Minerva felt in her outrage.

"You are scared of another kiss," he determined and smiled victoriously, as if her words meant nothing.

"Oh no, you are mistaken, I am not afraid of a *kiss,*" she emphasised the last word and realised that this was the most inappropriate and peculiar conversation she had ever had. It was also the most intoxicating, because never before had Minerva felt as alive as she did in that very moment, when her heart was filled with fighting spirit and fear. "I did fear you. I feared the liberties you might take. But I was wrong. You are nothing but a man who is bored and who doesn't know what else to do with his time, other than to delight in the sheer helplessness of a defenceless woman."

"Do you really call yourself defenceless?" Something in his eyes sparkled, and Minerva took it for joy that captivated his face in a fascinating way. "In that case, you should put aside your quill, or even better – burn it. A bunny-heart like you will never have the courage to write a book that will fascinate its readers."

"That… you can't possibly know. You have not even read anything I have written."

Ironically, he raised his eyebrows, and Minerva would

have liked to take her words back. Once again, she had followed him right into the trap he had laid out for her. "What makes you so proficient to think that you can pass judgement on me?"

The duke smiled, satisfied. "Well, I read," he answered simply and crossed his arms in front of his chest. "I would dare to say that Beaufort Castle is the home of the most extensive library in the entire county, maybe even in all of England."

Stars danced in front of Minerva's eyes as she absorbed his statement. Her face must have openly revealed her deep yearning for such a treasure, because he started to laugh. It was a surprisingly friendly laugh, which for a moment made her forget to whom she was speaking.

"Why don't you come by one day and have some tea," he suggested, as if they had been properly introduced by society, in the manner that it was supposed to happen. "You read to me from your book, and in turn, I will show you my library."

Minerva had not even noticed that he had drawn closer to her again, but this time she did not retreat from him. His wide, masculine mouth twitched ominously, and she felt an uncontrollable giggle start to rise up inside her chest, as she tried to answer.

"You know that that is impossible. My aunt and uncle would never allow us... I mean, me... to visit you."

"I have noticed that you are not exactly the most obedient young woman," he said deliberately. "... but, as I have already determined, you lack courage." He shook his head and looked at Minerva with a look of regret, before he turned around and left her standing without saying another word.

Minerva fought to suppress the disappointment and the urge to prove to him just how courageous she really could be. In vain. The Duke of Scuffold was about to leave the clearing, when she gathered her skirts and ran after him. "Wait!" She was well aware that this kind of behaviour was more than indecent, and yet there was nothing she could do. She did not even *want* to do something about it. The duke stopped in his tracks and slowly turned around towards her.

"I will visit you," she said breathlessly.

"You will visit me," he repeated quietly.

Hearing his echo created the biggest tingling inside

her chest, half fearful and half anticipating. For the first time, the duke looked at her seriously, and she thought she saw something in his eyes that resembled yearning. Then he blinked and the notion was gone. "I shall expect you tomorrow for tea."

Only after he had disappeared, did Minerva realise that her fear of him had also vanished.

CHAPTER 8

hat kind of secret was hiding behind those dark eyebrows, those mocking lips and those gleaming eyes of the man who had taken her captive against her will?

MINERVA WOKE SALLY UP, and she was grateful that the young woman was much too tired to ask any questions, that she didn't even reprimand her. Minerva's mind turned around the one question, over and over, and to which she didn't know the answer: Why would a man such as the Duke of Scuffold seek her company?

Surely, it was not just her appearance and even less her

considerable dowry. The duke owned vast tracts of land, and Beaufort Castle had an estate, which allegedly was not inferior to any of the castles of the royal family, in terms of luxury and splendour. With a painful stab in her heart, she remembered the conversation she had had with her Aunt Catherine, who had hinted more than once about the glamorous balls and dinners that had been held at Beaufort Castle. The female guests included visitors from France and Russia – beautiful and experienced women, who were of his age group and more suitable for him than a young girl such as herself. Maybe there was a tantalising widow who had lost her husband... no. She had started to concoct stories again, instead of focussing on the here and now.

What exactly had he meant by saying that she needed courage to write?

Minerva felt unbearably young and inexperienced. Unfortunately, she could not shake that feeling, all the way back to the Buckleys' house. Her aunt was already waiting for her in the salon, and she noted the sturdy boots and mildly soiled hem of her dress, with only a restrained shake of her head. Apparently, something far more important than Minerva's appearance occupied her aunt's thoughts, and Minerva's knees almost buckled with relief.

"Mr Benjamin Nicholls has announced that he will call tomorrow afternoon for tea," she began the conversation. Minerva tried, in vain, to wrack her brains to remember a gentleman with this name, whilst her aunt smiled at her expectantly. The more time passed with no response, the more her smile faded, until nothing but two laboriously held up corners of her mouth remained.

"How lovely," Minerva said, which earned her a chiding look. Her aunt had figured out her little manoeuvre.

"Mr Nicholls is the young gentleman who will pay his respects, with the approval of your parents," Aunt Catherine reminded Minerva. "Surely you remember our conversation?" Her voice had changed to a much more disapproving tone and was a sign of her tense nerves. "Your uncle has to speak to him about a business proposition, and once the two gentlemen have finished their discussion, the young man will keep you company for a while, whilst you both enjoy a cup of tea."

Minerva knew her aunt well and assumed that in place of a simple "cup of tea", the cook was already preparing an opulent meal with Anna's help.

"How lovely," Minerva repeated, somewhat absent-mindedly, just to gain more time. The Duke of Scuffold and his impertinent, yet compelling proposal took up so much space in her mind, that there was little room left for anything else, in particular another unwanted marriage candidate. On top of that, tomorrow the duke had ordered her to come to Beaufort Castle, of all days! If she were to pretend that she was indisposed, then it would be impossible for her to sneak out of the house unnoticed. His lordship would have to wait for her, whether he liked it or not. It would do him good, but regardless of that, Minerva felt a touch of disappointment. She would have loved to see his magnificent library. But no, it was simply not possible to avoid this forced tête-à-tête with Mr Nicholls. "How was your visit at the duke's castle?" she asked, to distract her aunt.

The answer was rather evident, judging by her aunt's harshly pressed lips, and at first, Minerva expected her aunt to brush her off by merely pointing out that this was not an appropriate topic for a young lady like her.

But to her surprise, Aunt Catherine answered, only after a short moment of hesitation. "Oh child," she sighed. "We did not even get to see him for very long. He pretty much instructed your uncle to help him with the writing of a contract, which your uncle will conclude with Mr Nicholls, and he gave him all the relevant paperwork. After that, he asked *me*," her voice sounded incredulous, "... to help him choose new servants." She frowned and ran her fingertips across her forehead to smooth the deep lines, as if she wanted to wipe her insubordinate thoughts away behind them. "Shortly afterwards, he excused himself and did not return."

"Uncle James must be very pleased to be able to work for such a wealthy man," Minerva offered, hesitantly. At least she now knew how the duke had managed to get away during the afternoon and to make it possible for her to escape the house. He had arranged for her aunt and uncle to be occupied for as long as had been necessary, without having to be present himself.

"Yes, you are right," her aunt replied. Her gaze fell upon Minerva's hands, lying idle in her lap. Without uttering a word, she grabbed the needlework basket and handed her the maltreated embroidery she had been working on earlier. Minerva took it and stared at it with little hope that she would ever be able to produce a satisfying result. Aunt Catherine's nimble hand, even with her slightly swollen fingers, was faster and more skilful than Minerva ever expected hers to be.

"Have you agreed to help him?"

Aunt Catherine snorted. "Your uncle assured him of my help," she said sharply. Sudden sympathy with her older relatives made her heart feel tight.

"I could help you with your task," she suggested, which earned her a sharp look from the piercing blue eyes.

"No," her aunt denied her completely. "I do not want you to spend even one minute in the same room as that rotten and corrupt man. Your opportunity for a marriage with Mr Nicholls would be ruined, even before he had a chance to propose to you."

"But..." Minerva began – she wanted to say that she and Mr Nicholls had not even met each other yet, let alone talked to each other. It was not only very premature, but indeed outright hasty to be speaking about marriage so soon. Then she had another thought.

"Since Mr Nicholls also has business dealings with the

Duke of Scuffold, he can't possibly have any objections if I come and support you during your uncomfortable task."

"You really are still a child, Minerva. Have you not learned yet that there are different rules for men than there are for women?"

"But Uncle James doesn't seem to mind that you are seen in the company of the duke." She did not add that she was very well aware of the difference in treatment between men and women, even though it was only a few days ago that she had begun to accept these observations as actual facts.

"Nobody, who has their five senses together, could assume there was anything disreputable between me and the duke." Her aunt replied coldly. "It almost seems as if you are trying to completely ruin your chances of getting married." She paused for a moment and began to stab at her own needlework. "Or is there another reason for your behaviour?" She let the hand that was holding the needle and thread sink into her lap. "Should I find out that you are associating with this man behind my... behind our, backs, I will notify your parents immediately. Do I make myself clear?"

Minerva felt her desperation growing. She was entangled in a web of lies, which she had created herself. At this point, she could no longer bring herself to confide in her aunt. However, she did need to meet the duke, if she wanted to prevent a scandal. Now, the question was, how would she be able to do that? For most of the evening and, unfortunately, also most of the night, she evaluated possible scenarios. In the end, she could think of nothing other than sending Sally to the duke to deliver a message. Minerva was angry that she had spent so much time with her fruitless pondering – it kept her from exposing Marianne de Lacey to new adventures, as well stopping Minerva from adapting her villain more to a likeness of the Duke of Scuffold. This man had stolen those precious hours from her – the time when she was allowed to write – and now he even prevented her from getting a good night's rest. All of this was so annoying! Even the message, which would inform him that she could not come, demanded all her attention. It was important not to anger him, at least not too much, as she did not want him to expose her to the Buckleys. On the other hand, she wanted him to feel a slight sting when he read her short letter.

After many fruitless attempts at writing that wasted precious paper, Minerva had to admit that she was unable to combine the desired esprit and rebellion against his behaviour in just a single letter. So, today, it turned out to be just a short message, in which she asked him to postpone her visit for a couple of days, since her family was adamant about her meeting his business partner, Mr Nicholls.

Dissatisfied with herself, she sealed the letter and instructed Sally to hand it to no one other than his lordship, himself. "Do not let them push you around – this is important," she reminded the young woman.

"Don't ya worry, Miss," the maid said and grinned mischievously. "I can do that – I made the acquaintance of one of 'is closest servants whilst working in the Dog & Bones, and I shall ask for John, immediately. He still owes me something, if you know what I mean."

Minerva did not fully understand, but she had a suspicion that Sally shouldn't disclose any more information regarding her encounter with the servant. The young woman hid the letter inside her bodice and patted it as if to show just how important the mission was to her. Yes, it almost seemed as if Sally's regard for Minerva had risen, and she was visibly pleased to know the name of Minerva's supposed secret lover.

For the first time, Minerva felt that she could actually trust Sally. It seemed to her as if she now understood the responsibilities of a maid – but, in addition, Sally's knowledge of what she thought was the truth, had turned her into a more serious and trustworthy person; it was such a far cry from the former barmaid, that Minerva almost did not recognise her anymore.

"Run," she said and decided, there and then, to increase her efforts to keep Sally in her employ, or to gift her one of her dresses. No. No more either/or – she would do both. She imagined Sally's face, when she gave her the green muslin dress and noticed her very own content smile as she passed her dressing table. It felt good to think of doing something for someone else and to do it gladly.

THE POSITIVE FEELING did not last long. It disappeared the moment Anna came to inform her that her aunt wanted to see her downstairs. Sally had not yet returned and that was more unnerving for Minerva than any harsh words from the duke.

The palms of her hands were sweaty, and it cost her all of her self-control not to wipe them on the fabric of her dress. When she walked past her uncle's study, she could hear some murmuring voices. It sounded as if two gentlemen were engaged in a conversation. Attracted by the one warm voice, which seemed strangely familiar to her, she stepped closer to the door.

Just in that moment, they all fell silent.

The door opened.

Her uncle looked at her, wonderingly, with raised eyebrows, while she could not do anything other than stare at the broad-shouldered person, for whom her uncle held the door open.

The Duke of Scuffold. What on earth was he doing in the Buckleys' house? Her heart beat all the way up to her throat, and Minerva wished that the earth would just open up this minute and swallow her whole. It dawned on her, only slowly, that her uncle was saying something. "May I introduce my niece, Miss Minerva Honeyfield, Your Grace? She is staying with us for a short time."

Minerva felt hot, and she silently implored him not to give away their secret. In that very moment she would have done anything to escape the wrath of her relatives.

"It is very pleasant to make your acquaintance, Miss Honeyfield."

He did not show any attempts to lean over her hand, but instead he sketched a short and brisk bow. She released her breath, which she had been unaware that she had been holding.

"Are you not feeling well, Miss Honeyfield?" He asked sanctimoniously while his eyes sparkled at her. Without the enhancing light of the outdoor sun, they had an entirely different colour. Now they seemed much less golden and hazelnut-coloured, and were darker.

And more threatening, as she noticed.

With every minute that she remained silent, the secret between them grew and with that his power over her. She swallowed twice to clear her tight throat. This rather narrow hallway was much too small for even three people. The duke was much closer to her than would have been considered decent. There was no way she could ignore his presence or act as if it was perfectly normal that the Buckleys had received a duke in their house.

"T-Thank you, my Lord," she replied. She could almost not bear her uncle's expectant silence – he expected more than just this meagre response. He saved her from her embarrassing situation by waving towards the salon. "I am sure my wife is already expecting us," he said with rather forced courtesy. "His lordship honours us tremendously by taking tea with us." That sounded much more sincere.

The duke entered the salon first, followed by Uncle James, who was leaving a respectful distance between them. Minerva, who would have very much preferred to run up to her room, did not see her aunt's reaction, and she was grateful that it was hidden behind her uncle's round figure and the larger than life back of the Duke of Scuffold. She really did not want to see her aunt's face right now, as she was obliged to receive the much-hated Duke of Scuffold, instead of the eagerly-awaited Mr Nicholls. Minerva was afraid that her own tension might have surfaced in an uncontrollable laugh or some other inappropriate reaction. However, hiding behind the two gentlemen, she gained valuable moments that enabled her to deal with her composure, before she sat down beside her aunt, with an expressionless face. Only after she had sat down on the sofa, did she notice that this position had significant disadvantages – she and the duke sat exactly across from each other. His eagle-eyes favoured Minerva with a passing glance. Was she the only one who saw the mocking sparkle in them, or could her relatives see it too?

It took everything in her to not slide restlessly back and forth in her seat, and instead to just sit there, daintily sipping at her tea. At least the duke had the decency to pretend to try one of the delicacies the cook had prepared, originally for Mr Nicholls' arrival.

Aunt Catherine did not say anything, but she sat on the soft sofa with a painfully straight back. Minerva's uncle was the only one trying to make conversation; however, at some point, even valiant Uncle James fell silent.

The duke cleared his throat. Minerva raised her gaze, since she had respectfully (and not in an embarrassed manner, she hoped) been looking at the ground up until now. At first she felt hot, then cold under his seemingly relentless observation. She breathed in as deeply as her tightly tied corset would allow and prepared herself for what he would say next.

At this very moment, any ensuing storm of outrage from her aunt and uncle seemed to be a much easier fate to suffer than his steely piercing gaze continuing to bore into her, straight to the depths of her soul.

"Mr Buckley," the duke said. Despite him addressing her uncle directly, his words were aimed at Minerva. She knew it, she felt it.

"I will need Miss Honeyfield at Beaufort Castle."

CHAPTER 9

*S*he would never give in and yield to his *ironclad demands.*

ONLY MOMENTS after the duke had left, aunt Catherine cried and raged, one emotion following the other. Uncle James tried to calm her, but after three failed attempts to do so, he fled to his study. Minerva wanted to do the same and disappear into her own room upstairs – however, her empathy for her aunt got the better of her. "Will you not tell me what upsets you?" She took one of the older woman's hands and winced, as her aunt ripped her fingers away from her.

"How could you?!" Never before had Minerva seen her aunt this angry. "What on earth were you thinking? You have been flirting with this man, behind my back, and after I particularly warned you about him!"

"It is not how it appears, Aunt Catherine," she objected, but her aunt shook her head vehemently.

"Are you honestly going to tell me that you didn't know anything about his intentions?"

"This is as much of a surprise to me, as it is for you," Minerva answered quietly. "You have to believe me. I did not know that he would..."

How could she put it, when she did not even know what was behind his mysterious invitation?

Her aunt moaned quietly. "So, you got involved with him, even though you had to assume that he was not interested in taking you as his wife?"

"No, that is not what I meant!" Minerva protested strongly. What a poor author she was, if she was not even able to have a clear conversation without being misunderstood. "I met him accidentally, that was all. Two times only! Please, Aunt Catherine, you have to believe me. I did not get involved with him, as you put it." Both her bad conscience and her patience began to vanish. Why did nobody believe her?

"And I am supposed to believe that?" Bitterness spoke in Aunt Catherine's voice, as she echoed Minerva's own thoughts back to her. "You have abused my trust, and with that you have manoeuvred your uncle and me into an impossible position. How am I supposed to explain to your parents that I was unable to protect you from your own stupidity, which will ultimately ruin you – if not cost you your very life?"

"I... I..." Minerva stuttered. She couldn't come up with a single answer to her aunt's statement.

Aunt Catherine snorted. "As you already know, the Duke of Scuffold is suspected of killing his first wife. What do you think will he do to you, once he has had enough and grows tired of your attention? At best, he's fond of you now, but do not fool yourself into believing, not for even one second, that his feelings are strong enough to last a whole lifetime."

There was no point in talking to her aunt right now. All of Minerva's attempts to right the wrong fell on deaf ears, as her aunt dismissed them one by one. The shock was obviously too great to overcome in just one afternoon. Only the fact that Aunt Catherine was genuinely worried about her, prevented Minerva from replying with a sharp answer. The worst of it all was that she really had not known anything about the duke's intentions, and now she was unable to form even one clear thought in her mind.

"Please, calm down," she said in a soothing voice, which only had the opposite effect on her aunt. "The duke has never mentioned anything to me about his feelings, nor shown that he has some unhealthy interest in me. It is more than possible that he actually spoke the truth and that he requires my presence at his residence solely for the purpose of visiting with the duke's oldest daughter and the Duchess of Evesham."

Aunt Catherine shook her head vigorously. "I do not trust that man. I do not know what to think of you either, Minerva. I am so very disappointed in you and your waywardness, which has led me to have to accompany you to the place of profligacy itself... Beaufort Castle!"

The way she emphasised the name of the duke's residence left Minerva in no doubt about Aunt Catherine's repugnance. "I shall write to your father immediately and not leave him in doubt as to what role you played in this disgraceful arrangement."

Minerva swallowed down her own rebellion, got up, curtsied, and left the room. She was relieved that she was going to be able to be alone with her thoughts.

However, her aunt was not finished with her yet. "I do hope that you understand that the duke is also responsible for Mr Nicholls' interest in you coming to an abrupt end. Mr Nicholls has asked to be excused and has explained to your uncle that the duke has made it clear to him, in strong words, that it would be better if he did not hope for your hand in marriage." Her lips were pressed into a thin line; however, Minerva was too excited to pay any more attention to her aunt's obvious displeasure.

Her heart was racing as if she had run up a steep hill. What were the duke's true intentions?

* * *

AFTER SHE HAD CLOSED the door to her room behind her, Minerva saw that Sally was waiting. The young woman had busied herself sorting Minerva's wardrobe, which she did with more enthusiasm than knowledge. Sally was brushing Minerva's second-best blue silk dress with a brush that Mary, back home, regularly used for shoes.

Minerva sat down on the edge of her bed. "Please put the things away for a moment," she instructed Sally. "Tell me if you have received a reply from Beaufort Castle for me." For some odd reason she was unable to say the duke's name. To say out loud that she was expecting a letter from the Duke of Scuffold would have given the entire situation (and the duke particularly), much more weight than she deemed appropriate. The only thing she truly expected from any lines he might have written, was an explanation for his irrational behaviour and for his strange request.

Sally shook her head until her red hair came loose. "No, Miss. 'e 'asn't given me a response for ya." She was biting her lower lip and seemed to hesitate for a moment. "If ya wish, I could go back there again," she offered, but Minerva just shook her head.

"No, that will not be necessary," she said gracefully.

The duke had not mentioned where they had made their acquaintance, but nevertheless, he had put her in tremendous trouble. Her aunt already assumed her to be a woman of compromised morals, and it was highly likely that her uncle thought the same. How skilfully the duke had suited the actions to his plan! One could almost suspect that he was a true master in manipulating people. It had been unmistakable, at least to Minerva, that he found great pleasure in doing so. He was a man who loved challenges.

But not with her! Whatever was behind the invitation, she would stand up to him, in her own way. For now, there were two things – no, there were three things she had to find out about his lordship. Minerva took out her notebook and opened the last page. To avoid any confusion in her work on Marianne de Lacey's adventures, she had decided to write notes about the duke and his strangely captivating personality on the last pages, near the end of the notebook.

She asked Sally to go and get her tea from the kitchen, before she dipped her quill into the ink and started to think. The order of the key events was not of importance at the moment. First, she needed to try and order her own thoughts. Didn't her father always talk about doing things strategically, like a soldier, as he planned a painful counter strike against one of his business competitors?

If the Duke of Scuffold believed that he could just use her, as he had with all the others, and whenever he saw fit, then he was in for a big surprise. She would comply with his request, which was nothing other than a thinly disguised order. The biggest mystery was the question of whether he had actually killed his wife or not. That was the first item she wrote in her notes, along with a reminder to ask Sally about it. As she wrote the word "killed", her hand trembled so badly so that the individual letters of the word were barely distinguishable.

The next question was: what were the Duke of Scuffold's intentions in inviting her to Beaufort Castle? When he had asked her uncle – or rather, when he had informed her uncle – that he was expecting the Duke of Evesham and his oldest daughter, his voice had sounded honest. She chided herself – of course it was the truth. Even a man such as him, who called an immense fortune his own, and who possessed a pronounced self-confidence, would not dare to invent something like that. Minerva felt dizzy at the thought of the Duke of Scuffold engaging an entire ensemble of actors just to get his hands on her. No, this was merely a product of her overheated imagination. With energetic strokes of her quill she crossed out her corresponding notes, rendering them unreadable.

She had written down two points on her list when she had a thought. What if it turned out that it was not she who was the object of his attention, but the daughter of the Duke of Evesham? He had said that he needed her to keep Lady Annabell Carlisle company, as her mother was unfortunately indisposed.

Apparently, Lady Annabell was somewhat clumsy – or as he had put it, the young woman seemed a little slow – and he hoped that Miss Honeyfield's presence during Lady Annabell's visit would have a refreshing influence on the young lady.

She realised that she was chewing on the end of the quill and laid it aside, unnerved. Tired, Minerva rubbed her eyes and only then noticed that her fingertips were covered in ink. *Tomorrow is another day,* she thought wearily, as she heard Sally's footsteps approaching her room.

For tonight, she would let the duke and everything concerning him, rest.

CHAPTER 10

And yet, there was something about the duke that drew her attention to him.

THE NEXT FEW days passed rather quickly. After the duke's fateful visit, time had seemed, at first, to be ticking by torturously slowly, but soon it had turned into a storm of hectic activities. First, a letter from her father had arrived. Aunt Catherine's stiff facial expression had straight away told her that Chester Honeyfield had given his permission for Minerva to stay at Beaufort Castle. Once more, Minerva felt pity for her aunt, when she saw that every one of her objections disappeared unheeded. She assumed that her Uncle James had also sent a letter to her father, telling him about his point of view. Aunt Catherine had not held back about her displeasure regarding Minerva's upcoming stay at Beaufort Castle, and Minerva believed that her aunt had not restrained herself from telling her father about her opinion of the duke. She felt nauseous – her aunt had most likely also informed her father about the rumours that were circulating behind his lordship's back.

Was her father prepared to deliver his daughter to a man who had pushed his first wife down the stairs? Thanks to Sally's eager support, she had been able to find this much out: After a furious argument with her husband, the duchess had been found at the bottom of the stairs the next morning – dead. The subsequent hastened burial had fuelled the rumours surrounding her sudden passing, much as the widower's behaviour afterwards. For over one year, the duke was nowhere to be found, and when he returned to Beaufort Castle, the pleasant, sociable, and cheerful man he had once been, had vanished completely. He dismissed most of his servants, including all of the female servants, from his townhouse in London. Everyone who did not see fit to move into the sinful pool of the main city, was placed elsewhere by his administrator. The duke closed off the east wing, where his dead wife had once resided and used only the west wing of the house, employing only male servants. Even his cook was a man and a French one at that! Sally had told her that she had served him a couple of times in the Dog & Bones, and she had pulled a face as she remembered his foreign chef de cuisine. She had said that he seemed a proud and conceited man, and that he had not once given her any gratuities.

"What about the festivities that take place there every full moon?" Minerva had asked and immediately added what had come to her mind. "The ghost in the forest cannot possibly be that of his wife, if she died in the *house*." She had noticed that her voice sounded somewhat triumphant and she wondered where the feeling of relief, deep inside her chest, had come from.

Sally had eyed her cunningly and smiled as if Minerva were some naïve little child.

"Ah, but that little building in the forest was her most favourite place," she had replied. "I know nowt about festivities – I mean, I do not know anything," she corrected herself. "John, the duke's servant, doesn't tell me that much, not even when I..."

Minerva raised her hand as a warning. Over the past few days, she had learned that her maid either spoke too little, or she said too much. Sally did not seem to be able to walk the path between those two extremes.

Nevertheless, Minerva had grown fond of her in the short time, almost against her own will.

AT NIGHT, Minerva often lay awake, thinking about the Duke of Scuffold. Now that she knew that he associated the magical place in the forest clearing with his late wife (and where he may even have kissed her), she began to understand his anger at their first encounter. Although she knew that she did not bear any resemblance to the black-haired beauty that the former duchess had been, she still had to admit, in hindsight, that she had overstepped her boundaries with her recklessness.

Much to her despair, she did not have enough time to work on her manuscript during the day. Two days after the Buckleys had informed her parents about the duke's intention to have her stay at his castle, her days were engulfed in a whirlwind of activities. Whenever she sat down to adapt the figure of her novel villain to match her living and breathing model, the preparations for her upcoming visit made her presence indispensable.

SHORTLY AFTER HER father's letter, her mother arrived in Scuffold. She brought two huge luggage chests, holding most of Minerva's wardrobe – from her very best evening dress, to a modest morning gown. Her mother apparently assumed that she would spend the rest of her life at Beaufort Castle, since she had even brought her older jewellery, which Minerva had long considered to be too childish, and which she had not worn in years. When she asked her mother why she had taken it upon herself to travel all the way to Scuffold, her mother smiled mischievously. "Your Aunt Catherine has a good soul, but I can tell from her letter that she does not approve of the Duke of Scuffold." She gazed at her sister-in-law, who had fallen asleep and she whispered: "Nobody is better equipped than a mother to assess a possible marriage candidate thoroughly."

A moan escaped Minerva's throat, which her mother, who was overly excited about her daughter's possible prospects, did not take note of. "Even *if* this gentleman refuses to fall under your spell, you will have the unique opportunity to make friends with Lady Annabell Carlisle. If all else fails, there is still Mr Nicholls, to whom you could still give a chance."

In all the hustle and bustle, Minerva had completely forgotten about Mr Nicholls. She had wiped out the poor man from her memory, ever since her relatives had invited him for tea, and before the duke had displaced him so ruthlessly. She could not imagine that even the most good-natured fool – should Mr Nicholls turn out to be one – would feel the desire to meet her a second time.

"Mama," she began, but her mother shook her head and put a finger on her daughter's lips, before putting her through a painstaking examination of her table manners, for the third time. This enraged Minerva more than anything – after all, her social manners were impeccable. Her mother even took the liberty of asking Minerva's uncle to dance a few steps with her, which was a more than strange experience, since the music was missing entirely. Her aunt had been right – her uncle really was a formidable dancer, and since neither her mother nor her aunt played the pianoforte, the silent performance remained an odd affair.

On day six, her nerves were so tense that she longed for the Duke of Evesham and Lady Annabell Carlisle's arrival with every fibre of her body – even if that meant that she would be completely and utterly at the mercy of the Duke of Scuffold. She had no illusion about his lordship's intentions. She suspected that much more lay beneath his invitation than the mere request to keep his guest's daughter company.

Minerva was a fly that had landed in the spider's web voluntarily.

CHAPTER 11

He had taken away her husband, and now he wanted to take away her virtue.

SALVATION ARRIVED in the form of a letter. The duke expected Minerva, her mother and her aunt for tea, on the afternoon of the following day. It had only been a short note, respecting the required etiquette, and was addressed to her uncle as the male head of the household. Her mother pressed the letter against her heaving breast, as if it was a promise to a solution for all of her problems.

On their way to the castle, Minerva attempted one last time to explain to her mother that the duke had not actually invited her there to court her – however, her words fell on deaf ears. Each in their own way, Aunt Catherine and her mother could not be deterred from their beliefs that they knew the true intentions of the Duke of Scuffold better than Minerva did. Her aunt anticipated the worst of him, whereas her mother expected the best.

During the past few days, Minerva had noticed how similar the two women actually were, despite their radically different points of view. Similarly to Aunt Catherine, her mother had not missed any opportunity to prepare Minerva for her anticipated encounter with the duke. Aunt Catherine had implored her to try not to speak, ever, with the duke in private, if she did not want to ruin her reputation even further than she already had. The invitation itself was not considered scandalous, only the fact that the duke and she had met without any chaperones being present. Her aunt had warned her that, should this secret become known, along with his bad name, it would ruin Minerva's reputation for good. Her mother had adopted this particular advice into her own repertoire – but with the opposite intention. If Minerva wanted to encourage the duke's plans to marry her, then it would be all the more important to present herself as virtuously as possible.

She generously ignored the facts of Minerva's original encounter with him, which according to the rules of society had never actually happened. A random encounter in a forest was considered scandalous, but she excused the duke's faux pas by conferring on him a sudden and irrevocable passion for her daughter, which could not be contained by conventions. Minerva suspected that it was not her mother's hidden romantic disposition that caused her to turn a blind eye on the matter, but rather an overwhelming combination of desperation and relief. Relief that a gentleman of his ranking would show any interest in her daughter, and desperation because Minerva had rejected every single man who had asked for her hand in marriage, so far, except the duke.

But how could she reject something that had never been spoken about?

Yet again, she wondered why neither her aunt nor her mother ever mentioned the rumours about the murder. It was highly unlikely that her aunt and uncle, or her parents, had not heard the particularly dangerous whisper. Yet, all her Aunt Catherine ever spoke about was the dark morality of the Duke of Scuffold. Minerva would have liked to question her aunt about what exactly constituted his supposedly immoral conduct, but she did not dare to awaken her aunt's quietly simmering rage. When she had asked her mother why she had accepted an invitation from a gentleman who was suspected to have killed – and she had emphasised the word carefully – his first wife, her mother had just rejected it with a casual wave of her hand. "The Scuffolds are one of the oldest families in the country," she said, and she seemed genuinely appalled at the idea that a duke might have killed anywhere other than on a battlefield. "Of course, I made some enquiries, when I received the good news," she added. "The current duke is a good friend of the Archbishop of Canterbury, and I cannot imagine that a man such as the Archbishop would tolerate a murder, even if the murderer was coincidentally considered a good friend of his." She frowned. "As you very well know, some people are just malicious." She rolled her eyes towards her sister-in-law. "If you do not have anything to do all day, gossip and tittle-tattle are the usual ways to distract yourself and to keep occupied." Minerva had to agree with her mother, even though she would not have expected such wisdom from her mother's mouth.

Nevertheless, she was still worried.

Minerva peeked outside and could not help a small yelp of excitement. The lush forests that surrounded Beaufort Castle, had given way to a beautiful park. The closely-trimmed lawn harmonised with the changing colours of the leaves in the big old trees, which lined up randomly along the winding path. Some blossoming bushes and flowers deepened the impression of a thoroughly vibrant garden, which almost resembled a natural paradise in its randomness.

The first impression of Beaufort Castle was breathtaking, and Minerva felt that she could almost forgive the duke his pretentiousness.

The residence was built on a soft hill, and much like the surrounding park and gardens, the building seemed to have a life of its own. The house had the stocky style that was typical for noble families who could follow their ancestors all the way back to the time of the Norsemen. Minerva remembered the magnificent paintings she had seen when she and her governess had visited a museum in London a few years ago. She could not recall what Miss Frost had told her back then, but she did remember the slight shiver she had felt, when she had taken a closer look at the dark and defensive castles. Although the soft rays of the autumn afternoon sun painted Beaufort Castle in a warm glow, the residence still seemed to have jumped straight out of a Gothic novel. Minerva could see and feel Marianne de Lacey running through the hallways, searching for a way out – away from the clutches of the duke.

"That is right, my dear," her mother said, as she squeezed Minerva's hand. "With such a smile on your lips, the duke will not be able to resist you. I already feared that..." She fell silent as the carriage drove through the rather imposing gate of the outer ward, before it came to a stop in the inner castle courtyard. Immediately, a liveried servant came running out and opened the coach door. Minerva was the only one who accepted his helping hand. Her legs were shaking. She realised that she would spend the next days in the company of the very man who occupied most of her thoughts.

The major-domo was already waiting for them in the entrance way, and he ordered two servants to take care of the guests' luggage. He looked at Sally, who had travelled atop the coachman's seat, and who now attempted to follow Minerva, with an inquisitive gaze. Although the man did not move a muscle of his face, his disapproval was almost palpable, as if he had uttered the words aloud. Minerva pushed out her chin defiantly. "Please show my maid to my room," she said loudly and turned her back on the man. Her mother looked at her with a reprimanding gaze, which told her that this matter would be discussed thoroughly later.

Before she entered the castle property, Minerva turned around one last time. The mighty tower that was looming threateningly from the fortress wall, as well as the high walls, seemed to belong to an entirely different building than the one she had admired from her coach just moments ago. What had seemed imposing mere minutes ago, now felt oppressive. How was this even possible? Her breathing quickened. She and Marianne de Lacey were in the exact same situation! Well, she was being accompanied by her own mother and Aunt Catherine, whereas Marianne was completely on her own, but she realised that this was the only difference between them. She raised her hand to her eyes and blinked up towards the sun.

For one crazy, gobsmacking moment, Minerva was certain that art imitated true life, and she believed that she had actually mysteriously written herself into her own story, which was dominated by an atmosphere of fear and terror.

"Minerva, darling," she heard her mother say, "... are you coming?" Her voice sounded muted from the entrance hall, where she and Aunt Catherine, who persistently shrouded herself in disapproving silence, were waiting for her. The major-domo guided them towards the parlour where, he assured them, tea would be served shortly. Minerva expected to find their host and his other guests in the room, but there was nobody there. She took advantage of this opportunity to look around. The contrast to the dark and cold entrance hall, where she had been greeted by two suits of armour, which flanked the massive staircase, could not have been greater.

A fire crackled in the fireplace, and expensive carpets covered the floor. The main colour in the room was pale blue, which appeared not only in the heavy curtains and wallcoverings, but also in the randomly placed decorative items. Porcelain figurines surrounded a precious little clock and competed for the attention of the beholder with vases and statues of heathen goddesses, who completed the somewhat strange collection. Above the fireplace was the portrait of a woman, whom Minerva thought must be the duke's former wife. It was a most indecent portrait of a woman and would never have been hung in the parlour of anyone who valued etiquette. The woman's black hair fell unrestrainedly over her shoulders and she was dressed in the type of dress that wrapped itself unseemly around her feminine curves. The woman was almost certainly not wearing a corset, which was obvious in her relaxed posture and rounded waist. However, the most disconcerting thing was her eyes, which had a colour somewhere between violet and blue, and which seemed to stare at Minerva maliciously.

A quick glance assured Minerva that her aunt and her mother were busying themselves with their tea, so she walked over to the fire, closer to the source of her uneasiness, and stretched out her hands, as if she wanted to warm herself. The mocking eyes still gazed at her; however, the signature revealed to her what she had hoped for – it was not a portrait of the Duchess of Scuffold. This painting was dated around one hundred years ago.

Relieved, Minerva returned to her mother and sat down beside her, where she took a sip of the delicious tea. Her aunt, who most likely remembered this room from her first visit to Beaufort Castle, had hardly touched her tea, nor the light pastries that lay untouched on her plate. If the circumstances had been different, Minerva would have gladly eaten them, however, in this tense state of expectation, she only managed to take a bite of one of them, and now it sat, indigestible, in the pit of her stomach.

She steered her attention to Aunt Catherine, as she was saying something in a low voice, which sounded suspiciously like an impolite remark about their host's character.

At that moment, the door opened, and he entered the room.

Minerva gasped for air.

She had made his acquaintance in unfavourable circumstances –she was sure of that – however, his transformation from a man who had resembled a gamekeeper, to a man whose every move demonstrated his noble background, was nothing short of astounding.

Someone, most likely his personal valet, had cut his hair and, undoubtedly, his clothes came from the best tailor in London. At first glance, his suit seemed modest, almost plain. Not the slightest embellishment distracted from the perfectly crisp cut. Instinctively, Minerva's eyes wandered back to the portrait of the woman, whose figure-hugging dress she had just admired. The duke's clothes hugged his body in a similar fashion, and yet, they didn't hinder his movements. Broad shoulders and... Minerva blushed, as her gaze wandered lower... long and elegant legs were accentuated by the black fabric. A bright white shirt, starched cuffs, and buttons that only revealed their modest shine at second glance, completed the appearance of a perfect gentleman. Even the artfully bound necktie – there was nothing dandy-like about it – emphasised the masculinity of his face.

"Please remain seated," said the stranger who had slipped into the duke's skin, politely. Was her mind playing tricks on her, or did his voice even sound different? "No need for excessive formalities, since we are *entre nous.*"

Minerva had been the only one who had remained seated, and she awoke from her trance and saw her mother and aunt both blushing – the one surely for joy and the other purely out of anger.

"It is my pleasure to welcome you to Beaufort Castle, Mrs Honeyfield. You too, of course, Mrs Buckley. It is extremely kind of you to help me with my little problem regarding the servants."

"I will keep my promise," Aunt Catherine replied. She did not seem to glower anymore, and Minerva wondered if the duke had magical powers or animalistic magnetism. His deep, soothing voice was uplifting, and her imagination lead her to see a young Duke of Scuffold – one who had travelled with the gypsies, back in the day, where he had learned all kinds of shady tricks. After all, he had disappeared for a year after his wife's death!

"Miss Honeyfield," the seductive voice reached her ear. A treacherous heat made her cheeks glow. "Are you ready?" the man, whom she had pictured at a funfair mere seconds ago, asked. Unsure, she turned around to her mother, who nodded encouragingly. Minerva got up and walked over to the duke, who politely offered his arm to her. She would have loved to back out, as she did not know what she had just committed herself to. "Mrs Honeyfield, Mrs Buckley... my servant,

Johnson, will accompany you to my administrator's office, with whom you will be able to discuss the first steps. Please be assured, madam, that your daughter is safe in my hands. I shall see you later tonight at dinner."

Just as he had said, a liveried butler stepped into the room. This had to be Johnson, for he bowed before her mother and her aunt, before asking them to follow him. She gazed at the man with interest, but also with a little fear. His nose was crooked, as if it had been broken more than once, and his fists looked huge and rough.

Minerva had expected that the duke would now lead her out of the parlour, but instead he waited casually until the door had closed behind Johnson and her two chaperones.

At once, Minerva removed her hand from his arm and took a few steps back. "What have you done to my mother? And where is Lady Annabell, whom I am supposed to keep company?" After all, he was not the only one, who could break any rules.

"Where were you when I told your relatives about the unplanned delay?" He shook his head, partially amused, partially reprimanding. It was a shame that the valet had cut the hair that had fallen into his face during their first encounter, Minerva thought and was startled by herself. He leaned towards her – a gesture already familiar from her two meetings in the forest. Hazelnut-coloured eyes with golden sprinkles eagerly took in every single detail of her appearance, whilst he spoke. "The visit of the Duke of Evesham and his daughter is unfortunately delayed," he announced.

"And you did not find it necessary to inform us about this change of plans?" she asked. Unfortunately, her voice didn't sound as self-confident as she had hoped. "That means that we can leave now," she declared and did not know whether she should feel relief or sadness.

A mocking smile accompanied his reply. "Unfortunately, the letter from my good friend arrived only an hour ago." She wanted to snort derisively to express her disbelief, but he was able to read her reaction in her face. "If you would be so kind as to accompany me to my library, as I suggested, you will not only be able to see my collection of books, but also have a look at the letter," he assured her and, once more, gallantly offered her his arm. "I would be delighted if you would take advantage of my hospitality for a few days longer."

Reluctantly, she laid her hand on his arm and regretted having taken off her gloves again and forgotten them. His skin was warm, and even though her fingers didn't touch it, she could feel the warmth and muscles underneath the fabric of his jacket. Carefully, she repositioned her hand, until her bare fingers rested on his starched cuff. She saw a dark fire blazing in his eyes – but, he allowed her to do it.

"Shall we," she suggested and gazed up at him. "But on our way there, explain to me what you have done with my mother and my aunt."

He adjusted his steps to hers and led Minerva up the wide marbled staircase. How often had he led his wife up these stairs? Minerva tried to shake off her thoughts of the dead woman, which gave her a soft sting.

"All I did was ask them to help me choose a few servants."

"But why?"

He opened the door himself and for a moment he let

go of her arm. It was a strange feeling, when she realised how much she missed the warmth that she had wanted to get away from only moments ago.

"I am planning to get married," the duke announced.

Minerva, who had meant to step over the threshold into the library, stopped, rooted to the spot. Her heart started beating twice as fast and a haze seemed to fall over her eyes. Had her mother been right after all?

Apprehensive and excited at the same time, she looked up to him, unsure of what her answer would be.

The duke cleared his throat.

If he wanted to ask her for her hand in marriage, why had he not asked her father, or at least her uncle? Why had he acted out this charade, luring her here to his castle? Why was he now avoiding her gaze?

"My good friend, the Duke of Evesham, has agreed to give me his daughter's hand in marriage."

CHAPTER 12

The duke was an unscrupulous scoundrel, who routinely broke the hearts of many delicate young women, just to consume them entirely afterwards.

MINERVA DIDN'T KNOW where she found the strength to endure the following hours.

Her first thoughts were to escape.

All she had to do was to pretend some kind of sudden indisposition, or the hint of a headache, and she could escape his presence – and yet she was unable to speak the words. So, she followed him into his library and mechanically answered the few questions he asked her, whilst her eyes wandered across the many titles of the books, which were arranged on numerous shelves.

Only when she discovered the novels by Mr Walpole and Mrs Radcliffe, was she able to think about something other than the duke and Lady Annabell Carlisle, who would soon be married.

The weird, stinging pain inside her chest faded when the duke handed her a copy of "The Castle of Otranto", before he took, in a fluid motion, yet another novel from the shelf and handed it to her.

"I recommend you read both books at the same time, alternating one with the other," he said. "Oh, and only read Mrs Radcliffe's work during the day – it is not good for someone with weak nerves."

"I do not have weak nerves," Minerva answered through gritted teeth before gazing at the second novel. It was "Childe Harold's Pilgrimage" by Lord Byron, a book she had long yearned for and which her parents did not allow her to read. "Thank you," she said quietly and with some difficulty. She did not understand why he, who was as good as engaged to another woman, handed her a romantic, dark novel such as this. Any other man would have won her heart forever with this gesture. Through a small gap in the curtains, the setting sun sent its rays through the window into the room. The duke's face was hidden in the shadows, but his hair seemed to be surrounded by a devilish glow. He stood there motionless, seemingly deep in thought, and looked at her.

The spell broke when her mother and aunt, both in the best of moods, joined them. Minerva looked at the two women and wondered what had caused the mood change, which bordered on exuberance.

Was one small task in the house of a desirable bachelor all it took for them to forget everything around them? Even though it seemed as if everyone had forgotten the possibility that his lordship, the high-born Duke of Scuffold, could potentially be a murderer, *she* had not. How could she, since he was the most inscrutable man she had ever known?

Not without fear, she thought to have caught a glimpse of her future. She saw herself growing old at the side of a boring but reliable husband. He would take all responsibility away from her, and would make all decisions for her, until the day she even left it up to him to choose the colour of her embroidery silks.

Another realisation hit her with full force.

No man would ever allow her to write. Should she be fortunate enough to marry a gentleman with a more liberal mind, he would perhaps allow her to write a guidebook for other women. About the art of running a household or even about etiquette – yes, those were the only topics she would be allowed to address as a woman.

She almost wanted to cry. She was filled with a strange feeling of endearment towards her mother and her aunt, who did not know any better, and she replied attentively and lovingly to their chatter. They only wanted what was best for her, Minerva realised. Up until now, she had dismissed their efforts with little to no gratitude. Should she immediately inform her mother about the duke's marriage plans? She hesitated. For one, it had been a long time since she had seen her mother so lively and excited, and it was probably inappropriate to volunteer any information that his lordship had given her in confidence. Or was she silent because of the quiet hope that his upcoming engagement was nothing but a made-up ploy to get her to…

she could not come up with a reasonable answer. She was more or less forced to stay here at Beaufort Castle and play along with this charade. Hopefully, she could think of a valid reason to speed up her departure by the time Lady Annabell arrived.

The thought of having to sit through multiple dinners for multiple hours, with him and his entourage, and having to lead meaningless conversations and not be allowed to show her true feelings – all that was almost enough to give her a real headache.

To her immense relief, two more guests had also arrived. The brother of the Duke of Scuffold, Lord Beaufort, and his wife ensured that not all of his attention was focussed entirely on her. Lord Beaufort was everything that the duke was not – polite, friendly, and not at all arrogant, despite his nobility and title. Like his brother, he also had brown eyes, although his were a touch darker, and so was his hair, which had a slight reddish shimmer to it, and which reminded Minerva of chestnuts. His figure was slightly more slender, his skin was paler and his fingers were the sensitive fingers of a man who knew how to play a musical instrument. In fact, he moved his hands around as if he did not really know what to do with them, and as if there was a tune in his head to which his hands were already half-responding.

Secretly, Minerva thought that he resembled the picture of what she had envisioned a duke would be like. It should have been the other way around, she thought, and she let her eyes wander back and forth between the two brothers. This title would have befitted the younger brother much better. It was her direct comparison of the two men that showed her, now, what she had not seen before. The duke did not seem to be comfortable in his beautiful and tailored suit. Of course, he looked the part, and she could also very well imagine how he would lead Lady Annabell across the dancefloor – however, he seemed much more comfortable in himself in those worn gamekeeper clothes.

After they had moved from the library into the dining room, she had not paid attention to the conversation, once more. All eyes were on her expectantly. "Lady Beaufort is interested in what you are currently writing," her mother repeated patiently. Minerva blushed and flashed the duke an angry look. Had it been necessary to mention her secret pastime in front of everyone? She saw that her aunt was obviously embarrassed for her, and her mother was just as uncomfortable, since the conversation had revealed her rather unlady-like pastime. She started when Lord Beaufort let his fork fall onto his plate with a loud chink. Compared to his brother, his lordship had a very pale complexion, but now he looked as white as a sheet of linen.

"Oh, it is nothing," she pretended, and shrugged off her novel, trying to gloss over the awkward moment, in which she had stared at Lord Beaufort so blatantly. "You can hardly call it writing, and there has not been a lot of progress yet anyway."

"I really do admire Mrs Radcliffe a great deal," Lady Beaufort said. She seemed to sense Minerva's discomfort, and gave her a genuine smile. "Have you ever read any works by Mary Godwin?" A tiny and almost inconspicuous hesitation, as well as the way she put her words, revealed that she had not been born in England. If one were to take into account the slightly understated elegance of her wardrobe, one could assume that Lady Beaufort was most likely French.

"Oh yes," Minerva replied and heard her mother inhale sharply, next to her. She wished the ground would swallow her whole for she had kept her reading, written by the well-known women's rights advocate, a secret from her parents – until now. Beneath the disapproving eyes of her mother, who now took a second serving of dessert, Minerva smiled shyly at Lady Beaufort.

"Certainly, you agree with Miss Godwin and her notion that women and young ladies should benefit from a thorough education, just as young men do, do you not?" the duke asked. He had leaned back, and his eyes seemed to glare at Minerva provocatively. This man was absolutely impossible!

"Of course," Minerva replied and drank a sip of the marvellous red wine to win some time. "Every rational person would have to agree with her opinion."

"However, wouldn't women, almost exclusively, act out of passion, whilst men are guided by common sense and rationality?" He spoke the challenging words casually. "After all, it was the German philosopher, Kant, who said that women…" For a moment, he closed his eyes and for mere seconds Minerva felt relieved, until his eyes opened again with a new-found fire in them, "… draw their wisdom solely from their feelings, whereas men retrieve it from calculating considerations."

"It is of course your prerogative, to trust the works of a dead German philosopher more than your own observations, my Lord," countered Minerva. "Surely you can think of women, even within your own immediate surroundings, who are not guided by their feelings alone." From the corner of her eyes, she saw that Lady Beaufort nodded approvingly. Her mother did not seem to be listening anymore and had busied herself with the sugary confectionary that Lord Beaufort now offered her. Much like her mother, Minerva also loved sweets. When the duke noticed her gaze, he offered her a piece and Minerva accepted it graciously.

Whilst she savoured the sweet treat on her tongue, she decided that she would no longer be guided by her emotions and that she would, from now on, act rationally. "What of the woman you plan to marry one day, my Lord? Do you expect her to display reason or emotion?" As soon as the words had left her lips, Minerva wished she could take them back. Just a few seconds ago, she had determined not to let her emotions get the better of her and to act rationally, and in the next minute she had ignored her very own decision. Mr Kant would have taken great delight in watching her.

"You are getting married?" Lord Beaufort interrupted the conversation. "Congratulations."

"It isn't yet official," the duke replied, and he glanced at Minerva in such a way that she was unable to interpret. "I would prefer not to speak of it just yet."

From here, the conversation turned to other topics, as Minerva noticed with great relief.

SHE WAS glad when the dinner was over, and it was time for her to go to bed. All the other guests seemed to feel the same way. She could not even retell what she had eaten. Most likely, it had been something delicious – however, she could not remember the taste or the appearance of any of the foods that had been served tonight. Sally came to help her undress, and once the young woman had finally left, Minerva allowed herself to cry the tears that she had held back for so long. There were not many, because as her head fell onto her pillow, she felt something hard underneath it. She jumped up into an upright position, relieved that she had not yet blown out the candle. Her hands pulled out a wrapped little parcel which bore her name, written in bold letters. "Miss Minerva Honeyfield, promising author," someone had written on the paper.

There was only one person who knew about her hopes and would have titled her this way. Her hands were trembling so much that she could barely open the loosely tied riband holding the package together, in order to pull the paper aside. She caught her breath when she realised what the Duke of Scuffold had gifted her.

It was a new notebook, bound in the finest and smoothest leather that felt almost like silk beneath her fingertips. There was also a selection of quills in different grades and two brand-new sealed inkwells, each with a different coloured ink.

This was worse than the works of Lord Byron – so much worse – because this gift hit her right in her heart. It was the gift of a gentleman to his chosen one, with which he would court a woman he hoped to marry.

At the thought of his strong hands writing her name onto the wrapping paper, she felt a wave of genuine joy flood her body and soul. In the next minute, her excitement was replaced by anger. She had been upset with the Duke, unsettled by his demeanour, and had been thinking for days about his inscrutable motives for seeking her company; and in the moment when he had revealed that he was planning on marrying another, he had begun to court her.

This was reason alone to be angry at him.

What was he thinking?

She jumped out of her bed and ignored the cold that touched her feet. Besides, Minerva thought, as she rummaged for her woollen shawl inside her trunk, it was better to feel anger than this strange all-consuming pain. She grabbed the unwelcome gifts, wrapped them back in the paper – making sure that her name was now hidden on the inside where nobody could read it – and tied the ribbon over it.

The silent regret she felt as she touched the magnificent notebook, Minerva pushed aside.

She put on her slippers, then opened the door and peeked into the hallway. As she expected, there was no one to be seen. With a candle in one hand and the package in the other, she sneaked out of her room. Since she had no idea where to find the duke's private chambers, there was only one way she could show him that his attentions were unwanted. She would have to deposit the package inside the library. The possibility of his finding it there was good, even without her writing his name on it. The part of her that always was on the lookout for intricacies and grand gestures for her novel, regretted that she was unable to return his gift directly to his doorway. Well, she had no other choice than to be satisfied with the options that presented themselves to her.

It was not as easy as she had thought, to find the way in the darkness. The house was huge, and the silence that surrounded her seemed to pull on her already tense nerve strings. The flickering light of the candle did not really help to locate the library, and she was equally disoriented, because she had – due to her inner turmoil after the duke's revealing of his disastrous plans – not paid attention to her surroundings. The wind had grown colder, and it howled around Beaufort Castle as if it had jumped straight out of Mrs Radcliffe's imagination.

Hesitantly, she kept toddling forward and regretted that she only wore thin slippers. But was not this the portrait of a man whose face she vaguely remembered?

Minerva lifted her candle up until the light fell on his well-proportioned features. His cheekbones were slightly less striking than those of his descendant, and he had a terrible beard, including some wildly out-of-control sideburns – however, the resemblance was uncanny. She had compared that face with the duke's, when he had led her to the library earlier in the day. Minerva tiptoed further along the hallway. She was certain that she was going into the right direction. And there it was finally – the massive door that hid the incredible collection of books. She pushed the handle down and entered the room.

What she had not sensed during the afternoon, now washed over her like a wave. The smell of paper engulfed her, a known scent and intimately familiar in a way that only a scent intertwined with the most precious memories could be. The soft, lightly worn carpet beneath her feet swallowed any sounds from her steps. How wonderful it was to be surrounded by all these exquisite and selected treasures. In the far corner, near the window, she saw a sofa. It had been placed there without any regard for a harmonious interior, but simply because the light would still be bright enough to read there, even in the afternoon. A small table stood nearby, where one could place a book down or a drink.

Soft cushions ensured that it was comfortable to sit there, whilst preventing any unpleasant stiffness in the neck from reading too long.

This was the room of a man who preferred the company of books to that of people. She carefully placed her package on the table next to the sofa. He would almost certainly find it here. It was not necessary to write to him that his attentions were not welcome. A man who made such a thoughtful gift, would understand the meaning of the unspoken message. With a sigh of regret, she placed the parcel down and looked longingly at the sofa. How nice it would be to just sit there for a few minutes and to escape in the soft shine of the candle, into another world. She could forget what had happened and also what might happen tomorrow. Maybe... just a short moment, only to warm up her frozen feet?

Minerva walked over to the shelf from where he had pulled out Mrs Radcliffe's work and observed the titles. Apart from translations of the passionate German poet Schiller, she found the notorious work by Mr Lewis, right next to the works of Shakespeare, and "School of Widows" by Mrs Reeve. She could not help but smile. Someone should bring some order here, she thought, as she ran her finger across the spines of the books. Should she dare? Her heart pounded in her chest treacherously, and her hand stopped right at the book by Mr Lewis. Nobody besides her would ever know that she had actually had a glimpse into a book, which was labelled by critics as "sensationalist" and "rotten".

With a dry throat, she pulled the book off the shelf and blew the dust from its back. This work had not been read by anyone in a long time. It was highly likely that it was one of the first publications. Her aunt would have probably taken her straight back home, if she knew of the existence of the book in the duke's collection; and her mother would have... a hand lay on Minerva's shoulder from behind. She yelped and dropped the book and the candle at the same moment a dark voice sounded behind her.

"That book is not a suitable lecture for a young lady," the duke said as he bent down to retrieve the candle from the floor. Fortunately, nothing had gone up in flames, and the candle was still burning. With shaking legs and feeling short of breath, Minerva turned around and stared at him.

"What on earth possessed you to scare me like that?" The tone of her voice had jumped up by at least an octave. She felt how the rage inside of her started to boil again. Here he stood, with a self-satisfied and smug smile on his face, and his hand did not tremble in the least.

"No, Miss Honeyfield, the question is a different one. What were *you* thinking, sneaking around my house in the middle of the night, gaining access to my library and…" He went silent, as his eyes fell on the treacherous little parcel. She could not really make out his facial expressions in the faint light of the candle, but Minerva thought that he looked surprised.

"I just meant to return something," she answered and deliberately ignored the other book lying at her feet. Once again, he stood much too close to her, which made it impossible for her to relax. Whenever he was present, she had the feeling that she was the centre of his attention, much like a rabbit who was the prey of a hound.

"What are you talking about?"

Impatiently, she nodded towards the package with her head. "The notebook, ink and quills that you left beneath my pillow."

He seemed to take a minute to understand what Minerva was talking about. It was highly peculiar. Had he already forgotten what he had done?

"Does this mean that you have given up your writing?" He underlined his voice with mocking regret. "What a shame. I was looking forward to stimulating conversations with you."

"It only means that I do not find it acceptable to receive gifts from a man," she had not used the word *gentleman* on purpose, "... who is engaged to another woman."

"It angers you that I am planning to get married?"

"Not at all," Minerva returned and pulled her shawl tighter in front of her chest. "You are a rational man, whose actions are not guided by his heart, but who is dictated by his calculating mind instead. I am most certain that it is the right decision to marry Lady Annabell Carlisle." Where did the certainty that her words would resonate with him, come from?

"So, you mean to say that I never follow my heart?"

The intimacy of their night-time encounter caused Minerva to say the first thing that came to her mind.

"I believe that your wife's death has hurt you much more than you realise and that, for this very reason, you are striving to not enter your next marriage with a deep connection to the woman who is going to be your second wife."

"You really should write novels," he determined, before he fell silent. This silence between them stretched out to the point where Minerva could no longer take it. She lifted her head. She wanted to say something, but she could not find the right words, as the duke had lowered his head. She noticed every single detail she had not noticed before. The shimmering golden stubble of his beard and the colour of his lips, which even a young lady would envy. His eyebrows were shaped in perfect arches, she thought dreamily, and she regretted that his eyelids were slightly lowered. Seeing the sparkling gold spatters in his hazelnut-brown eyes this close would have been a true spectacle. Where did the sudden heat she felt come from, the closer his lips came?

A quiet sigh escaped her, and in this long and yet much too short moment, even if she had wanted to, she would not have been able to move. It was good that his hands circled her waist, for Minerva's legs threatened to collapse under her.

Long after she had returned to her room, she could still feel his lips on hers.

CHAPTER 13

H is gaze burned like fire, his eyes shimmered diabolically.

IT HAD ONLY BEEN A KISS, but it had changed everything.

Minerva only noted her aunt's departure in passing, as if it happened in a dream. Her aunt had realised sour-heartedly that she was no longer needed, now that the Duke of Scuffold could accept the help of his sister-in-law. Minerva's body made all the correct moves, her mouth said all the correct things, but none of what was happening around Minerva reached her inside.

Her mother had decided to stay. "Although the duke regrets that your aunt had to go back home, he was still kind enough to renew his invitation to you and me both," she told Minerva during their breakfast. They sat alone at a grand table, and their conversation was only broken when one of the servants asked what their wishes were. "I am so very glad that you have finally made the acquaintance of a gentleman, whom you like. And what's more, he is a duke, no less!" Her mother seemed to accept Minerva's requirements for a husband, which – so far – she had found rather unnerving.

"Mama, he has not proposed to me," Minerva replied, "... and he will not, because he has asked the Duke of Evesham for his daughter's hand in marriage."

"Oh, I am sure that he will present the question of all questions to you very soon," Lady Beaufort said, as she joined them at the table. "Good morning to you, Mrs Honeyfield, Miss Honeyfield."

A servant appeared at her side and filled her cup with steaming hot tea. In the bright daylight the woman had not lost any of the beauty that Minerva had noticed the evening before. Lady Beaufort had already passed the peak of her youth, and she was closer to forty years of age than thirty, but she took her place in the bright light of day without any reserve. Her hair had almost the same colour as her husband, a warm tone of brown with a slightly reddish shimmer, but on her it looked elegant. Neither her figure, nor her attitude followed the current fashion. With her voluptuous curves, deep voice, and unusually outspoken and direct manner of address, she was more than just a particularly fascinating personality.

Minerva found her extremely likeable, and she was pleased when Lady Beaufort asked her to accompany her on a short walk in the park after breakfast.

"Of course you may go," her mother agreed, when Minerva looked at her with pleading eyes. "I still have to speak to the duke's administrator about some details regarding his servants. The duke's servants, not the administrator's, of course." She laughed nervously when she realised that with the arrival of Lady Beaufort, who was a female relative of the duke, her interventions were no longer necessary.

Minerva noticed how she was trying to find escape, not to have to face "the question of all questions", as Lady Beaufort had called it, as the future mother-in-law of the Duke of Scuffold.

The lady laughed loudly when she realised the unfortunate situation into which Minerva's mother had manoeuvred herself. It was a cheerful laugh, without malice. "Please do not worry, Mrs Honeyfield. I am more than grateful to you for relieving me of this rather tedious chore." Minerva noticed that she had not eaten anything but only taken a few sips of her tea.

"Ah, here is my husband," Lady Beaufort said and held out her hand for him to kiss. Minerva saw his eyes light up and felt a slight sting of envy. These two had such a strong connection, and it was based on more than just "rational" or even economically beneficial considerations.

The way he held her hand, how his eyes searched for her face and how she half closed hers – all this told of a marriage of love. "I shall kidnap your daughter and take her into the park, if you will allow me, and I shall leave you in the company of my husband. Please, do not bore Mrs Honeyfield with your stories from the club, Thomas," she advised her husband facetiously and rose from her seat.

"Oh, there can be no question of it," Minerva's mother objected. "I like listening to a gentleman telling stories about his experiences. It widens a woman's horizon, wouldn't you agree, Lady Beaufort?"

"I do believe that it all depends on the stories. The ones my husband likes to tell," she gazed at him with a penetrating look, "... are most often unsuitable for a woman's tender ears."

At that moment, the duke entered the room, which meant that her mother did not have to answer, and Minerva forgot everything she had wanted to ask Lady Beaufort.

The kiss had changed her perception of him completely, maybe even the way she viewed the world. Her heart beat longingly at the sight of him, and she had the feeling that even the sun was shining brighter than it had earlier.

Today, he wore his comfortable clothing again, which she had secretly called "his gamekeeper outfit". Soft breeches, the tweed jacket she was already familiar with, and some old, but still immaculate leather boots. Although his necktie was correctly tied, it still had something unexplainably casual about it.

He looked wonderfully vibrant – the way he entered the room with long, far-reaching strides, his eyes passing over the assembled guests, only to stop and linger on her. Minerva swallowed hard. Why did she realise only now how intriguing she found him, after she had learned that he was promised to another? At the next available opportunity, she would have to demand that he clarify the situation. His brother and his wife, as well as her mother, all assumed that he, in his own strange way, was courting Minerva. The longer this game went on, the more disappointed her mother would be, not to mention the fact that he – and for as long as she played along, she too – were deceiving his relatives.

Silently, she decided to give him two more days, before she would announce the truth to the world, which was the fact that he had only invited her as entertainment for his future wife.

In the meantime, she had to find out why he had kissed her last night. Because today his face showed no signs of the intimacy they had shared yesterday. How could he keep himself under control like that? Her knees were buckling beneath her, her heart hammered painfully against her chest and corset, and her breath was shallow and taken in short agitated intervals.

"Good morning," he said, greeting everyone after a

seemingly endless pause. He only noticed now that Minerva and his sister-in-law had gotten up from their seats. "May I ask, what are your plans?"

"Miss Honeyfield and I will take a stroll through the park, which will give us an opportunity to get to know each other a little better," Lady Beaufort replied, before Minerva had the chance to utter a word. The hazelnut-golden eyes turned towards his sister-in-law's lovely face.

"I advise against it," he grunted. "There are clouds mounting, and it will start to rain soon." This was utter nonsense. Through the terrace doors Minerva saw bright sunshine. His ill humour seemed to disintegrate with every minute that passed without an answer. Was she the reason behind his distant behaviour? No, Minerva could not and did not want to believe that. After all, he had been the one who had initiated the touching of their lips. She had not provoked him in any way.

"We will not stray too far from the house," she said and realised how breathless she sounded. Her gaze was glued to his face, desperately searching for a sign of recognition. Robert had kissed her, but the man that stood before her now, was the Duke of Scuffold again.

A dangerous man, as her aunt had never grown tired of reminding her.

Maybe Aunt Catherine had been right all this time.

Only a man of dubious morality would kiss a lady at night and act as if nothing had happened the next morning.

Another thought came to her. If Aunt Catherine had been right in her poor regard of the man, maybe her suspicion that the duke had murdered his wife was not far from the truth. Suddenly, and despite the warm sunshine, Minerva felt ice-cold, and she wanted to get away from this man, who had the ability to confuse her more and more with every hour she spent in his company.

"I do have a parasol with me, which will shield us from the worst weather conditions." Lady Beaufort went to push past the duke, who had no other choice but to let her and Minerva pass, if he did not want to appear disrespectfully impolite.

Long after the two ladies had left his view, Minerva felt his eyes burning on the back of her head.

"Please tell me dear... how did you make the acquaintance of the duke?" Lady Beaufort enquired. She had linked arms with Minerva and taken the lead. Even though she was half a head taller than Minerva and walked with a forceful step, she did not give her the impression that she was an unwelcoming afterthought.

Should she speak openly to a woman she had just met and who stood so far above her in rank? Minerva had never really cared much about titles, and in the safety of her wealthy parents' house, she had always looked upon them rather carelessly – that was until she had met the Duke of Scuffold.

"It was an accidental encounter," she said evasively.

Lady Beaufort's head turned away from the beautiful surroundings and towards her. Her piercing green eyes sparkled when she spoke. "How old are you, Miss Honeyfield?"

"I am twenty years old."

"So young," her companion sighed as she slowed down her steps. "Please allow me to speak openly to you." This was not a request, but merely a statement. Minerva looked at the woman beside her, curiously, and she wondered what kind of warning and what kind of advice she might hear now.

"I am six-and-thirty years old," the woman announced. There was unmistakeable pride in her voice. The short pause would have given Minerva the opportunity to assure Lady Beaufort that nobody would ever consider her that age and that she looked radiant still, but she let the moment pass in silence. "I met my husband in Budapest." Her eyelids lowered as she recalled a memory too precious to share with others. "I was standing on stage, playing the role of Cupid, after the original cast member had fallen ill. It was the first and last time that I was in a leading role on the stage. That same evening, Lord Beaufort gained access to my dressing room and asked me to become his wife." Proudly, and yet slightly sadly, she lifted her head and stared out into the lush green landscape. "As you can see, I gave in to his courtship. It truly was a whirlwind romance, and to this day, I do not regret a single moment – with one exception." It seemed fitting, Minerva thought, that this woman had once stood on a stage. She wondered if her mother knew anything about Lady Beaufort's colourful past and if she generously ignored it, now that her daughter had the opportunity to become a duchess. "I was a good singer – a very good one, actually – and I could have gone a long way. I do not have a life of my own, if you will, besides being the wife of my husband. I have not received any children, which could have made me something else but Lady Beaufort, the wife of Lord Beaufort."

They had reached another fork in the pathway, and Minerva realised that they had walked further away from the house than she had anticipated.

"So, are you trying to advise me against marrying the duke?" Not that it would ever happen, no. It was curiosity that led Minerva to ask the question, not hope.

"Not if you genuinely hold him dear," Lady Beaufort replied. "But, if you ever want to achieve something in your life, if you strive for more than being the property of your husband, then my answer would be yes. Then I would advise you against marrying him."

Minerva felt a strange coldness, not only because the sun had disappeared behind the clouds – just as *he* had predicted. "The duke does not seem a man who would disallow his wife a pastime, such as writing, purely for conventional reasons," she tried to answer tentatively as she watched her companion's reaction.

"Oh no," the duchess replied, and for a moment she

released Minerva's arm to open up the little parasol that she had brought. As if she had jinxed it, the first drops of rain fell from the sky. "He does not care much about the opinions of the Beau Monde. However," she leaned her head trustingly towards Minerva and lowered her voice, "… if you give him your hand in marriage, you will be his. Wholly, completely, body and soul, or neck and crop, as they say back home. He is," her green eyes bore into Minerva's, "… a *rather* possessive type of man, if you understand what I mean."

So, all in all, Lady Beaufort advised her against marrying the duke, even though she had seemed so pleased less than half an hour ago. Minerva felt hysterical laughter rising in her chest. Her mother was already planning her wedding that would never take place, and Lady Beaufort was trying to warn her against a man, who had no intentions but to play with her feelings. How much more did she yet have to learn, before she would be able to walk the thin ice that accompanied choosing a suitable husband? Another thought sent shivers down her spine. Every single person seemed to have a different opinion of the duke. He had shown a different face to each individual, but which one was his true countenance?

He appeared arrogant and sometimes even dangerous; he mocked and challenged her. He was a man like no other, who had shown her his dark side at their first encounter, and now he was planning to marry Lady Annabell. At the same time, she was standing here, in his grounds, wondering if she had not been wrong about him. A man who could kiss in a way that she would never be able to forget for the rest of her life and compare every future kiss with the touch of his lips against hers – could not possibly be an entirely evil person.

She had remained silent for a long time, but now it could no longer pass as a mark of polite consideration. "But maybe I am wrong about him and he has changed," Lady Beaufort said.

"Have you known him for a long time?" The answer to the question was obvious, but Minerva wanted to steer the conversation in a different direction. "Please forgive my directness, Lady Beaufort, but you give me the impression that I may speak to you freely." She paused for a moment to see how the tall woman would react. Encouraged by her friendly, although slightly reserved smile, Minerva continued. "How did the duke react when he learned of your marriage to his brother? I am not asking out of curiosity alone, but because I find it difficult to read him. Anything that will help me understand his personality, would be very much appreciated," she tried to explain.

"At first, and just like everyone else, he thought of me as too adventurous," Lady Beaufort admitted. Her voice sounded as calm as before. "I have to thank his late wife for changing his opinion about me. She was very similar to you, you know – not on the outside, but very much in her equally free spirit and ready to give any person a chance regardless of their background. She was also writing a novel. Did he tell you about that?"

"No," Minerva replied calmly, despite the thoughts that were racing through her head. "Maybe we should go back to the house," she suggested. "The cold wind is harsher than I anticipated." The hem of her dress, as well as her shoes, were soaking wet by now. Lady Beaufort did not seem to mind the cold, or the light rain. Quite the opposite, she seemed to enjoy it and held her face defiantly into the drops. For what purpose she had brought her parasol along at all, exceeded Minerva's knowledge.

"I do believe that my brother-in-law is already

searching for you. Look there... that is him, is it not?" She pointed at a man who was coming towards them from Beaufort Castle with rapid pace. "Do you see what I was trying to tell you? He does not allow you to give your attention to anyone other than him. I urge you not to give your consent to giving him your hand in marriage."

Minerva looked from her to the man, who was closing the distance between them. With a smile, Lady Beaufort said goodbye to her, shortly before he reached them. She wanted to stroll a bit further, she said, and that the cool air and rain did not bother her. She was not worried about Minerva, since, after all, she was now in the care of a man who wanted to protect her from every little brush of air.

Since the Duke of Scuffold had stepped into her life, it had been a constant up and down. Fear was replaced by hope. Dejection was pushed aside by an exuberant joy for life.

In the presence of this man, mediocrity was not an option, there were only extremes – and if she was entirely truthful to herself, that was exactly what she liked about him. There were too many boring men in this world, such as Mr Meade, whose face she had already forgotten.

Now he stood beside her. He watched the departing figure of Lady Beaufort, before he took his jacket from his shoulders and draped it around Minerva's. Her mother would have been delighted, and Minerva was not immune to his gesture either – at least until he spoke.

"What has my sister-in-law told you?" The words came out of his mouth harshly and in the same harrying tone that she had heard him use before.

"She has advised me to give good thought to whether a potential proposal should be accepted or denied," she replied. She saw all kinds of different emotions rapidly flash across his face, only to give way to an expression of complete emptiness.

"Your visit to Beaufort Castle ends, here and now," he said, without replying to her words. "It was a mistake to invite you and your mother to come here."

The sudden feeling of rejection burned like fire, deep inside her chest. At first, she just wanted to do nothing but walk back in silence, but then she could not stand it anymore and stopped abruptly in her tracks. She was wet through from the rain and felt so cold that her teeth chattered, but she ignored her physical feelings. His scent, which rose from his jacket, engulfed her entirely, and Minerva felt almost compelled to close her eyes and dream herself into another world, where there were no dark secrets.

"You have no heart," she said and found the strength to hand him back his jacket, but he shook his head and draped it across her shoulders for a second time.

"We should go back to the house. I do not want to be responsible for your ending up catching a fever and having to stay in bed. Just for your information – I *do* have a heart, as you should know by now."

Was he referring to the kiss? "If that is true, then why are you playing with me?"

"Who says that this is a game?" he remarked and pushed her forward relentlessly as he quickened his own step. "Something quite the opposite is happening here. If this had any entertainment value whatsoever for me, comparable to a game of chess, then you would be in danger of being knocked off the board."

Minerva did not appreciate the comparison, and even less the direction his thoughts took, since they were much too similar to her own from the beginning of their acquaintance. "In this regard, you seem to have a lot of practise," she said. "You have manipulated me from the beginning – you have lied to me and, as if it were not enough, you have used my family to achieve a goal of whatever kind. Was it really absolutely necessary to employ my uncle in the task and to request my aunt's help, just so they would be favourably inclined towards you?"

"Would you have preferred, instead, if I had forced you to come and meet me in secrecy behind your family's back, as I did before?"

Minerva exhaled slowly, to calm her nerves. "No, but there would have been a thousand other opportunities," she said, and she noticed that he slowed his pace the closer they got to the house.

"Of course, your family would have welcomed me with open arms, as the Duke of Scuffold – the man who murdered his wife out of jealousy, and who now lives his sinful life for everybody to see," he retorted mockingly.

"Do you honestly believe that I was not aware of that?" He was right, but none of that explained his reasoning and why he had started this disturbing charade in the first place. When was the best time to ask him about this, if not now? "You have purposefully awoken hopes of marriage in my mother that you will not fulfill. You know exactly, how much some people care about a noble title."

"Some people, or your mother?"

"Of course my mother is not free of faults, but she is exactly that: a mother, and as such, she and my father want what is best for their only child. I assume that you can understand that."

He fell silent and frowned, but this was the only reaction Minerva received from him after her passionate words.

"Very well. I shall inform my mother, at once, that we are no longer welcome at Beaufort Castle," Minerva returned to the beginning of their conversation. The relief in his eyes was so intense that she felt the emotion as if it were her own. Suddenly, Minerva realised what she had been doing: She had spoken privately with a man, who was ominous at best and probably unscrupulous in all interpretations. Did she even want to know the true reasons for his invitation or to be told his perfidious plans? She closed her eyes. Her thoughts went around in circles, without giving her the slightest clue or logical reason for his skittishness.

However, it was too late to take it back now.

The Duke of Scuffold had also remarked that their time together was nearing the end.

"Will you promise me that you will leave promptly?" He studied her carefully, and it seemed as if he was fighting some inner struggle. "Very well," he murmured more to himself than towards Minerva. Golden eyes found her blue ones and held them captive. "I *would* like to get to know you better, Miss Honeyfield. Would you allow me to court you, when all of this is over?"

The shock flooded her body like a surprising wave. At first, Minerva felt cold, then warm. There was nothing but sincerity in his voice, and he turned his body, leaning slightly towards her and shielding her from the rain. She tried to say "Yes", but she only managed a curt nod. He raised his eyebrows and did not wait for her answer, but instead he held her hand to his lips. Whilst Minerva savoured the warmth of his touch, she also realised that she actually believed him; however, his question had not answered any of hers. In fact, it had only raised even more questions than before.

They both turned around as they heard footsteps. A man – was it Johnson? – was running towards them. Visibly agitated, he stopped at a short distance from the duke. His gaze was mostly calm, but his voice vibrated with urgency. "Sir, your presence is required." Johnson's eyes flicked nervously towards Minerva. "Mrs Honeyfield isn't feeling well. We have already sent for Doctor Springfield. She... it is best to see for yourself. Sir, Miss."

Minerva started to move the second he had finished his sentence. The duke followed closely behind her. She felt his presence like a shield at her back, and she was grateful that he was there. Everything that had begun to blossom between them would now have to wait. Without looking to her left or right, she ran up the stairs towards her mother's room, but the duke caught up with her and grabbed her by her wrist. She was pulled around, and she tried to extract herself from his grip, but he held her tightly.

"I will come with you."

She was much too nervous to pay attention to any conventions. The duke reached the door before her, and he did not waste any time to knock, but he blocked her view of her mother, as she entered the room. What she heard was bad enough – the sound of fevered movement – but seeing it was even worse. Her mother lay in bed, her face was as white as a sheet of paper and shimmering from perspiration. Worse, her body was jerking in excruciating convulsions. Beside her bed stood a small bowl and its sour smell made Minerva's stomach turn. She rushed to her mother and wanted to push aside the servant, who was holding Mrs Honeyfield up, just when she had to vomit another time.

"Come," the duke said and took her arm, in an attempt to lead her from the room. "There is nothing you can do for your mother. The doctor is on his way."

"No," Minerva objected harshly and pulled a chair to the side of the bed. She did not speak another word after this last syllable, but it was enough to make the duke realise that she would not leave her mother's side.

The following two hours could not have been worse, even if Minerva had descended into hell itself. The doctor came and vigorously shooed her out of the room, only allowing her back in after he was finished examining his patient. When Minerva re-entered the room after what seemed like hours, she realised why the doctor had kept her away at all costs. The room smelled so much of bodily fluids that Minerva had to fight a rising nausea. Pillows, blankets, and sheets were soiled, and Minerva was grateful when Johnson came and began to exchange the bed linens, with the help of another man and under the doctor's supervision. They took the greatest care to transfer the sick woman onto new sheets. Before Johnson left, he discreetly opened the window a crack.

Minerva held her mother's hand, even though she was not sure if her mother even knew she was there. She grabbed a cloth to dab her mother's forehead, when she noticed a small piece of paper that had fallen to the floor. Instinctively, Minerva bent down and picked it up. The paper was sticky from confectionary sugar and chocolate. This was typical of her Mama, she thought, and almost smiled. She had always said, "I cannot go to bed without my bedtime sweets." Even here at Beaufort Castle, she had not let go of this habit of indulging herself at night. Minerva put the piece of paper aside and turned her attention towards the doctor, who was making arrangements to leave.

"Thank you, Doctor," Minerva said with tears in her eyes.

Her mother was far from being in any kind of state that could be considered healed, but her breathing sounded slightly less laborious, and the horrifying convulsions seemed to have ceased. She lay in bed with her eyes closed, in a slightly elevated position, because this would make it easier for her to breathe, the doctor explained. He also said that he would send a nurse, who would keep watch over the patient, before he said his goodbyes.

"Just a moment please," Minerva whispered, not wanting to wake her mother from her much-needed rest. "Can you say what has caused this strange attack on my mother's health?"

The man tried to avoid her gaze. "Unfortunately, I am unable to tell you, Miss Honeyfield," he said and walked towards the door. "I would advise you to speak to the duke, but without his permission I am not allowed to tell you anything." He disappeared, before she could say a word. Her first thought was to run after him, but she did not dare leave her mother alone. Although Mrs Honeyfield seemed as calm as was possible, under the circumstances, who knew what would happen if her exhausted body suffered another convulsion?

The long wait began.

CHAPTER 14

*B*etrayal was his daily bread.

AT SOME POINT, Sally slipped into the room, with deeply reddened cheeks and wide-open eyes. "Where have you been?" Minerva spoke quietly, so as not to awaken her mother. She turned away from the woman, for fear of losing the last remnants of her self-control.

"I... I am so very sorry, I was..."

"Enough," Minerva cut her off, sensing that Sally had

busied herself with something that would prove disagreeable. "We will talk later." She wrung out a cloth and dabbed her mother's forehead.

"Can I count on it that you will stay by her side, regardless of what happens?" She rose from her chair and looked at Sally. "I will not be gone for long."

"I am sorry, Miss," Sally tried quietly once more. There was hardly anything left in the face of the usually vibrant young woman, who took everything lightly, who was prone to impudence, and who ran after every possible and naughty liaison. But she was the only one Minerva could trust in this house. Sally might be somewhat reckless, but she was not malicious, Minerva thought. She also had to admit that it was partially her fault that Sally took so many liberties. She had neither kept a healthy distance as her parents kept their servants at arm's length, nor had she made the young woman a real confidant. Instead, Minerva had juggled too many balls all at once, enjoying secrets and philandering with a man, whom she had not been properly introduced to... And what had it gotten her?

A heart that had realised too late, what it wanted.

And a mother, deathly ill and bed-bound, for reasons Minerva could not yet fathom, but which, she suspected, were somehow linked to the duke's apparent courting of her.

She had overestimated herself so completely, that the mere thought of her presumption made her blush to the roots of her hair. Everything she had done and thought circled around her like the earth turned around the sun. She had wanted to become an author, and she had wanted to teach the Duke of Scuffold a lesson – at no time had she thought about her parents and what it might mean to them, to have to deal with a rebellious daughter.

That was over with now.

She would speak to the duke and then take her mother away from here as quickly as possible. As soon as her mother was able to travel, they would leave Beaufort Castle. She would marry the first candidate her parents put forward, and she would try to be a good daughter and a good wife.

"Miss?" Sally's hesitant voice interrupted Minerva's thoughts. "Is everything all right? Would you like me to send for the doctor for you? You do look a little pale, if I may say so." When had Sally stopped swallowing half of her words?

Well, that was not important right now.

"Yes," Minerva said, "... everything is all right." Nothing was all right. "I shall go and speak with the duke and ask him what the doctor told him. We will depart as soon as my mother feels well enough to travel. In the meantime, ..." she gazed at her mother, who did not show any signs of life, apart from the regular rising and falling of her chest. Seeing her waxen face confirmed Minerva's decision to behave like a grown woman from now on. "In the meantime, you will look after Mrs Honeyfield. The doctor informed me that he was sending a nurse, but you will stay with my mother until I return – regardless of what the nurse might tell you."

She closed the door behind her quietly, after she had watched Sally take her place by the side of the bed and remove the damp cloth from her mother's forehead.

The search for the duke did not turn out to be difficult. He was in the library, writing. When Minerva entered the room, he rose from his chair. She did notice that he turned the paper over, despite the fact that the ink had possibly not dried yet, which would render the document unreadable.

A few heartbeats went by, while they both silently looked at each other until he pointed towards the sofa. Minerva sat down with a stiff back. Her mother's mysterious illness had changed everything – even the way she perceived the Duke of Scuffold. For the first time, she noticed the shadows of exhaustion beneath his eyes. His mouth, usually ready to pull into a mocking smile, was now a narrow line. The masculine features of his face, the high cheekbones, and the striking chin, had taken precedence over any emotion. He was still the same man, and yet he was a different one. An aura of recklessness, which she had only assumed before, now came to light. To Minerva, he seemed like a man who would do anything to reach his goal and would relentlessly hunt down anyone in his path. What had caused this change in him?

Was it the sudden illness of her mother that had brought this other side of him to the surface? A cold hand seemed to reach for her heart. There had to be a reason. Feverishly, she tried to sort out her thoughts. The connection between what happened to her mother and his immediate character change was too obvious to ignore. His coldness and mercilessness indicated that he believed himself in danger – a danger that was posed by her mother. No, Minerva corrected herself, not by her mother herself, but from what had happened to her.

She held her breath and closed her eyes. This was another mistake in her thinking. It was not a case of something happening to her mother – *someone* had done something to her. Minerva felt ice-cold and started to shiver. Poison. Someone had tried to poison her Mama.

"I see you have divined the truth," the duke said with a flat and strangely toneless voice.

Minerva stood up. Her movements were purposefully slow. As if from far away, she thought she had to ask the duke for the use of his carriage if she wanted to leave this place. She could not, and would not, stay here under his roof, one second longer. She needed to tell Sally to pack her and her mother's belongings. If the duke were to refuse her his carriage for flimsy reasons – maybe just to keep her in his house – she would have Sally smuggle a letter to her uncle, and he would almost certainly... the world began to spin.

Two strong arms caught her and laid her gently onto the sofa. At first, she wanted to protest as he touched her legs to put them up, but the words became stuck in her throat. He carefully lifted her head and pushed a pillow underneath it, before he pulled a chair closer and sat down beside her. The situation was much too similar to that in her mother's room, where she had watched over her mother's fragile state, so she sat up slowly and waited for the dizziness to pass.

"What has the doctor told you that he was not allowed to tell me?"

He remained silent and looked at her, as if he wanted to figure out if he could trust her.

"She is my mother. I have the right to know everything."

"Mrs Honeyfield has most likely been poisoned with arsenic. Doctor Springfield said that the dose was just big enough to bring her to the brink of death, but that she will not die."

The last part of the sentence echoed inside her head. The tension was released from her shoulders, and she lowered her head, which suddenly felt incredibly heavy. "Have you informed the magistrate?" She scolded herself a fool for not thinking of it earlier and asking the doctor herself.

"No," he replied after a little hesitation, which was barely noticeable. "I have asked Doctor Springfield to keep some of the... liquid and to examine it. If this sample turns out to contain arsenic, I assure you, I will notify the authorities immediately."

Had he reacted the same way back then, when his wife had died? He did not seem to find anything out of the ordinary in his methodical behaviour, whereas Minerva, if she was truthful with herself, didn't even have a clue what to do in this situation. Still, it seemed absurd to suspect the duke. There was no reason for him to want to poison her mother.

"Your mother needs a lot of rest over the next few days," he continued and gazed at her with an odd look. "But I have already arranged for the coach to be readied and that your things are packed." He wanted to get rid of her and her mother, at all costs.

Minerva's thoughts only led to one possible conclusion: he knew who had tried to kill her mother, and he wanted to protect him or her. Despite her first inclination, she couldn't leave Beaufort Castle. She needed to stay here until she was absolutely certain who had tried to murder her mother. She wanted the culprit brought to justice, even if his lordship tried to prevent it.

"You let a servant pack my things?" He sighed, and she understood what he meant to say with that.

She had long ago crossed the borders of propriety, and an attempted murder blew the remaining conventions wide open – much more than his kiss had done. "Under no circumstances will I leave without my mother," she declared determinedly and braced herself for his wrath.

"Oh yes you will – even if I have to carry you to the carriage myself."

"No," Minerva rejected. "Do you not understand? Someone has tried to murder my mother. Not for one minute will I leave her out of my sight, until she has recovered." *And until I find out who is behind all of this*, she added in her mind.

"No? Then what are you doing here, right now?"

That hurt. Purposefully, he had put his finger exactly on the one point where she had contradicted herself.

"My maid is with her. I…" she tried to get up, "… shall return to her room right now."

He thwarted her attempt and pushed her back onto the sofa. "Not before you realise what risk you are taking. Do you really want to sit by her bedside day and night? Do you want to test every bite, before she eats it?"

"Doctor Springfield has already arranged for a nurse to help me. Sally is also there. Between the three of us, we shall manage. She will be better soon – that is what the doctor said… and…" she swallowed. "… I am scared," she finished the sentence and watched his eyes darken even more than she would have thought possible. Her admission had left her lips without her wanting it to.

"So, it is decided. I will allow you to spend this evening and the night with your mother. Should she feel well enough tomorrow to manage the short trip without endangering her health, then all the better. If not, I will send you back to your uncle's care."

He got up. His decision was final, Minerva could tell by the resolution tightening the corners of his mouth. He held his hand out towards her. "I will accompany you back to your mother, and I shall instruct my servants to look in on you regularly. Should you need anything or should your mother's health decline, you will immediately let me know, regardless of whether it is in the middle of the night or early in the morning. Are we clear on this, Miss Honeyfield?" He reminded her of a raptor, ready to pounce and attack. At the same time, he radiated something that bordered on desperation. No, that was the wrong word.

The duke was *unsettled,* and that in turn unsettled Minerva more than she wanted to admit. Was it possible that he was actually worried about her? She pushed the thought aside. Nothing in his behaviour, so far, had indicated that he saw anything other than a means to an end in her.

If it had not been for the kiss, she would have trusted her thoughts, but now a small doubt about the truth remained inside her heart. She wondered, and not for the first time, if she could trust him.

Without paying any attention to his outstretched hand, she walked past him and straight up to the room where her mother was resting. It was better to have him believe that she was angry and intimidated, when in fact she was not planning on giving in again.

She was absolutely determined to only leave Beaufort Castle when she knew for certain who had done this to her mother. If that meant that she would have to endure her doubts about the integrity of his kiss for a little while longer, then so be it.

CHAPTER 15

O *nly death would be able to release her from*
her torments.

THE NURSE ARRIVED in the early evening, and she immediately took her place by Minerva's mother's bedside. Minerva's initial mistrust of the catholic nun subsided when she watched the older woman's calm, determined manner as she tended to her mother. Nevertheless, Minerva remained by her mother's side until it was time for dinner.

With difficulty, she forced herself to eat a few bites of the food that a servant had brought up for her and

Sister Mary Magdalene. Later, when she saw that her mother had dozed off, she asked Sally to take her place.

"I will try to sleep for a few hours," she said. "When I return, you may go back to your room."

"Very well, Miss," Sally replied and even curtsied. Minerva sighed and pulled the young woman towards the door, with her.

"I know that what happened to my mother was not your fault," she said. "However, I will no longer tolerate any escapades. I am willing to take you to London as my maid, but only if you do not let yourself be distracted by any entanglements. Do you understand?"

Sally's reaction let her know that she had been right in her assumptions. The young woman had dallied with one of the blokes, of whom there were plenty here at Beaufort Castle. She blushed deeply and tears welled up in her eyes, before she lowered her head. But at the same time, she could not suppress her excitement about Minerva's suggestion. Sally's eyes gleamed with quiet joy, and it filled Minerva's chest with a warm feeling. She had done the right thing.

"I will only ask you once, and it is important that you

tell me the truth," Minerva took advantage of the favourable moment between them. "Who was the man that you met with? Was it the duke's chamberlain?" Her heart beat loudly and irregularly. It was not very likely that the duke was behind the arsenic attack on her mother, but she needed to know for sure.

"Yes," Sally replied with a whisper. They both gazed at Sister Mary Magdalene, who sat by her mother's bedside reading a book. "It was the chamberlain of his lordship. His name is Giovanni. We met in the hallway accidently, when I was on my way to the kitchen. He offered to show me the park and…"

"I understand." Minerva raised her hand. So, Lord Beaufort's servant was Italian. It was well known that some of the most notorious chemists came from that country. One only had to remember the Borgias, who had preferred to get rid of their enemies by poisoning them. This was documented in many books, so maybe there was a kernel of truth in the stories. Still, she should not forget that the assumption could turn out to be untrue. "That is enough, Sally. Thank you," she added, and her maid thanked her with a smile. Was the only reason for Sally's change her realisation of how her own promiscuity had contributed to the unfortunate chain of events? Or was it also a result of how Minerva treated her now? Possibly a combination of the two, she told herself, when she reached her room.

Her tiredness was indescribable, and yet she did not sleep. Whenever she closed her eyes, her mother's face appeared before her, contorted with pain. If it was not this agonizing image, then it was the Duke's features dancing before her eyes – they were angry, then mocking and lastly, challenging. Even as she began to count backwards from one hundred, the unwelcome thoughts kept pushing into her mind.

IT DID NOT HELP – she couldn't sleep. Minerva got up, and this time she did not forget her slippers complementing her nightclothes along with her shawl. The fire in her fireplace had long since died out, and as soon as she crawled out of the warmth of her bed, she was surrounded by cold air. She padded towards her small desk and pulled her notebook out from its secret hiding place, which was not really a hiding place at all.

Since Lady Helen Fitzpatrick's scandalous correspondence with her lover had come to light, everybody knew about the so-called "secret hiding places" in desks. Minerva opened the last page of her shamefully neglected novel. Too bad, she did not have quills or ink at her disposal. A search in the little drawers and compartments of the desk were unsuccessful. However, she knew exactly where she had last seen ink and quills. She had once before found her way to the library in the dark, she should be able to succeed a second time.

She peeked carefully out into the corridor. A movement near the end of the hallway startled her, but when she gathered all her courage and peeked around the corner of her door a second time, everything remained silent. She was not afraid of the stranger who had poisoned her mother. A man (or even a woman – anything was possible) who used poison, would most likely try to avoid a direct confrontation. She kept telling herself this over and over, as she descended the stairs with nothing but a candle in her hand. In the flickering light, the two suits of armour on the stairs almost looked alive, especially since the duke had not just arranged them in a lifeless guard position. No, he had preferred to present the overly large metal limbs in the middle of an attack position, with their swords raised.

For a man, whose family motto was 'Attempto!' which meant 'I shall dare', this was hardly surprising.

Minerva let out the breath she had held when she finally reached the library. All her thoughts about the coward and his poisonous concoctions did not distract her from being afraid of her own shadow in the dark, cold building. Quietly, she opened the door. The scent of old paper never failed to calm her jittery nerves. She walked quickly through the room, stopped by the desk and began to search for the two items she needed. In fact, she found both ink and a selection of different sized quills and was about to reach for them when another thought occurred to her. She set her candle down on the desk, pushed aside the swanky oak chair and stared at the papers laid out before her with a racing pulse. Earlier, the duke had tried to hide a letter from her. What were the chances that the letter contained information that would reveal the name of the person who had poisoned her mother? It was not unlikely that the duke had already dispatched said letter by now. Worse, it may contain information of a deeply personal nature.

Should she and could she resort to such an immoral measure?

She would never find out, if she continued to stare at the table, wrestling with herself and her conscience. Determined, she searched through the small stack of papers that lay openly on the top of the desk. No, this would have been too easy. She sank into the sumptuous chair (which was surprisingly comfortable) and hesitantly stretched out one of her hands. There it was – the slight indentation underneath the desk's table top that she had been looking for.

With a sound that sounded deafeningly loud in the silence of the library, the secret compartment opened.

What she found was not a half-written letter, but an old book, bound in dark leather and adorned with a golden vignette. On its binding, she found the Scuffold family crest, as well as their motto. The initials, 'RS', were stamped into the leather.

Minerva's first impulse was to return the book to its original hiding spot, to lock the compartment, and to hurry back to the safety of her room.

Her second thought, however, made her hesitate.

What, if *not* his diary, would show her a true picture of the man who was constantly escaping her? Decided, she pressed it against her wildly pounding heart and sat down on the sofa, the candle right on the small table next to her. With her fingertips she opened the first page.

Tomorrow, I shall be the happiest man in the world.

Startled, she almost closed the book again. Reading the sentence and knowing that he had written it, made her think that these were the words of a man she did not know. A much younger, more cheerful Duke of Scuffold spoke to her from this very first line.

She brushed aside a string of her hair from her damp forehead and realised that her hands were shaking so much that the letters before her eyes danced.

Then Minerva thought about her mother and about the person who was responsible for her misery. She continued reading.

Tomorrow, Julianna Grey will become my lawfully wedded wife, and I cannot wait to call her mine. The exquisite joy she gives me, I shall reciprocate with a devotion that is unequalled on this earth. Her spirit shall guide me to joy and kindness; her body shall become my temple of pure devotion.

Minerva giggled nervously, and she felt heat creeping up her cheeks and spreading across her chest. What had she expected, on reading the duke's personal journal? Bravely, she scanned across the following pages, where the duke had poured out his heart in detail, regarding his future marital bliss. Apparently, the duke took his marital responsibilities exceedingly seriously, and it seemed that his attentions had been received with ample gratitude. Minerva skipped a few pages and was just wondering whether the duke had also filled the remaining pages with praise and extolments of Julianna's physical assets as well as her passion, when she landed on the latest entry. Confused, she looked back. No, she had not been wrong. The last entry before this one had been over a month ago. She lowered her head and began to read, more attentively.

I do not know what is happening with Julianna. Since she decided to emulate Mrs Radcliffe's success and began her work on her novel, she has changed. She is retreating from me more and more. Where at the beginning we still read what she had written together and come up with the next part of the story, she is now closed off and only reluctantly reveals what she puts on paper. I have considered gaining access to her work and reading it behind her back, but, I do not want to betray her (nor my dignity) by doing so. I shall be patient.

Hmm. Who had told her that the duke's first wife had also liked to write? She could not think of it – although she knew that it had been merely a few days ago, if not hours.

My brother and his wife came to visit. I was surprised at how pleasant the new Lady Beaufort is – I expected a more adventurous woman, who only married my little brother for his title and money. Despite her past as a stage actress (which she doesn't seem to be concerned about – quite the opposite, she seems outrageously proud of it), Julianna and I have enjoyed these past few days together very much. To see my younger brother cheerful and away from the gambling tables, which could have been his ruin, makes me indulgent in a manner our father would never have been.

Also, it is quite apparent by the way they interact with each other, that their feelings   for each other are heartfelt and true, as is the case between Julianna and me.

A thick blotch of ink had made the next two words un-readable. However, what followed after, was clearly written, although in an agitated hand.

... how it once had been, I should rather say. My wife is becoming more and more estranged. She is increasingly retreating from me and even denies me. It has probably been a month since we last shared our bed, and I must admit that it was a rather un-pleasant affair. Instead of accepting me with all of her passion as I was used to, she seemed to endure my affections, rather than to yearn for her release.

Minerva did not fully understand what he was talking about, and she would have gladly skipped this partic-ular passage, if it had not been for the feeling that she was closing in on something important.

I have asked her over and over why she was chang-ing, but she refuses to give me an answer other than "You will not understand". In a marriage, which started as lovingly as ours, is there any worse sen-tence than this? I do not understand her any longer, and she does not think it worthwhile to share her worries with me. All I know is that, in a bewitched way, it has to do with that book of hers. There are times when I catch her staring at the empty pages with despair, as if she hoped that they would magically fill with words. At other times she writes furiously to the point of absolute exhaustion, and she will not eat, and just drinks tea, all the while getting thinner and thinner.

This was followed by yet another long pause, where he had not written anything.

Thomas and his wife came to visit, but only stayed for a short time, before they left for Beaufort House in London. During their visit, it seemed for a while that Julianna was again the woman, whom I fell in love with. She was cheerful, almost happy, and she devoted only one or two hours a day to writing. But only a few days after Thomas and his wife left, everything changed. It seems to me that Julianna is seized by a strange restlessness that can not be re-strained. She cries, or she is unusually harsh to the servants – or she allows them a familiarity that is inappropriate. There are hours when I am certain that she is mentally unwell and in need of treat-ment, and yet I can not bring myself to consult a specialist.

Minerva swallowed hard. This meant that the duke's love for his wife was cooling off, even though it was not completely gone. Still, he did think about having her committed. A shiver ran down her spine as she remembered reading half an article in the newspaper, before her father had taken it away from her. Bedlam, the big insane asylum in London, had been opened to visitors for a viewing, which is what the unscrupulous reporter had done, and he had not held back about what he had seen. Hastily, Minerva kept on reading in the dwindling candlelight. There was another long gap before the next entry. She closed her eyes for a second, imagining the misery, the lack of love, in a marriage that had started so lovingly.

I forbid her to write.

It was just one sentence on that date, and it cut Minerva right to her core. After this, six weeks passed without an entry.

Thomas says that I should leave her be and that there is no point in opposing the will of a woman. This seems to be the secret of his marital bliss, but he has always been the more lenient of us. I cannot sit back and watch my wife sink into ill health and misery, without trying to do something about it. In a way, he might be right, since my writing ban has done nothing other than making Julianna even more restless and irritable. The presence of her sister-in-law seems to do her good, just as much as that of my easy-going, always cheerful brother. We spent a few days together and her carefree demeanour reminded me of our first year of being married. However, as soon as the two had said their goodbyes, she immediately fell back into her old ways and retreated from me.

Five weeks later, Julianna informed him that she was expecting his child. His exuberant words burned themselves into Minerva's memory, and although she knew the outcome of the story, she hoped for a happy ending for the two of them, regardless. His deeply honest, direct way of writing evoked so many emotions within her that it was hard to bear.

And of course, the next blow followed.

She told me that she wants to leave me. She does not love me anymore, I am not the man with whom she can be happy for the rest of her life. I am too shallow, and I do not understand her way of living. She says that she had to deny all her true feelings in my presence. I have asked my brother and his wife to come and visit, hoping that they can exert their moderating influence on Julianna and dissuade her from leaving me. The scandal does not scare me, but I worry that she will not be able to live without my help. Even now that I no longer love her the way I once did, I cannot look upon her with indifference.

The last sentence made Minerva cry.

Julianna was buried today, and I'm to blame for her death.

CHAPTER 16

W̶ho was this man, who acted dark and unapproachable, and who hunted her mercilessly like a hunter hunts its prey?

MINERVA'S THOUGHTS were making her dizzy.

How much of the loving man, who the Duke of Scuffold had once been, was still in him today? And how much had died together with his first wife? She closed the book and put it back into its hiding place. The journal had closed some gaps, but not all of them. Minerva finally had an idea what had sparked his interest in her. It had been the one similarity, the one thing she and Julianna had in common: writing.

The most important question remained unanswered, namely, whether he had murdered his wife. The duke had written that he was guilty of her death, but that only meant that he *felt* guilty. He had prohibited his wife from writing, and in the end, he had lost his love for her. These things were enough to burden a sentient man's conscious reason. After all, he had been capable of deep and passionate love. From each line, from each of his words, spoke a man who was not unfamiliar with emotions.

She shook her head when another thought came to her, and she quietly closed the library door behind her. A little more than three years had passed since his wife's death, and now he wanted to marry again. Not her, but Lady Annabell Carlisle – but apart from the two of them, no one else knew. Everybody considered *her* the bride of the duke. Her mother had been poisoned, and to Minerva, there was only one conclusion: Someone did not approve of his marriage plans. It seemed all the more obvious to Minerva that the death of his first wife, who had been hovering on the verge of insanity, was somehow connected to the events of the last few days. If only she could discover what the connection between the present and the past was! Another detail was clear to her: The duke could not have poisoned her mother, since he knew that their supposed engagement was not real. If he was not the murderer, it had to be someone else – someone who had been present – both back then and now.

She had reached her mother's room and knocked quietly before entering. Everything was peaceful. Sister Mary Magdalene nodded towards her, put her finger to her lips, and got up. Sally looked so exhausted that Minerva felt yet another stab of bad conscience. She had burdened Sally with too much in her new role, first as a maid, then as a chaperone standing guard by her mother's side.

Sister Mary Magdalene drew Minerva outside into the corridor. "Your mother is doing well. I think that she will wake up sometime tomorrow. If you wish, you may go to bed and rest."

"Thank you, that is very kind of you," she replied. "... but I would like to be with my mother, just in case she wakes up." In addition, she had promised Sally that she would switch places with her, which seemed necessary at this point. The young woman may have still been awake, but Minerva noticed that her eyes kept falling.

So, she sent Sally to bed and got comfortable in one of the chairs. The faint smell of camphor, the darkened atmosphere, and the regular, soft breathing of her mother felt like a balm for her shaken soul.

* * *

SHE FELT as if she had fallen only shortly asleep when sister Mary Magadalene gently touched her arm. "Your mother is awake, and she is asking for you," she said. Immediately, Minerva's tiredness gave way to relief. She suppressed her rising tears and went to sit by her mother's bedside.

Her mother gave her a weak smile, which she returned.

"Are you thirsty? Would you like something to eat?"

Sister Mary Magdalene cleared her throat. "I shall inform the kitchen personnel to send a broth or a light pudding. In the meantime, Miss Honeyfield, please be careful not to overly exhaust the patient. She is still very weak." This meant that her mother was not yet able to travel. Their departure would be delayed by at least one more day.

"Would you please also send for Doctor Springfield?" Minerva asked the sister and handed her mother a glass of water, which she drank in small sips, with Minerva supporting her. Her mother's appearance almost broke Minerva's heart. Mrs Honeyfield had always been a lively woman, full of vitality – but, right now, Minerva glimpsed how her mother would look as an old woman. The lines around her mouth had deepened, her face was pale, and there were dark shadows beneath her eyes. The quiet clicking of the door let Minerva know that she and her mother were now alone.

"How are you feeling, Mama?"

"Better," her mother answered, unusually sparing with her words. She asked Minerva to fluff up her pillow at her back, so that she could sit up a little more. "Thank you, darling." Not only Minerva, but her mother also seemed to be as soft and yielding as she had not been for a long time. For a short while, neither spoke, both sunk into their own thoughts. Minerva feverishly tried to think of a way to ask her mother about the events prior to her being poisoned, without upsetting her unnecessarily. Then again, it seemed almost impossible not to tell her mother about the danger she had been in – and possibly still was.

She was just about to say something, when there was a knock at the door and a servant appeared, closely followed by Sister Mary Magdalene. "His lordship requests your presence in the library, Miss," the servant said, seeming to wait for an answer. Minerva asked him to tell the duke that she would be with him in a short while.

She released her mother into the sister's care and was grateful for the delay that the duke's command had given her. After all, it was no easy task to tell her own mother that someone had tried to murder her. Minerva hurried into her room, washed her face, and put on a new dress, with Sally's help. The green batiste dress was light and quickly put on, without her and her maid having to waste endless minutes with long ribbons or tiring rows of buttons. Sally held out the matching slippers, and Minerva thanked her.

"Have you had anything to eat yet? If not, go to the kitchen and have them bring you something to my mother's room. I do not want you to pass out from exhaustion." Sally looked as if she wanted to ask Minerva if everything was all right but decided against it.

"Are you sure that you do not want me to accompany you to the Duke of Scuffold?"

Minerva shook her head. "No, that will not be necessary. My mother needs you more than I do," she said and left the room. Her feet almost found their way to the library on their own, or at least that is what it felt like to her. A servant was waiting in front of the door and opened it for Minerva.

The duke stood with his back towards her, and he was staring outside the window, engulfed in his thoughts. "I hear that your mother has woken," he said without looking at her. He reached out and motioned her to come to him. Hesitantly, she stepped closer. The blood rushed in her veins and as always in his presence, he claimed all her thoughts for himself. "I shall wait for Doctor Springfield's report, however, I would like to see you gone from this house sooner rather than later." His words sounded bitter.

In light of what she had learned about him during the past night, it was not surprising. Every room, every hallway harboured memories of his first wife and of their failed marriage, as well as her tragic death.

"I would prefer to stay," she replied, her heart pounding in her chest, moving so close to him that only an inch separated them.

"Even now, after your mother was poisoned and you read my diary?"

Minerva flinched and retreated back a step. "How did you find out?" she gasped.

The duke followed her. "I shall be damned, if I tell you. What were you thinking, doing such a thing?"

"I could ask you exactly the same thing," Minerva returned haughtily, and she refused to take another step back from him. She raised her head and looked directly into his eyes. "There is not one question that you have bothered to answer me," she said.

"Your claim is incorrect. You once asked me what I wanted from you, and I have answered that I would like to court you."

"Of course," Minerva replied, "... and you seem to have

conveniently forgotten that you promised to marry the daughter of a friend. That was just the kind of answer aimed at distracting a young woman from asking too many questions." The more she spoke, the lighter her heart felt. "I do not believe one word you say, your Grace. Please excuse me. I have to go and look after my mother."

"You will stay," he ordered and led her to one of the chairs. "You want to know the truth?" He laughed, but there was no amusement in the sound. "Then let me repeat the question I asked you at the very beginning of our acquaintance. Are you brave? More specifically, are you brave not only when it comes to the characters in your novel, but also to yourself?"

What did he mean by that?

"I do not understand what you are asking. Tell me why I am here. Please tell me what you are planning with this sick little game of yours."

"I am trying to expose the murderer of my wife."

Minerva was glad that she was sitting. Her head spun, but her uppermost feeling was the realisation that he had not killed his wife. Assuming it with her heart was one thing – hearing it straight from his mouth was another. She wanted to cheer, to cry, to reprimand him, all at the same time. The rising emotions were so intense that she felt dizzy.

"What role do I play in this scenario?" she asked.

"You, Miss Honeyfield, are the bait."

CHAPTER 17

*T*he duke sneered down at Marianne, who lay before him in chains. "Now you are finally mine," he said. His laugh echoed gruesomely off the walls of the dark dungeon.

"Explain yourself."

The sentence sounded much harsher than she had wanted it to, but how else was she supposed to react to his shocking admission? The Duke of Scuffold had an extraordinary talent for knocking her off balance. If she was completely honest with herself, she had anticipated something of this nature... just not *this* extreme.

It also meant that his affections towards her had only been a pretence.

Even the kiss had been part of his plan. As soon as the message had reached him that his friend, the Duke of Evesham, and his daughter's arrival would be delayed, the Duke of Scuffold needed someone else to play the role of his future wife. The realisation left a bitter taste on her tongue, but it was nothing compared to the acidity of the bitter treachery that spread throughout her body.

"At first it was nothing but a ploy," he said, and got up to instruct the man waiting in front of the door, in a low voice that she could not hear. When he returned, he moved his chair closer to hers and took her hand. "I saw you in the woods and was angry at the audacity with which you seized my wife's favourite spot. When I learned that you were also writing a novel, well... my first instinct had been to simply chase you off my land. However, then I saw that you were different – different from Julianna." He did not take his eyes away from her for a moment, as Minerva had expected at the mention of his wife. Again, Minerva wondered if he was perhaps versed in the art of mesmerism, because she was unable to avert her gaze away from him.

"Young and innocent and full of life. For you, writing is more than just a way to escape from life. You actually put all of your heart into your words – I can feel that."

Maybe it had been the same for Julianna, Minerva thought, and he had taken away the foundation of her life by forbidding her to write. But no, she shook her head – it had been different. Julianna's personality had already shown signs of change before that. His ban had been nothing but a desperate attempt to protect her from something. But from what? Had it really been just the writing that had had a detrimental effect on her, and which had caused her to become more and more estranged from her husband?

A soft knock sounded at the door, and after a discreet moment, Johnson entered the room, carrying a tray on his arm. Without a word, he served the tea and left silently. "However, we had not been appropriately introduced, and once I discovered that you were the Buckleys' niece, I saw only one possibility to get to know you better." Minerva felt heat rise in her body, which was not only due to the tea. Nervously, she put down her cup and folded her hands in her lap, so he wouldn't notice how much she was shaking.

He took a deep breath, a movement that set his body in motion in a way that was both indecent and beautiful. "I had no choice but to force you to meet with me again. As unusual as you were, I could not be sure that you would disregard the strict rules of society." He looked straight at her.

"I do not know what I would have done, if you had just suggested another meeting," she admitted. Minerva looked over to the window, through which bright rays of sunshine fell onto the carpet. Her fingers felt stiff from being intertwined. "I assume that you asked your friend for help in the meantime, and he agreed to assist you together with his daughter." She fell silent and thought about what she had just said, but the duke interrupted her thoughts.

"Do you think of me as someone who would carelessly risk the life of a young lady?"

"Unless you tell me otherwise – and tell me the truth – I have no other choice," she replied desperately. "I truly want to believe that you have done these things for good, even honourable reasons, but how can I?" She looked around, searching for something she could occupy her nervous hands with, but found nothing. His right hand reached out and he covered her cold fingers with his own. "How can I take this for any-thing other than a long-planned and cold-blooded mission? Surely you did not reassure yourself of the Duke of Evesham's support just a few days ago. And what does Lady Annabell say to all this? Have the two of you actually thought about introducing the lady into your plans at all?"

For the first time in days, an honest smile lit up the face of the man who was holding her hand. "Truth-fully, all of this was actually Lady Annabell's idea," he said and nodded when he saw the disbelief on Miner-va's face. "She is a very adventurous young woman, and she has a great deal of imagination. I am very fond of her, as one would be fond of a younger sister." Min-erva tried very hard not to blush, because she would never have asked the question so openly. "You will like her, I am certain of it."

"And the Duke of Evesham has no concern that you would put his daughter in danger?" Minerva found it hard to believe. Secretly, she debated whether she should feel sorry for the noble young woman, or if she should envy her, concerning her seemingly neglectful parents. She was overcome with a warm feeling to-wards her own parents, who worried about her future all the time. There were so many things she had not considered. She had been too quick with her judgement and had overlooked that there was always another point of view.

"My good friend, the Duke of Evesham, has no other choice. Once Annabell sets her mind on something, it is almost impossible, even for an overly loving father, to dissuade her." He laughed, and Minerva joined him. It was a precious moment of feeling carefree that brought them closer together. This was also in the literal sense, as she noticed. Their heads had turned towards each other, so close that she could feel his breath on her cheeks. "Minerva," he whispered her name, and his lips brushed hers so tenderly, so fleetingly that she would never have thought it possible. His eyes gleamed golden and feverishly, and her cheeks glowed in the heat. With obvious reluctance, he slowly pulled back from Minerva, but he still held her hand. It was difficult to think straight now, but she managed to remember the last point of their conversation – before his touch had nearly erased everything else.

"So, it was Lady Annabell's idea to play this dangerous

game, and she not only convinced her father, but you also. What was it that made you agree?"

He tilted his head to the side. Once again, Minerva wished that he had not cut his beautiful, long hair so radically, regardless of the current fashion. She had liked his long hair. Even now, she longed to let her hand run through those untamed locks of his. "Do you know that I was gone from here for a year?" She nodded, but refrained from telling him that people had started the wildest rumours. Even though she anticipated that the duke knew about them, she did not want to interrupt the story's flow. "Well, when I returned, I did so with the intention of finding a new wife and of returning Beaufort to its position as a true home again. I did not keep those plans to myself, and the results were disturbing. At first, I noticed only little things. I felt watched. It was as if someone was lurking in the shadows, just waiting for the right moment to strike. There was an attempt on my life, a rather pitiful attempt actually, that I could easily fend off. However, the second attempt took the life of one of my servants. That was not something I was willing to accept quietly."

Minerva remembered her aunt's warning to keep away

from the Duke of Scuffold. She, too, had mentioned a death, but wrongfully assigned the cause to the duke. "So, you know who is trying to kill you, and you have decided to lure this person into a trap. For that you needed bait."

"I swear that I would never have placed you, or Lady Annabell, in any kind of danger. As soon as you entered the stage, or better, the playing field, it seemed the perfect opportunity to spend some time with you. You were never in any danger, since everyone believed that Lady Carlisle would be my future wife. When their arrival was delayed, the damage had already been done. Everyone, including your mother, believed that there was something blossoming between you and I, and they expected me to declare myself. All I could do was try to protect you, but without your noticing. I will never forgive myself for not thinking that your mother would end up becoming the target of a murderer."

"She was not," Minerva declared. "I believe it was accidental." She closed her eyes for a second. She remembered the small piece of paper that she had found by her mother's bedside. "Everybody who attended our dinner, heard about my love of sweets," she said slowly, while trying to make sense of the many details inside her head. "It must have been easy for them to smuggle a box with confectionary, or something similar, into my room, hoping I would assume that it was a gift from you. All I can think of is that my mother saw the little box and was unable to resist. She was very fortunate to be found in time."

"I am not relieved," he declared with a dark voice.

"You do remember what you have asked me twice, don't you?" she asked. The duke nodded. Minerva took a deep breath. "You wanted to know how brave I am." She looked straight at him and tried to put all of her conflicting emotions into her eyes. "I am brave enough to assist you in your search for your wife's murderer." He wanted to say something, but Minerva audaciously laid her finger on his lips. "Now, I would like to ask you the very same question. Do you have enough courage to trust *me?*"

"It is not a question of courage," he objected. "I cannot knowingly put you in danger. This would go against everything I deem good and right."

"Not even if my help is the only way we can capture the person who murdered your wife?"

His face froze and it was wiped of any emotion.

Minerva had not wanted to be deliberately cruel, but she knew that this was the only way that she could convince him to let her play a new role in the dangerous game that they had started together. Only then would the man, for whom she felt more than she could ever put into words, face his own ruthless truth.

CHAPTER 18

Her feelings were swaying like a sleek boat that had lost its course during the storm of the century.

AT THAT ONE MOMENT, Minerva had been so certain that she had managed to convince the duke, that she, in fact, had meant the little word "we". *We will make this work*, she had thought, only to realise a moment later that he was looking at her with dark, gleaming eyes.

"I will not allow it, Miss Honeyfield," he said and got up from his chair. "I had hoped that the knowledge of the danger you have so recklessly gotten yourself into would make you wise. Your mother has already fallen victim to an attack that was meant for you."

He paused, and his face lost all expression, which told her that he was unwilling to discuss this matter with her any further. It took only two heartbeats before she saw the anger that lurked behind his emotionless façade and that manifested itself in his tense shoulders and the glare of his icy eyes. "I shall await Doctor Springfield's report. Should he assure me that your mother is well enough to travel the short distance to the Buckleys without endangering her well-being, you will leave Beaufort Castle immediately."

"And what happens if my mother still isn't well enough to travel?"

He smiled at her in a way that looked more as if he was baring his teeth. "In that case, I shall ask your aunt to come and help and to – should it be necessary – lock you in your room."

"You are not serious about this," Minerva protested.

"Do not test me," he challenged her. "And now, I will accompany you back to your room. You can have your meal there or in your mother's room. You will not eat a bite of anything that Johnson does not serve you, personally. You remember Johnson?"

"How could I forget him," Minerva muttered, partially stubborn and partially intimidated. The duke did not acknowledge her reply, but instead gave her a curt nod and asked her to follow him. Reluctantly, she did, trying to keep up with his fast pace. Minerva could very well imagine that he might simply grab her and drag her to her room, if she did not comply with his orders – hence her stumbling after him in a rather un-ladylike fashion. Just as they turned into the hallway leading to her room, Doctor Springfield stepped out of her mother's room.

One look at his face was sufficient for Minerva to re-lease a sigh of relief. Nobody with bad news looked as he did right now.

"Doctor Springfield," the duke greeted him. "How is the patient?"

"She is doing rather well, your Grace," the doctor replied with a respectful bow, before he turned to-wards Minerva. "Your mother will need a lot of rest over the next few weeks. I have already informed

Sister Mary Magdalene about the correct treatment plan and nutrition schedule."

"Thank you, doctor," Minerva replied.

"Is Mrs Honeyfield well enough to travel a short distance in a carriage?" the duke asked. "Obviously, I will see to it that she is not put under any additional strain."

The doctor shook his grey head regretfully. "I would strongly advise against that, your Grace. At her age, it is best to exercise the utmost caution, particularly since the overall condition of the patient isn't as I would like it to be. She..." He glanced at Minerva and swallowed whatever words he had meant to say about her mother. Minerva stepped up next to the duke and looked up at him. Behind his deep frown, thoughts seemed to be racing across his face.

"She will have to depend on your hospitality for at least one more week, if not two," the doctor finished his report; seeming to sense the duke's mounting discomfort, he quickly said his goodbyes and hurried away.

Minerva pushed past the duke and knocked on the

door. Before she entered the room, she turned around to him once more.

"I shall spend the next two hours with my mother. Therefore, I will be safe, your Grace. Do what you must, and do not let me keep you from whatever it is that you need to do."

But he would not let her get away that easily. He closed the door that she had already slightly opened and straightened himself up to his full height in front of her.

"Promise me that you will not do anything stupid," he demanded with a slightly muted voice.

"To what, exactly, are you referring?" Never before had she noticed just how provocative a blink of his eyes could be. For a short moment, she thought to memorise this gesture for Marianne de Lacey's next encounter with her duke, however, it seemed that she had crossed a line with her real-life opponent. With tightly pressed lips he grabbed her by her arm and pulled her, not exactly gentle, closer to him.

"You know exactly what I mean," he whispered. She pushed out her chin defiantly. Was he meaning to kiss her? The moment of indecisiveness passed, and he let her go, without kissing her. "Go to your mother. I expect to see you in exactly two hours. Should I not find you in your own quarters, I will not hesitate to remove you from your mother's room, myself, regardless of the state your mother might be in. One more thing – stay away from my brother."

She cast him a last puzzled look as she closed the door behind her.

* * *

AUNT CATHERINE ARRIVED SO QUICKLY, that the speed of her arrival astounded Minerva. She wondered whether her relative had come as a chaperone for her, or to keep her recovering mother company. Either way, she was happy to see her. Minerva also wondered if her father would take it upon himself to travel all the way to Beaufort Hall. She had no doubt that her aunt had already informed him about his wife's sudden illness. Would her father put aside his businesses to rush to her mother's bedside and to look after his daughter? Minerva did not think so, but she could not be certain. If her father could actually bring himself to leave London, then she had around two days left before he would arrive and restrict her movements even more than the arrival of her aunt had already done.

Her mother slept most of the time, or she dozed on and off, which was a good sign, according to Sister Mary. "The body needs time to heal from the strenuous effort of fighting off the illness," she explained calmly and with such authority that even Aunt Catherine seemed a little bit intimidated. The sister and the doctor both avoided calling her mother's state anything other than an illness. Had the Duke of Scuffold instructed them to keep the true cause a secret? As much as Minerva appreciated it, and since her mother was on the road to recovery, she was becoming impatient, as she urgently wanted to ask her mother about the events leading up to her falling ill. What had she eaten? Had someone mixed the poison in with her drink?

Added to her worry about her mother, Minerva was struggling with her feelings for the duke. Her contradictory emotions concerning this imperious, arrogant, and yet attractive man, caused all kinds of physical emotions, which were just as conflicting as he was, and Minerva felt everything from a light tingling on her skin, to a burning rage, as well as an unknown yearning that burned inside her tightened chest.

When she lay down in her bed and tried to get comfortable, she felt as if she were wearing a second corset made up of feelings, which sometimes made her feel claustrophobic and at other times light and free. Whilst she was tossing and turning with these thoughts rolling around in her mind, her eyes closed, and she fell into a deep sleep.

IT WAS ALREADY DARK when she awoke. Someone, most likely Sally, had lit up a candle that sat on a small table right next to a tray. Underneath the metal cloche she discovered an already cold dinner, which she listlessly pushed aside. Instead, she took some of the cheese and bread that the cook had sent up as a precautionary measure. A small bowl with sweetly scented pudding looked tempting, but after a moment's hesitation she pushed it aside. She padded over to the door and tried to open it.

It was locked.

The duke had been true to his word, and he had actually locked her in her room. Enraged beyond all measure, she ran over to the bell and rang it so furiously that she feared she would break the wide band on which she pulled. When Sally finally arrived to her room, she was unable to open it from the outside. It was completely locked shut!

"Please wait, Miss," Sally called through the closed door. "I will go and ask in the kitchen if there is a second key. I will be right back!"

It only took a few minutes, before Minerva heard the sound of a key turning in her lock, and her maid entered the room. She kept her anger at bay. After all, it was not Sally's fault that the duke had locked her in.

She asked Sally to bring her some fresh water, so she could have a nice bath. To her surprise, the warm water was actually scented, and the young woman carried in two big white towels, across her arm. With every stroke of the damp cloth on her skin, Minerva felt not only her tiredness vanish, but also the quiet desperation she had felt. When she had finished, she felt... not exactly like new, but certainly very refreshed.

"Who gave you the key, Sally? Has anybody said anything about me being locked in?" The red head of the young woman, who was busy cleaning the bathtub, shot up. Green eyes found her blue ones. "Of course, Miss," Sally replied. "The duke 'as ordered 'is chamberlain to only 'and me the key when I bring you breakfast."

He had thought about everything, and he had even ensured that no one, other than her maid, would be able to come to her room. Feverishly she tried to discern how much she could confide in the young woman about her mother's "illness", however Sally surprised her – once again.

"'as 'is Lordship locked you up..." she determined, "... for your own protection?"

"That is what he would like everyone to believe," Minerva confirmed. "Are you aware of what my mother is suffering from?"

The red lips pulled up into a mocking smile.

"I might not be as educated as the sister next door, but I am not deaf. If someone who is less than a few feet away from me, mentions the word arsenic, then I can very well imagine what must 'ave 'appened to your poor mama."

Relieved, Minerva sank back onto her bed. "Have you spoken about this to anyone? Maybe in the kitchen?"

"No, Miss," Sally replied and busied herself to remove the keys and the towels from Minerva's view. "It's not my place to do so."

"Sally, stop with the theatrics," Minerva said. "We both know that you do not really care about that." Sally tilted her head to her side and looked at Minerva attentively. "I advise you not to speak about this to anyone. Should someone ask you what my mother is suffering from, you will simply answer that you do not know." Her eyes burned with authority and she emphasised it as much as she could. "Arsenic means poison, and poison means that we do not know who did it... it could have been anybody." She gestured to Sally to stop with her nervous puttering about. "Now, would you please brush my hair? I would like to lie down. I assume that Aunt Catherine is with my mother?"

Obediently, the maid picked up the brush and released Minerva's hair from its pins. It was always a feeling of relief when her hair fell in open waves across her back. She could not understand how some women could add flowers or birds or other decorations to their already heavy and complicated hair-styles, in an attempt to look even more attractive. Her gaze found Sally's in the mirror. "After this, you should take this night as well, to get as much rest as possible."

"Would you like me to stay 'ere with you, Miss? I can sleep on the sofa. It's big enough for me."

"Actually, that might not be such a bad idea. I am certain that he will lock us in again, but maybe he will appreciate that I will not be alone in my room."

"You are talking about the duke, aren't you, Miss?" Her eyes began to gleam. "I do think it's marvellous, 'ow much 'e obviously cares for you. I mean, 'e is of course responsible for you after all."

"Do you think it is fine for him to lock us in?"

Sally shrugged. "After all, you lock away your jewellery as well, don't ya?"

"Well yes, but my jewellery is not really able to defend itself, if some thief wants to come and steal it," she objected.

"And you can, Miss?"

Minerva pulled her mouth. This conversation had taken a turn she did not like.

"I will tell you something, Miss, if I may speak freely. You should be 'appy that this man is looking after you the way 'e is, and that 'e is protecting you. If I 'ad such a man, I would never ever let 'im go ever again, and I would do anything that 'e told me to do."

"Why do I have trouble imagining that?" Minerva mumbled. "That may well be," she said a little louder. "However, I am not an object, but a grown woman. I can very well look after myself."

Was that a snort she heard coming from Sally's mouth?

"A woman needs a man like a 'uman needs air to breathe." This sounded like some irrefutable truth that Sally had picked up somewhere. Minerva closed her eyes. It made no sense to start an argument with her maid, right now. She was, after all, the way God had made her, and in her own way, Sally was good and right. She deserved respect. She had been working from a very young age, and she had been forced to look after herself – was it so surprising that she longed for a strong and decisive man?

And this very thought counted just as much for her, she determined, as she snuggled herself under her thick covers. Her whole life, she had been – well – spoiled. Her parents had fulfilled pretty much every one of her wishes and given her everything she ever wanted. Apart from the one thing they were unable to give her: independence or even freedom. Although she had already slept for quite some time, her eyes fell shut just as she heard the door open quietly.

In the darkness, she thought that she could make out the duke's unmistakeable stature, and her suspicion was confirmed when she heard the door close again and the sound of a key being turned in the lock.

CHAPTER 19

Now there was no more hope. Even her only ally, the servant with the disfigured face, had swayed, since he too had to face the raging anger of his master.

WHEN MINERVA WOKE the next morning, Sally was already awake. Neither she, nor Minerva mentioned the conversation they had had the evening before. Sally helped her to dress, and Minerva sent her to the kitchen to have breakfast. The maid knocked once at the door, and shortly afterwards, the key was turned from the outside. Minerva did not appreciate Sally being in this sort of cahoots with the duke, however, it was no longer surprising, given the short conversation they had had. It was a shame that her new-found leniency did not include the duke, she thought, whilst she knocked at the door. It seemed that the duke had ordered someone to stand guard in front of her room and to ensure, no doubt, that it would always be locked.

"Yes, Miss?" It was Johnson, whose wide face did not show any sort of emotion.

"Good morning Johnson," Minerva replied, as she pushed herself past him. She speculated that he would not dare to lay a hand on her – and she was right. She listened to his steps, which quickly followed her as she descended the stairs towards the breakfast room. But she had underestimated him. Just before she reached the room, he ran past her and put himself in her way. His eyebrows were tightly drawn together, and he silently shook his head. "My apologies, Miss Honeyfield, but the duke has explicitly forbidden that you leave your room without his consent."

She would not begin an argument with a servant and even less with a man who was as devoted to his master as Johnson. Minerva turned on her heels. Passing a window, she saw the figures of Lord and Lady Beaufort, who were walking in the park. A plan began to form inside her head – a plan that seemed too dangerous and yet...

On the stairs, she slowed down her pace, until Johnson was close behind her. "Please inform the duke that I will not, under any circumstances, stay in my or my mother's room all day. It is not for him to decide what I may or may not do, or to restrict my movements in this way. Please go, immediately."

"I am not allowed to leave you alone, Miss," Johnson retorted stoically. "In that case... please excuse me for getting you into trouble like this, but unfortunately, I have no other choice." She turned around again, lifted her skirts and ran, with a fluttering heart but determined steps, down the stairs. Towards her left, a door led towards the parlour, from where she would be able to get to the terrace. From there it was only a few steps into the gardens below. She was surprised at how easily she had managed to escape the heavily breathing Johnson, who struggled to keep up with her, but he finally had to give up his pursuit when she reached the double-winged terrace doors. She pushed them open and found herself face-to-face with Lord and Lady

Beaufort. Behind her, Johnson slowed down his pace –
she had feared that he would almost run into her – and
then he came to a halt when he saw the noble couple
in front of him.

Without saying a word, he bowed curtly to the two
and abruptly turned around. His outrage was obvious,
even in his usually controlled movements, since Minerva had now gained a few valuable minutes with her
smart little move, to test the waters.

With a breathless smile, Minerva stepped towards the
couple, hoping her appearance did not reveal too
much of her adventurous escape from Johnson.

At that very moment, she almost hated her imagination, because it was then, of all moments, that she had
an idea of how Marianne de Lacey could escape her
duke's clutches: simply with the support of the servant
who had started to feel pity for her.

"Are you feeling better, Miss Honeyfield?" Lord Beaufort's voice successfully dispelled all thoughts of her
starving heroine.

"Better? Me?" She needed a short moment to catch her
breath. "Oh yes, of course. Thank you, my Lord. It is
very kind of you to enquire about my well-being." He

exchanged an ironic look with his wife, which could have meant that he had reasonable doubts about Minerva's mental state.

Although the arrogance, familiar to her by his brother, angered her, it was beneficial to her at that moment. Let him think I am a dumb goose, she thought.

"And how is your Mama?" It was Lady Beaufort, who inquired. Compared to her husband, her smile was genuinely warm, and she released her husband's arm to link hers with Minerva's. "Come with me. We shall continue our nice little walk, which was so rudely interrupted last time. You will not mind if Thomas accompanies us, will you? If your... fiancé shows up, my husband's presence should calm him sufficiently. He is so very worried about you. Rightly so, I might add. You are such a precious child."

Minerva struggled to follow the barrage of endless words. What irritated her most was the short, but suggestive pause before the word 'fiancé' – however, the slight hesitation could just as well have stemmed from Lady Beaufort's search for the correct word.

"Yes, my fiancé," Minerva purposefully used the original French word and then regretted it, since it did not match the role she was playing, "... is extremely worried. It may not be official just yet, as you may have noticed," – only a complete philistine would not have noticed the still missing announcement – "... but he is acting as if we are already married." She giggled girlishly and hid her mouth behind her hand. Of course, she was not wearing any gloves, since Johnson had chased her around the house this morning without them, and on top of that, she had left her scarf and her coat upstairs in her room. "My Lord, would you be so kind as to ask one of the servants to bring me my coat? Or they should just send Sally, since she knows where to find it. The coat, I mean of course." Oh, it was not easy to play the silly goose, and the lord's sceptical look told her that her attempts were not all that believable. "Only if you don't mind, of course," she added and shivered theatrically. Marianne de Lacey would have been proud of her.

"But of course," Lord Beaufort demurred. "If you would excuse me, please. I shall return very quickly, ma chére." He kissed his wife passionately on her gloved fingers and disappeared towards the house.

"What would you like to talk to me about, Miss Honeyfield? Or may I call you Minerva?"

"How do you know... how gracious of you, my Lady. Of course, you may – it would be an honour." Hopefully she did not seem too exaggerated. Fortunately for Minerva, the beautiful and collected face of the French woman did not show any signs of her having noticed anything untoward. Minerva wrung her hands, which was not easy, as they left the terrace with linked arms.

Minerva glanced back towards the house.

Neither the duke, nor Lord Beaufort could be seen. Now she had to say what she had meant to say, quickly, and in a way that Lady Beaufort would understand. "As you know, the Duke of Scuffold has honoured me by asking for my hand in marriage." Lady Beaufort nodded and waited, patiently. "He... well... we met each other under rather unconventional circumstances. I... he..." She blushed, which was not to her detriment, because Lady Beaufort stopped in her tracks and looked at her inquisitively.

"Are you telling me that you are in trouble, my child? Has my brother-in-law overstepped his boundaries in a way that is only appropriate for a husband?"

"I knew that you would understand me," Minerva

sighed, relieved that she did not have to say the words. Once more, she glanced back at the house.

They were still alone, but time was of the essence. "I do not know what to do," she wailed quietly and despondently. "Obviously, the duke has acted like a true gentleman," she added quickly, when she realised that Lady Beaufort could potentially misinterpret her words. That was not her plan.

"It is my father who is unwilling, you know. Aunt Catherine has told him about the rumours that surround the duke here in the shire. You know, the ones regarding his first wife's suspicious death. Now he, I mean my father, wants me to marry the next man who crosses my path."

"And what can I do for you, my dear? I don't know your father." This was the moment where Minerva had to be very careful. Under no circumstances could she hint at Lady Beaufort's past in a derogatory manner or let her know that she possibly thought of her as a promiscuous woman, who would be familiar with means and measures not deemed appropriate for a lady.

"I have no idea," Minerva sobbed believably. Behind them she heard steps approaching rather quickly.

The gravel beneath their feet almost rose like dust, as the Duke of Scuffold marched towards them, closely followed by Lord Beaufort and Johnson, whose face was bright red.

Minerva almost felt sorry for him.

"Quickly now," Lady Beaufort said. "Just tell me this – are you in love with my brother-in-law, and do you want to keep the child? Or are you seeking my help in finding another solution?" Minerva was shocked at the brutality with which Lady Beaufort had steered her awkward mumbling into a different direction.

"I do love him," Minerva said hesitantly. It was a strange moment, which lasted but a mere heartbeat, and yet it seemed to stretch out endlessly. She repeated the words once more in her thoughts: *I do love him.*

It was the truth. God help her, she was in love with the man who now came running towards them – rage written in his eyes. He had her coat in one hand and the other one was balled up into a fist. His short hair, which she still was not really used to, glowed in the sunlight like a freshly polished coin. His movements were strong and yet graceful, much like a dancer, just... different. More dangerous, Minerva thought, and she was barely able to take her eyes off him.

Why had the earth-shattering realisation, which turned her entire world inside out, occurred at that particular moment?

"Let me do the talking," Lady Beaufort whispered to her and pressed her hand. "I will discover if he loves you. I believe that you may have hope. If not – there is always a solution – all you have to do is be brave and follow the path all the way until the end."

"Oh, there you are," she greeted the men so cheerfully as if Minerva had not entrusted her with a terrible secret. Minerva had to remind herself that her secret was not actually real, but one that had sprung from her imagination. Lady Beaufort pressed Minerva's hand once more, before she handed the young woman over to her obviously resentful 'fiancé'. All of this was handled with a certain pomp, as if she wanted to pre-empt the ceremony that her father so cruelly wanted to deny her.

He had no other choice but to play along and keep his game face on. He assisted Minerva, as she slipped into her coat, and he bowed down to her. "Come with me, Miss Honeyfield, I shall bring you back into the house. It is cold, and your mother has requested to see you."

She gave Lady Beaufort one last smile, before the duke was able to steer her back towards the house. "Follow me straight into the library," he growled, and he immediately let go of her arm as soon as his brother and sister-in-law were no longer able to hear or see them. He must have been truly angry, because he did not say a word to her, not even to reprimand her. When Minerva objected, saying that her mother demanded to see her, it was Johnson who answered her.

"Your mother is doing fine, Miss. This was but a ruse to get you back into the safety of the house."

"Bring tea," the duke said harshly to poor Johnson.

Up until now, the duke had remained firmly silent, but as soon as the door had closed behind them, the long-restrained raging storm erupted in a barrage of angry words. "What on earth were you thinking, Miss Honeyfield?" She flinched. Never before had anyone spoken her name in this manner, so cold and at the same time full of contempt. "I know exactly what game you are playing, and I am telling you right now that I will not allow it." He paused for a moment. Minerva saw that he was balling his hands into fists. "You have nothing better to do than to present yourself to my wife's murderer as a dumb rabbit to a hunter." His voice was now a whisper and sounded more threatening than his raised voice ever could have been.

"I had a good reason–," Minerva defended herself with tears in her eyes.

"I do not want to hear your so-called reason," he cut her off immediately.

"It is not necessary that you worry about me," she dared to reply defiantly and raised her head. She did not care if he saw her tears. It did not bother her in the least.

"Pah!" The duke said icily and poured a rather generous portion of whiskey into a glass. "Do you honestly think that all of this is about you?" He drank and put the glass down so hard that it broke as it hit his desk. In the semi-lit room, the shards shimmered as seductively and coldly as his eyes. "Allow me to enlighten you."

He took another glass, and Minerva saw that he had

cut himself. A thin red line ran down the back of his hand, but he paid no attention to the injury.

"My brother is a gambler. He is up to his neck in debt, and he has no scruples about getting hold of money in any way necessary – which you would know, if you had paid close attention to what I told you, and had taken my warning seriously. On top of that, he is also a regular consumer of laudanum and opium, whichever he can get his hands on when he requires it."

Shocked, Minerva held her hand in front of her mouth, unable to express her horror and pity.

He suspected his very own brother of murder?

She felt how her body slowly began to shiver, and how it started to spread through every inch of her.

"I…" Her voice sounded much too quiet. "I cannot believe that your brother is a murderer."

He laughed quietly. "Who else could it have been? He has always been a creature with no backbone, and he has always envied all I have – my status as the oldest son, then my title, and finally, the woman I once loved more than anything."

Minerva rigorously pushed aside the pain that she felt

at the mention of his first wife. This was not about her or her feelings. "Why did you not hand him over to the authorities? Or at least confront him with your knowledge about his deeds and have him undergo treatment?"

"Blood is thicker than water," the duke replied curtly and brutally, before he closed his eyes and breathed in deeply. He exhaled for just as long. "He is my brother," he said in a tone of voice, in which she clearly heard desperation and inner turmoil. "I can still see him as a little boy – how he tried to impress our father, over and over again. Without success. In my father's eyes, Thomas was always just the one who was born after me. Unimportant, because he would never inherit and carry on the title of the Scuffolds." He shook his head. "God forgive me, but I simply could not bring myself to hand him over. Not even when I saw her lying there at the bottom of the stairs. I swear to God, I will do everything I can to not give him the chance of robbing me of my love a second time."

Minerva's heart jumped inside her chest, when she heard him say that. He was talking about her!

He emptied his second glass and then set it down in the midst of the other shards of glass, before he crossed his arms in front of his chest. "You should never forget that my brother is not only a very desperate man, but also an extremely smart one, despite his... condition. He has been able to get away with murder once already. Surely, he thinks he can get away with it a second time, because there is no one who suspects him."

His mouth had become a white, hard line in a face that seemed to be nothing but rough edges. "Then you go and throw yourself into his and his wife's arms, with some far-fetched, although possibly well-meaning plan. Did you honestly think that you would be able to find and confront a cold-blooded murderer all by yourself?"

"I am sorry," Minerva gave in quietly.

The trembling had now reached her limbs and she sank to the nearest seat, unable to stand upright for another second. The silence between them expanded. "But if he has laudanum and opium at his disposal, why–" ... *did he resort to using arsenic*, she had meant to say, but the duke did not let her finish.

"You might have courage, but you are a very foolish creature," the duke said.

There was a knock at the door, and Johnson entered the room. This time, the tray contained only tea and two cups. Johnson gave Minerva a calculating look after exchanging a look with his master, and then took it upon himself to serve the tea.

The duke waited until Johnson had left the room, before he continued. "Now I have no other choice but to send you away, and once and for all bury my hopes of holding him accountable for what he did. Either that, or I have to accept your childish plan."

Minerva tried desperately to read his face. The initial rage the duke had felt seemed to have vanished, and now he looked tired and exhausted. Her own shaking disappeared. Now it was up to her to make a decision and convince him that she could support him, if he allowed it.

"My Lord," Minerva said and got up from her chair, not really sure if her legs would carry her. Surprisingly, they did. "You are hurt. Please let me have a look."

She walked over to him. "Do you have a handkerchief?" she enquired and took the one he pulled from his breast pocket. She took his reluctant hand into hers, dabbed the almost dried blood from the back of it and tied the formerly white cloth like a bandage around his hand. He looked at his hand and its new bandage, and then he looked up to her. A second time, she reached for his hand, with a pounding heart and the certainty that she would not be able to take back what she was about to do.

She laid the palm of his hand against her cheek and snuggled right into it.

"I trust you completely," she whispered. "With you I am brave and even more than that. I am sorry that I..." how could she best describe it, "... have destroyed your plans. Please let me make it up to you."

The hazelnut-brown specks in his golden eyes started to dance. "I believe I have no other choice, if I do not want to lose you too." It took almost two heartbeats before Minerva realised the true meaning of his words. At first, she did not want to trust her own ears, but when she looked up into his face, she read the answer to her never-asked question.

"Minerva," he said with a hoarse voice and kissed her a third time. It was like a fairy-tale, she thought in a rather far-removed part of her mind – or was it her heart?

This third time tipped the scales. Everything she had meant to say was erased by the feelings that his lips caused within her. When he released her, her mouth was burning, she was gasping for breath, and she was as happy as she had ever been in her life. The Duke of Scuffold smiled cautiously, but it was the most beautiful smile she had ever seen. She could have stared at him forever, soaking up all of his expression and remaining in his arms for eternity. But his next question brought her back to reality.

"What exactly have you told my brother and his wife?"

She told him everything.

First, he turned pale and blushed, and then paled again, when the strong emotions got a hold of him. Fearfully, she looked up into his face and sighed with relief, when she saw his lips twitch treacherously.

Minerva could not have expected what happened next. He fell onto one knee, right in front of her, took her hand in his and pressed a kiss onto it, before he spoke. "Miss Honeyfield, would you do me the great honour of giving me your hand in marriage?"

CHAPTER 20

*B*ut that was not the end of her ordeal, yet.

IN THE END, he agreed to her plan, although only after numerous arguments and objections. For three days they were meticulously checking all the clues again and again to make sure they were not mistaken. Only when they were absolutely certain that they had discerned the suspect, beyond doubt, did they begin to concoct their ironclad plan.

Minerva loved him for the way he worried about her

and his eagerness to protect her at all costs, but she also knew that he would never find peace as long as just a little speck of doubt remained in his mind. Maybe her own desire to help him was the female version of his protective instinct. Not that he would approve of such a notion – he was much too masculine to do so. What had ultimately convinced him, had been the fact that he would be able to help his brother and still be able to resolve the events that had occurred that night.

"What are you thinking about," he asked her as they sat in the library, side by side in a precious moment of peace and privacy. "I am thinking about your brother and his wife and about what we are planning to do tonight."

"Are you scared? You can voice your fears to me at any time. I shall find a different solution, which will not put you at risk." He pulled her close until her head rested against his chest, allowing her to listen to the regular beating of his heart. "I am not scared, because I know that you will be with me at all times," she replied. "Johnson will be there, too. On top of that, we have discussed every detail over and over again. We can no longer delay the execution of this plan, because it will eventually become obvious that I lied," she added, remembering the piercing look Lady Beaufort had cast on her belly. Of course, there was no trace of what nature had allegedly given her, but Minerva had been in favour of not delaying their plan much longer. Lord Beaufort and his wife could decide to leave Beaufort Castle, at any moment. That meant another wait for the right opportunity to elicit a confession from Thomas.

Their plan was for Lady Beaufort to tell her husband, the murderer, about their imminent marriage. Lord Beaufort would then be forced to act, as he had when he murdered his brother's first wife, because she had stood in the way of his inheritance. Thomas was known to be a notorious gambler with a mountain of debt, added to which was his need to numb himself with all sorts of substances. Robert himself had said that his brother envied everything that he called his. Whether it was his brother's urge to destroy Robert's happiness, or his pure greed for the wealth and title that would come with an inheritance, Minerva was not entirely sure. However, when Thomas heard that his brother was planning on marrying a second time, and on top of that to a woman who was supposedly carrying his child, then the younger man would be forced to act immediately. Or lose everything.

Something flashed in the duke's eyes, a memory perhaps. "I still do believe that you deserve to be put across my knee for your recklessness." He shook his head, but in a loving way. "How on earth did you come up with the idea to create such a ludicrous story? What do you think would happen if your parents heard about it?"

"Don't you dare," she said with a warning look. "My parents do not have the slightest idea about any of it, and the only man who has ever physically reprimanded me, is my father. I do not intend to change that."

It seemed as if he was willing to continue this short battle of words, however he straightened his posture without loosening his hold on Minerva. "You are right. We cannot change it now, anyway. You have planted the seed, and tonight is the time to harvest." His mouth had taken on a bitter cast as he thought about the trap they had concocted for his brother. "All right, let's go through everything one more time and from the beginning."

"Do we really have to? We have discussed this over a hundred times already." Minerva pulled a face, but then quickly straightened out her features, as she remembered that she was now an engaged and soon married woman. "I shall take the opportunity right after breakfast, whilst you distract Lady Beaufort on a pretence."

"I shall ask her to watch Beaufort Castle whilst we are on our honeymoon in Italy. They are supposed to believe that we want to avoid the rumours that will inevitably arise in the face of a hasty wedding." She was still rather uncertain as to whether Lady Beaufort would believe such a story, but Robert made her understand that he would make sufficiently dark comments, until Lady Beaufort had no other choice but to believe him. His tone of voice sounded confident, and she assumed that he had some kind of secret knowledge about the mechanisms within a marriage, of which she had no idea. Therefore, she let the subject rest and decided she would simply trust her man.

"At the same time," she continued, "... you will let her know that you are aware of your brother's financial and health struggles, which is the reason why you are asking her and not Thomas for her presence at Beaufort Castle. Of course, you shall ask Thomas officially at the dinner tonight, to keep everything in order." She smiled a little desperately, for she really knew every step of his plan by heart. "In the meantime, whilst you will inform her about all of the upcoming tasks, I shall mention to Thomas that the impending wedding and the duties of becoming a duchess are making me nervous. I shall pretend that I would like to confide in him and talk to him about my biggest fears –that you still love Julianna more than you will ever love me. I shall play the helpless and scared little woman."

She did not like that part very much, but it would give Thomas the impression that he had nothing to fear in her presence.

Robert took her hand in his. "It's very important that you don't show your true feelings at all," he warned her. "Thomas has a very sharp nose for lies. It would be useful if you whispered a mixture of truth and lies into his ear. You can ask him if I will allow you to continue writing your books, just as Julianna did back then. This will steer his thoughts in the right direction. He is supposed to see parallels between you and Julianna, which might cause him to react impulsively."

As he uttered the last words, Robert's look turned dark, and he pulled his eyebrows tightly together.

He didn't like the idea that Minerva would present herself as a victim to his brother. However, she believed that his brother's addiction would cause him to confuse the present and the past, and thereby also her and Julianna.

Then Robert only had to catch him red-handed, so that he could demand a full confession from his brother.

Minerva rolled the plan back and forth in her head. Something did not sit right with her, but she could not really say what it was.

"Just do not overdo it," Robert warned her once more.

The thought, which she had almost been able to grasp, was gone again.

"You only have to get him to meet with you, somehow."

"I could lure him to the pavilion," Minerva suggested. "I think that the calmness of the place will give him a false sense of security, and I might be able to get him to confess. I will tease him with my knowledge, until he admits to what he has done, or until he tries to put his hands on me. That is the moment when you and Johnson intervene. Voilà, he confesses, and you have the undeniable assurance that your instincts have not deceived you."

She gave him a gentle kiss on his mouth. "Robert, given the circumstances, this is the best you can do. Do not forget that those substances have made him ill. You will help him to get well. Once he has recovered from his terrible addiction, he can go to the colonies and start a new life there."

"I am not so much worried about the scandal, as I am about him falling back into old habits, once he arrives in the colonies. What if he keeps murdering there? Here, I at least have some control over him. But there..." His voice trailed off.

"There, he no longer has a reason to come after your life," Minerva reminded her future husband. "You will be thousands of nautical miles away, and your wife is expecting a child, do not forget that."

"As if I could ever forget that," he murmured and finally returned her kiss. "This day will be the most exhausting of my life. Johnson and I will not let you out of sight for a second. In my case, you must take my words in their strictest sense."

"Come, my love," Minerva said, tasting the unfamiliar name like a candy on her lips. "We have a few minutes before breakfast is served."

"And we should use them wisely," he added to her sentence and pulled her towards him.

CHAPTER 21

He put his hands around her neck and squeezed her throat.

HAVING to get up after a night like this and dining with the others was bad enough. What made matters worse for Minerva was not being able to show her nervousness. She asked Sally to put her hair up in a nice little bun and slipped into her dark-blue muslin dress. It had a modest style, as was currently the fashion, and Minerva loved the colour. She found that it gave her blue eyes extra depth, and her light hair shone even brighter, to the point where it almost seemed colourless. This unusual colour, as well as the tight hair style, would help her to play the role of being someone else. All in all, Sally had done well in the short time she had been in Minerva's service as her maid.

It would only be this one morning, she told herself. She just had to be brave this one more time in her life. After that, she and the duke would be able to begin a new life – one they would share without having Julianna's ghost hovering around them or his brother's evil intrigues poisoning their love. Minerva looked at the portraits of the ancient Scuffolds as she walked down the long corridor. Some of them, like the gentleman with his pointy beard and lavish hat, seemed to gaze down at her disapprovingly. In turn, there were those, like the voluptuous woman in an enormous skirt with a greyhound's intelligent eyes peeping from underneath it, who seemed to wish her good luck in her endeavours. Deep in thought, she realised too late that there was someone standing around the corner. A collision could barely be avoided, and she took a clumsy and unladylike step backwards. She stumbled and was caught at the last minute by her future brother-in-law.

For a moment, the two of them stood in the hallway, inappropriately pressed against each other. With her sensitive nose, Minerva could not help but notice the unpleasant smell of an unwashed body emanating from Lord Beaufort. He seemed to look even paler than he usually did, and his eyes were gleaming feverishly.

She swallowed hard. Not even the few minutes to reach the breakfast room remained for her to find her composure.

"Good morning, future sister-in-law," he said and gave her a watery and somehow cautious smile. "I hope, you are feeling well?"

"Thank you for asking, Lord Beaufort," Minerva replied, and she pondered what she should say next. Whenever she had played the planned conversation with him in her head, she had been the one in charge of the situation. She had spoken, and he had given her the correct answers. Robert had warned her that it wouldn't be as easy as that, and of course, he had been right. Instead of saying anything, she lowered her gaze and wrung her hands.

"You do know that you may speak with my wife at any

time, should there be anything that concerns you, do you not?" he said in an almost concerned tone.

The offer was so unexpected and friendly that Minerva stared at him with a startled look. She would have expected anything from this man, but not the sensitivity and delicacy with which he addressed the possible distress she might feel, and on top of that, in such a discreet manner.

"You are too kind, my Lord."

"Thomas," he corrected her with the hint of a smile. "I think that – for the time we are alone – we may forget about formalities such as lords and ladies and dukes and future duchesses."

He hid his shaking hands behind his back and offered to walk the rest of the way to the breakfast room with her. "My wife is already there," he said. *Not if Robert has been successful*, Minerva thought, and realised that he had relinquished the idea of holding out his arm to her. Minerva knew that Robert had been up early this morning, since he knew that his sister-in-law would always be the first one to arrive in the breakfast room. Minerva had always thought this to be odd. For a woman who had once been an actress, but also for her habits and by the way she looked, one would assume she was a lady who slept in late and had her breakfast brought to her bedside. However, Lady Beaufort was of those people who would go to bed last, and in the morning rise first. It could very well be due to Lady Beaufort's burdens, she thought whilst Lord Beaufort led Minerva towards the stairs. After all, the lady had to be strong for herself and her husband, which most probably took every ounce of strength in her.

"Thank you, Thomas," Minerva said timidly and walked as slowly as courtesy allowed. They reached the stairs, and she felt a cold shudder when she remembered that Robert had found his wife at the bottom of these very stairs, which she was about to descend herself, with the murderer himself! Sometime the night before Julianna's death, the first duchess must have stood here with her brother-in-law, alive and unaware that she would soon die.

Minerva felt dizzy. Almost automatically, she searched for the banister and shivered as she touched the cold stone. The world turned blurry, and it seemed as if a fog lay in front of her eyes. She only perceived her brother-in-law only as a dark shadowy figure, whose face shone brightly and yet hazily.

She knew he had said something to her, because his mouth was moving, but she didn't understand the words.

"Minerva!" Without further ado, he grabbed her by her arm.

Minerva was unable to suppress a scared gasp. Now, he would push her down the stairs, just as he had done to his previous sister-in-law.

In that exact moment, someone behind them cleared his throat. It was but a quiet sound, discreetly and un-doubtedly from a man accustomed to making his presence known in this understated manner.

Never before had Minerva been so happy to see John-son's face. The grip around her arm loosened almost un-noticeably, but her brother-in-law still held her tightly.

"May I be of assistance, my Lady? Sir?" His deep rum-bling voice felt like a rescue rope that he had thrown to a drowning Minerva. The confines of her world widened a little, and she was able to breathe again.

"Thank you, Johnson. I felt a little dizzy," she replied, with as much dignity as she could muster at this point. She hoped that Thomas would believe that her indisposition stemmed from her delicate state, and not from her fear of him.

"Would you prefer to lie down?" Thomas asked her, and his face seemed to have lost some of its paleness. Was her mind playing tricks on her, or did he look guilty?

"No," Minerva replied and smiled at him, but obviously not very convincingly, because he narrowed his eyebrows. At that moment, the resemblance to his brother was uncanny. He was a more slender, younger version of the man whom she had promised to marry, and maybe he was also a slightly more vulnerable version. Her heart tightened painfully, when she realised that she was about to lure him into a trap.

With all the strength left, she reminded herself of the danger she had just escaped (and probably was still in). This man did not deserve her sympathy. He had pushed his own sister-in-law down the stairs, and he had tried to poison her own mother. He would not hesitate to push... the same fate upon her. "I am in need of some fresh air," she whispered. Then a little louder: "Johnson, please ask Sally to bring me down my coat, hat, and gloves. I would like to take a short walk through the forest. I am sure I will feel better afterwards."

"My Lady, you should not walk these grounds alone," Johnson objected. "Please allow me to accompany you." She looked at him sternly, but Johnson did not flinch at all.

"No, thank you, I said I wanted to be alone," she repeated, craned out her chin and started to descend the stairs carefully, but with shaking knees. "I am sure, Lord Beaufort will be happy to accompany me," she added and gazed back up at her future brother-in-law with, what she hoped, was a complicit look. Minerva did not have the slightest inclination of trudging through the forest in the late autumn cold, but if there was no other way – well, what had one of her tutors always said? The end justifies the means. Although this was only ever mentioned in connection to the desirable status of a married woman, the statement remained true – all the more so, as she had a noble cause, which would ultimately bring her husband well-deserved peace of mind.

"Well, of course," Lord Beaufort murmured, even

though he didn't really seem particularly excited about the idea. Johnson gave her a last look from the landing and withdrew, undoubtedly, to notify Sally. "Are you sure that you wouldn't much rather be in the company of my wife?" It was his last meagre attempt to get away from her presence, but Minerva linked her arm under his, determined to not let him escape so easily.

Not ten minutes later, she and her brother-in-law were outside in the park. She took a deep breath. Now that they were alone, she could think about how to apply the next step: persuade him to a secret meeting.

Then she realised that they were alone already. Her future husband was not exactly hiding somewhere nearby, but instead he was inside the house, trying to distract Lady Beaufort. Dammit! Why did the events not follow the plan that she and Robert had set so carefully?

Robert had warned her. "The best plans have a tendency not to work out," he had said to her, and by the way he had pulled his mouth into a thin line, he had been close to excluding her from it. It had been a wise decision to tell Lady Beaufort that she was pregnant – without this aspect, which put the duke under pressure, she would never have managed to convince him to let her help.

"Tell me something about Julianna," she heard herself say. "Sometimes I feel so incredibly close to her, Thomas. She must have been a brilliant mind. Your wife told me that she was also writing a book. Is that correct?"

At first, he didn't answer her. "She was a wonderful person," he said in a strangled voice. Minerva glanced up at him from below and quickly looked away again.

"Julianna was... like a beacon in a dark night. She had a gift of making someone else's life bearable, even when you were completely lost."

"I wish I could have met her," she said quietly when Thomas paused.

She had purposefully taken the narrower path that led from Beaufort to the pavilion, where she and Robert had had their first encounter. Thomas seemed to be becoming more and more restless, at her side. He continually glanced back over his shoulder, as if he felt someone was following him.

"Is everything all right with you?" she enquired.

"Yes, it is just that… this path is leading us to Julianna's favourite place," he replied. "I… do not know… but I find the place eerie." Minerva pushed him gently on-wards, ignoring his obvious reluctance.

"Why so? Do you believe her spirit haunts the site?" She purposefully spoke with a light-hearted, almost joking voice. He glanced at her suspiciously. Minerva noticed that his forehead was covered in tiny beads of sweat, and once more, pity for this weak, lost man threatened to overcome her.

"Well, it is possible, don't you think?" His voice sounded stifled. "Do you believe that the souls of the dead show themselves to those responsible for their death, sister-in-law?"

"I do not really know," she said after a moment of re-flection, avoiding a branch that reached far into the path. Her feet were cold. As always, she had thought about everything, but not to put on the right shoes for her trip to the wilderness. Her blue slippers would probably be ruined after the walk.

"When I found the pavilion for the first time, I wanted to hide from my aunt and uncle, to work on my story in peace," she told him with a smile, which he reciprocated hesitantly. "Even before I met Robert for the first time, I thought that I had sensed a presence there. Something that you cannot put into words, but still feel clearly. It was a woman, of that I am certain."

The derelict building came into view. Her future brother-in-law stopped abruptly and moaned quietly at the sight of the small pavilion. In the cold light of the early morning, the signs of neglect were all the more visible.

"My aunt later told me that the people around here speak of a crying woman who haunts this place; it is said that it is the first Duchess of Scuffold. I assume that you are aware that they suspect your brother of her murder?"

She did not think it was possible, but his face turned even paler.

Minerva released her grip on his arm and stepped into the pavilion, whilst he stood outside as if his shoes had grown roots there. She hardened her heart against his obviously deep desperation, and after a moment of inspiration, she added, "I do not believe that Robert is the one behind her murder."

Their eyes met across the short distance. For a moment, she thought that she had gone too far, for his eyes were completely empty as he stepped closer.

Now, it was only the rotten wood of the floor that separated them from each other. Minerva thought that she heard a shout, and then there was the sound of something or someone making their way through the woods in great haste.

"It was *you*, was it not?"

Thomas awoke from his stupor and raised his hands in a gesture that could have meant anything – surrender, relief, or the desire to silence the person who knew his secrets, forever. "God help me, but you are right. I am as much responsible for her death, as if I had killed her with my own bare hands." His face seemed to fall apart under the sudden wave of emotions that overcame him. Even before Minerva was able to make sense of his strange choice of words, she saw tears pouring down his face.

"You have to understand," he said desperately, seeming far away in thought. "I liked Julianna a great deal. She was… like me, in a way." He was now sobbing openly. "There was a true artist hiding inside of Julianna, and when Robert forbade her to write, she became ill." His words poured out in jerking gasps, and Minerva did not dare to disrupt his speech. "She was unable to sleep, unable to eat. So I introduced her to opium."

With shaking hands, he wiped away his tears.

"You have no idea just how guilty I felt, when they had found her dead. I immediately knew that she had lost her balance in the opium rush and fell to her death... and I had believed that I was *helping* her."

Minerva did not understand how he – of all people – who was trapped in the claws of his opium addiction, had believed that he could help Julianna with it, but that had probably been part of his twisted view. However, what she saw on his face was torment that she didn't even wish on her worst enemy. She held her hands out to him, no longer able to suppress the feeling of empathy towards him.

An explosion disrupted the air. From somewhere in the distance, smoke rose. Thomas's face took on a strange look that she could not understand. Only when she saw his shoulder starting to turn red and Robert came rushing towards them, face pale and tense, did Minerva understand what had happened.

The duke had shot his brother.

Thomas sank to the ground, strangely gracious in the way he fell. Robert was with her instantly, pulling her into his arms and covering her face with kisses as he took turns swearing and reassuring her that he loved her. The next second, he pushed her away from him and searched her body for any injuries.

They had found the man responsible for Julianna's death.

CHAPTER 22

*F*or a moment, Lady Marianne de Lacey was inclined to let the duke do as he pleased.

ONCE MINERVA REALISED JUST how much she had overestimated her own capabilities, her entire body began to shake uncontrollably. Even though she had been certain that Thomas would not harm her, his reaction to her words had been so sudden and strong, that anything could have happened at that point. "Are you all right? Are you hurt?" her love kept asking her, and Minerva forced a smile.

She would never forget the expression on his face, when he thought that his brother had harmed her. She would remember that for the rest of her life, and she considered it the most precious gift he could have given her.

"I am fine," she confirmed with a weak voice. "Nothing happened to me. Everything is all right." She said the words with an expression of surprise, almost as if she could not believe that she was alive – but so it was. Her racing heart and light head were a welcome assurance that Minerva was still amongst the living, but what about Thomas?

Robert followed her gaze and turned even paler. "Can you stand?" he asked, and his eyes bored into hers. In that moment, something happened between them, which Minerva was unable to put into words. Suddenly, everything seemed simple and in a strange way, clear. There was no doubt between her and Robert. Whatever had happened and whatever would happen in their future, they would conquer it together.

"Of course I can," Minerva said determinedly, but he still released his hands only reluctantly. "We should look after Thomas," she said and put her fingers on his. "Your brother is alive."

Minerva did not say what she was thinking out loud, because she saw the same emotions flashing across Robert's face: relief, that he had not killed his own brother, combined with the knowledge that he and his brother were now at the beginning of a long journey, which possibly could lead to a reconciliation.

Robert knelt down beside his brother, and Minerva did the same. This was also because her legs were not yet able to carry her, despite her defiant declaration a few moments ago, as well as because she wanted to be near Robert and share everything with him. Thomas's eyes were wide open, and his right hand was pressed to his left shoulder. "I'm so sorry," he croaked, his face distorted in pain.

Robert didn't say anything. The muscles in his jaw were hard, his lips tightly pressed into a thin line, as he removed Thomas's hand from his shoulder. "Let me see your wound," he ordered, ignoring his brother's words. Minerva forced herself to look, although the smell of the blood made her feel nauseous. "It's just a flesh wound, but we should bandage it and get you back to the house." He looked down at himself and pulled off his spencer from his shoulders.

"Wait," said Minerva, realizing that he was about to

rip his shirt to shreds to bandage his brother. "My skirts are probably better suited." She got up, lifted her dress a handbreadth and instructed Robert, with a look, to rip the fine batiste. She did not even care that Robert was able to see her ankles. It was not the time to worry about the appropriate decorum.

Thomas was still conscious. He was white as a sheet, but his chest rose and fell regularly. He would live and face the consequences of what he had done. Justice would be served, even though he would not feel the full force of the law. Was his urge for opium reason enough to exercise leniency, even though he was morally guilty of the death of his sister-in-law? Minerva thought about her mother, who was still recovering in her room.

"Why did you try to poison my mother?" she asked loudly, to overcome the sound of the shredding of fabric. Robert looked at her in astonishment, and Thomas's eyes widened as well.

"Your mother was poisoned?"

There was no doubt – the expression of surprise on his face was genuine, Minerva thought. Nobody was that good an actor, especially not in circumstances such as these, wounded on the ground and in agonising pain. She avoided Robert's inquisitive eyes and concentrated on the face of the man who lay before her.

"Someone gave her confectionary laced with arsenic," Minerva said, never taking his eyes off him. It was only a suspicion, since she had not yet spoken to her mother about the chain of events, but after careful deliberation this seemed the most probable solution. "Tell me the truth and I shall never again mention it to you – why did you want to kill my mother?"

"I did not do that," Thomas stammered, beads of sweat breaking out on his forehead.

Robert did not exactly handle him gently – however, Minerva took it as a good sign. If Thomas really had been in mortal danger, Robert would have treated him differently. He had lowered his head, so she could not see his face, but the posture of his shoulders revealed that he did not miss a single word of the conversation between Thomas and Minerva.

"I swear on all that I hold dear and sacred that I did not have anything to do with it."

As strange as it was, Minerva believed him. So, if it

was not him, who else was behind the cowardly attempted murder?

***

The way back to the house was exhausting, but they managed to get there eventually. Robert had half-carried his brother over his shoulder, whilst Minerva had followed them. She kept her distance from the brothers to give them a little space, but also because she wanted to be alone with her thoughts. Every now and again, Robert glanced back to assure himself that she was fine. Minerva enjoyed his attention, wondering if there could ever be a real reconciliation between the unequal men. The snippets Robert had told her about their childhood touched her more than she could put into words. Robert was the stronger of the two, there was no question about that, but could Thomas have withstood his wretched addiction if his father had loved him? The realisation of just how much her own parents loved her broke over her and cut into her heart like a knife. She had not been a good daughter to them, she thought ashamedly. Instead of finding a compromise for their arguments, she had stubbornly insisted on her view of things, without even attempting to understand the concerns of her mother and her father.

The thought brought Minerva back to the starting point of her reflections. Who had poisoned her mother? They left the forest behind them and reached the park. Johnson came running towards them and took over Robert's position. The duke immediately fell back to Minerva's side and took her hand.

"Do you believe him?" he asked unceremoniously.

"Yes," Minerva replied without hesitation.

"So do I," Robert said heavy-hearted. "It's most aggravating that your mother is still too weak to be able to tell us anything that happened." He gently squeezed her hand and slowed their pace until Johnson and Thomas could no longer hear them.

"Could it have been an accident?" Minerva asked, even though she didn't really believe in this theory. Robert shook his head.

"It is possible that she ingested arsenic by an unfortunate chain of circumstances, but it is highly unlikely. Here at Beaufort Castle, we only use arsenic to keep the rat plague at bay, but everyone here knows it is poisonous. On top of that, my administrator keeps the supply within a locked cabinet in his study. He said that none was missing since he had last used the arsenic over a month ago."

"That means our search is not yet over," Minerva said.

Abruptly, Robert stopped in his tracks and shook his head. "Oh yes, it is," he said determinedly. "As soon as I have taken care of the situation with Thomas, I shall inform the authorities – something I should have done much sooner," he said grimly. Silently, Minerva agreed with him. Why had Robert simply not asked his brother, instead of quietly fuelling his suspicions? Thomas, too, had suffered from the continued silence he had imposed on himself. Julianna's death was irreversible, but he could have spared himself and his brother much suffering if he had admitted his unfortunate involvement. He was morally guilty, but he had not pushed her down the stairs, as Robert and she had initially suspected. Surely law would take this into account, or would it not?

"It will take a few days before the Bow Street Runners arrive, and until then I will ensure that you and your mother are under guarded protection."

"You are willing to involve the Runners?" The London magistrate, Henry Fielding, had established this police force in the last century. Their reputation was not exactly the best, however, even the fiercest opponents to the group could not deny that they had the most experience in the field of criminal investigations. A simple constable from the country would undoubtedly have been utterly overwhelmed with an attempted murder by poisoning – therefore, it was a logical decision to seek help from the London police. "Is there no other solution for Thomas? I cannot help myself, but I do have the impression that he is not responsible for the death of your first wife."

"Do you mean because the opium has clouded his mind?"

"That too, but did you hear his words?" He nodded. "I cannot put my finger on it, but something doesn't seem right. Your wife's death, Thomas's alleged involvement – all this sounds so…" She searched for the right word.

"Perfect," Robert finished her sentence with a dark face. "I know. I did fear that my judgement could be clouded by relief, if one can call it that, that there was no evil intent behind Julianna's death, at least not from Thomas's side."

Minerva placed her hands onto her hips. All at once she felt terribly angry, not at Robert, but for his sake. "Why are you telling me that now? So many mistakes could have been prevented, if only you and Thomas had spoken to each other. Will I now have to extract every single word, every consideration from you individually?" She shook her head, and her hair flew in all directions. "Please promise me one thing – do never keep anything from me, just because you assume that I cannot bear it. I am strong enough to carry my share of suffering and happiness in a marriage." She paused for a moment. That last sentence reminded her of something she had seen recently, and Minerva was almost certain that it could be important. What was it? She closed her eyes and concentrated. No, she had not seen it, she had thought about it. She gasped and held her breath, then opened her eyes again. She felt nauseous, and her heart was pounding heavily in her chest. She was just about to say aloud, whom she thought was the responsible for the treacherous attack on her mother and why, when she read the exact same realisation on Robert's face.

Beaufort Castle was but a few minutes away by foot, but when the two of them started running towards it, Minerva knew that every second counted.

CHAPTER 23

*B*ut then her survival instinct prevailed,
and she wrenched herself from his grasp.

ROBERT REACHED Beaufort Castle before Minerva did.
She watched him run up the stairs and stumbled after
him, longing for the freedom of movement that the
male clothes offered him in comparison to her imprac-
tical shoes and narrow cut of her dress. Where was
he? She looked around, but he had already disappeared
inside the house. Minerva forced herself to think
calmly, even though she was completely out of breath.
Behind her, she heard Johnson's voice, talking calmly

to Thomas. She turned around and ran back towards the odd pair.

"Where can I find Lady Beaufort?" she gasped. Thomas's eyes were surprisingly clear for a man who had just suffered a gunshot wound. Did he suspect what his wife was involved in?

"If she is not in her room, you may find her in the parlour or in the park. She always liked to be outside, where she could feel the force of nature." He spoke about his wife in the past tense, as if she had died. Minerva shuddered. The impression that she could be irrevocably too late, intensified. She pondered her thoughts. Should she first go to her mother, or should she instead search for Lady Beaufort in the places her husband had named? No, it was more important to look after Mama and to ensure that she was fine. Without acknowledging Johnson, who was calling something after her, which she thought to be something like a curse, she darted up the stairs. Minerva did not take the time to knock but burst into the room unannounced. Lady Beaufort sat by her mother's bedside and held Minerva's mother's hand in her own. Minerva did not stop, but rushed towards the beautiful woman, who had not even bothered to raise her head when Minerva had stormed into the room.

She was the very epitome of a benevolent lady, looking after the sick, Minerva thought absentmindedly. Her eyes flew back and forth, but apart from an untouched glass of water, nothing seemed to be out of the ordinary, and nothing indicated another attempt on her mother's life.

Without looking at her, Lady Beaufort raised her hand. Minerva stopped in the midst of her movement, and the momentum almost pulled her off her feet. "Please don't do anything to my mother," she said and was quite surprised at how calm her voice sounded. Her mother seemed to be fast asleep, because her breathing was regular beneath the blanket.

"Do you honestly believe that I meant to harm your mother?" Lady Beaufort's voice sounded hoarse from unshed tears, but when she lifted her head now, nothing but hatred shimmering in her eyes. "You silly child. *You* were the target, not your harmless old mother."

Minerva took a step towards the bed. She almost anticipated that Thomas's wife would be hiding a dagger in the folds of her dress, but she did not see anything that indicated that.

"It was about the inheritance, was it not?" If she could involve her in a conversation for long enough, Robert would have enough time to come and find her. Surely he knew what Thomas had told her a few minutes ago, which was that the park was one of his sister-in-law's favourite places, and was looking for her there. Hopefully he was fast enough to stand by her side in the event of an attack. Minerva believed that she was able to defend herself against Lady Beaufort, however, she doubted that she was fast enough to save her mother, should danger threaten.

"What else could it be?" the woman said mockingly. Her face was nothing but a rigid mask – pale and lacking any kind of emotion. Her beauty had become that of a doll, who absorbed her surroundings with an expressionless look. "I have sacrificed everything for my husband: my career, my youth, and my beauty. And how does he thank me? By spending all of his fortune at the gambling tables, in drug dens, and in brothels... and if that was not enough, he is letting his substance addictions turn him into a wet wimp."

Minerva cringed. It was not just the bluntness with

which Lady Beaufort spoke of her husband, but about the violence with which she spewed out all the hatred she had bottled up for so long. Carefully, keeping an eye on her sleeping mother, she took another step forward. This time, Lady Beaufort did not react or ask Minerva to stop. Only three, maximum four steps separated Minerva from the woman. "And there was no other solution other than to murder me?"

"It is not like I haven't tried different things. I did warn you, did I not, during our walk in the park? I have to admit – the second time it was not that difficult, albeit ultimately unsuccessful."

Minerva felt how the colour drained from her face. The true meaning of Lady Beaufort's words, and what she had just admitted to her, hit her. "*You* were the one who pushed Julianna down the stairs," she whispered, and the harsh laughter that escaped Lady Beaufort's chest confirmed her suspicion. Her eyes fell on the neatly folded hands lying in the woman's lap. The knuckles were tightly white, and the veins on Lady Beaufort's neck protruded, becoming clearly visible as she gasped out the next words with tremendous effort.

"The silly goose was completely senseless from the drugs that my husband had given her," Minerva's opponent sneered. "It was nothing but a stupid coincidence that I encountered her that night. She could barely walk straight. All I had to do was give her the tiniest push with the flat of my hand, and everything was taken care of. At least, until..." Her face lost all colour, and the hands in her lap began to shake.

"Until I appeared in the picture and told you that I was expecting the duke's child. You were forced to act upon the new revelations," Minerva completed for her. She took a deep breath and dared to step up to her mother's bed. Slowly but surely, the devastating confusion in her head gave way to a calm order. Anything that had been said or heard in passing, suddenly made sense to her.

Minerva started to see the structure that surrounded the puzzle of the attempt on her mother's life.

Where she had felt fear before, she was now overwhelmed by a feeling of utter disgust. "Surely you were aware that your husband felt guilty about Julianna's death? What would you have done if he had confessed to the murder? He could have ended up on the gallows, which would have left you with nothing, and even worse, with the scandal of being the widow of a murderer."

"That was a risk I was willing to take," Lady Beaufort dismissed Minerva's concerns with a shrug. Her breathing sounded laborious. "Nothing ventured, nothing gained."

Minerva felt sick when she heard her father's business philosophy coming from this unscrupulous woman's mouth. Running a business with this motto was one thing, but applying the phrase to the lives of others, was something else entirely. She was just about to ask what her plan was to remove the duke from her path, when Lady Beaufort raised her eyebrows and tilted her head sideways.

"Ah, there he is, your knight in shining armour. Right on time, just as the villain is dispatched." She stood up unsteadily, stumbled, and tried to lean against the bed post. Minerva watched out of the corners of her eyes how Robert darted forward, to catch the falling Lady Beaufort in his arms. "Too late," she smiled, and she seemed almost to embrace her own death with relief. "I have decided to determine the time of my departure from the big stage, myself."

How was it possible to feel so much disdain for someone who was about to take their very last breath? Towards Thomas, she had felt such pity and empathy that it had almost torn her heart apart. For Lady Beaufort, she felt nothing at all.

She watched as Robert let his sister-in-law slide to the floor. He felt for her pulse and shook his head.

A small sigh from the direction of the bed startled Minerva. Her mother had decided to choose that particular moment to wake up. Minerva didn't know if she wanted to laugh or cry, or maybe both, which she ultimately did, as she ran towards her mother and threw her arms around her neck. When her mother spoke, her voice sounded muted, but happy. "Oh child, why are you crying?" Robert stood up, and Minerva's mother first looked at him and then glanced at her daughter with a firm look. How she still managed to do that after everything she had been through, would forever be a mystery to Minerva.

"I do not even want to know what the two of you were doing on the floor, here in my bedroom."

Minerva blushed bright-red – however, before she could straighten out the misunderstanding, her mother continued, "Please, just tell me one thing... when will the wedding take place?"

EPILOGUE

All is well that ends well, Lady Marianne thought, looking into the face of the man who was now her husband. Never again would she have to feel the incredible fear that she had felt in his presence for almost half a year. Everything had turned out to be so very different than she had initially anticipated.

HER FATHER'S chest was swollen with pride, as he led Minerva down the aisle towards the altar. Her mother was only able to retain her composure and not cry relentlessly out of pure happiness, because the attendance of Robert's aunt, the Marchioness of Queensberry, showed her the virtue of being reserved.

Minerva was nervous, but in a very positive way. She believed that she felt Robert's presence and sensed him walking down the aisle in the small chapel with long strides. Indeed, there he was, and smiled at her modestly. To outsiders, he probably looked content and calm. Minerva looked into his hazelnut-brown eyes, and she saw the deep, unwavering love he had for her. Her father gave the bride's hand – she was the *bride*, she still could not believe it – into his, the *duke's* hand.

In a few minutes she would be the Duchess of Scuffold.

She didn't really care about the title. Her gaze wandered up to meet Robert's. He was the picture-perfect groom. He listened to the words by the priest who married them, in a relaxed and yet attentive manner. Robert had obtained their marriage licence through a friend of the family, the Archbishop of Canterbury, which allowed them to marry at any given time and place. Of course, at first, her parents had protested when Minerva told them that she wanted to get married as quickly as possible, however, these protests had only been half-hearted attempts. She had tried to explain her feelings to her mama and papa, saying that she could not bear to be separated from her future husband for a day longer than absolutely necessary. Her mother had sighed, her father had uttered a satisfied grunt, and with that, the question regarding their wedding date had been settled.

The priest had already asked the formal question, if anyone had any objections to the two of them being married. Unlike Lady Marianne's duke, Minerva's duke did not have a mad wife living in the top of the tower, so all people present remained blissfully silent.

Minerva tried to pay attention to what the priest was saying, but only when he raised his voice and turned towards Robert, did she really prick up her ears. Minerva had no doubts about what his answer would be, but she wanted to savour every second of it.

"Do you, Lord Robert Beaufort, Duke of Scuffold, take this woman to be your lawfully wedded wife, to enter into the holy bond of matrimony according to God's will? Do you promise to love her, honour her, and be faithful to her, until death do you part? Then, please answer with 'Yes, I do'."

"Yes, I do," Robert said loudly and clearly.

Minerva noticed that one of the wedding guests behind them burst into tears. That could only be her mother, or Georgiana, who had travelled together with her parents all the way to Kent to attend the wedding and to see the eternal bond with her own eyes.

Now it was Minerva's turn to answer the question – an answer that would unite her and Robert in the eyes of God and the church, forever.

"Do you, Minerva Lucille Honeyfield, take this man to be your lawfully wedded husband, to enter into the holy bond of matrimony according to God's will? Do you promise to obey him, serve him, honour him, and be faithful to him until death do you part? Then, please answer with 'Yes, I do'."

"Yes, I do," she said clearly.

Only after she had spoken the words aloud, did she realise that she was now the duke's wife. He bowed his head, and the priest cleared his throat. Minerva felt all eyes staring at her, and it did not matter to her at all.

"Until death do us part," he repeated their vow inaudibly for the rest of the congregation. It was a private promise – one he made only to her for the both of them, a moment of intimacy in the midst of the publicity of a noble wedding such as the duke's.

That is what Robert did, short and tender. His kiss was sweet, even though Minerva longed to feel his lips on hers for longer. His eyes promised her that he would heed her wishes very soon. But first they had to sign their names in the church's register and take the traditional wedding breakfast, before they could leave for their honeymoon in Italy.

"I still cannot believe it," Georgiana whispered into her ear, when they found a short moment alone together.

"Neither can I," Minerva admitted. "I sometimes look at him and think to myself that I must be dreaming."

"I would feel the same way. He really *is* a very handsome man," her friend confirmed. Minerva suppressed a proud smile, but she had to agree with Georgiana, nonetheless. Robert was everything she had ever dreamed of in a man.

The one drop of bitterness was the absence of his brother, but after everything that had happened, Robert was not yet ready to face him. After long consideration, he had decided not to send his brother to the colonies, but to give him a second chance. First, he had to overcome his addiction. Currently, Thomas resided in a private sanatorium, which Doctor Springfield had recommended. Minerva still remembered his raised eyebrows, when he treated the 'hunting injury' of Lord Beaufort and verified Lady Beaufort's accidental death. Robert had told him the truth, however, and asked him to keep it confidential – not for his sake or because of the feared scandal, but to enable his brother to return to a normal life more easily. Doctor Springfield had agreed, on the condition that Lord Beaufort undergo a treatment and distanced himself from the use of opiates.

Minerva squeezed Georgiana's hand one last time, and she promised her that she would write to her from Italy every single day. She hugged her happy mother, who could not stop her words as they said their goodbyes, and she embraced her father, who tried to hide his emotions, as usual, behind a grouchy grunt.

"Are you coming?" Robert asked and stretched his hand out to her.

"In a moment," Minerva replied. She slipped unnoticed out of the large tent and waved over to Sally, who had taken advantage of the festivities to flirt with the coach driver of the marchioness. Minerva would have to have a firm talk with the young woman, but not today on this joyous day. Robert had offered to hire a French lady's maid, who would be more skilful than the often still rather clumsy Sally, but Minerva had rejected his offer vehemently. The more time she spent with the girl, the more she grew fond of her. She would never forget the look on Sally's face, when she had told her that she was allowed to stay with her at Beaufort Castle and not as a kitchen maid, but as her personal maid. Sally had repaid her by burying her nose into the magazines and periodicals Minerva owned, and studying the different images in them. Sometime soon, Minerva planned to teach Sally how to read, but for now she was happy that the young woman immersed herself in the drawings. By now, she had developed a remarkable skill in dressing Minerva's hair in a manner that was in no way inferior to the hairstyles of the ladies of the finest society.

Out of the corner of her eye, Minerva saw a dark-haired woman yelling at one of the servants, who was desperately trying to hold on to her. The woman was moving around wildly, with flailing arms and stomping feet. Driven by curiosity and also because the woman seemed familiar to her, Minerva approached the two people. It was just at the right moment, as the servant's face looked desperate. "I am telling you, I do know the duchess," the woman insisted. Minerva nodded to the young man, who was relieved to let go of his wild captive.

Minerva cleared her throat and smiled when the woman turned around to her. The clinking armbands, the long hair falling freely down her back, and her colourful dress were unmistakable.

"Good day to you, Marie-Rose," Minerva said politely. "As you can see, your prophecy has come true."

"Your Highness," the Roma woman said and sank to her knees. Up until now, Minerva had never anticipated how triumphant a gesture of respect could be. "I never doubted it."

"Did you come to collect your reward?"

To her surprise, Marie-Rose shook her head so vehemently that her black locks flew in all directions. "No," she replied. "I just wanted to catch a glimpse of you and make sure that those shadows that darkened your fate have disappeared for good."

Minerva did not really know what to say. A part of her wanted to believe that the woman was telling the truth, but the rational part of her nature remained sceptical.

Either way, Marie-Rose had not only been right in her prognosis about Minerva's rise in social status, but she had also been correct in another part of her prophecy.

She raised her hands and removed the diamond encrusted earrings she was wearing. "These are for you," Minerva said.

Majestically, Marie-Rose took the two pieces of jewellery into her hands and looked at them briefly, before she stuck them into her bodice. "That's very generous of you," she declared.

"Do not mention it." Minerva played down the issue. She had the feeling that she owed fate something. Her family, particularly her mother, were doing well. Robert's brother was on his way to recovery. She herself had found the man of her dreams, whom she loved and honoured.

She was aware that she had been very lucky, and earrings were just a small price to pay, to keep it that way. "Farewell," she said to the woman and nodded towards her, before she turned around. She didn't fancy hearing yet another prophecy.

Minerva called for Sally, who reluctantly left the coach driver behind, and asked her to bring her the notebook with the now finished novel. It just about fit into her little bag, and she wanted to use her honeymoon to begin her next book. She had finished Lady Marianne de Lacey's story. In her new book, she wanted to try and honour Julianna's memory by writing down her story – unrecognizable, yet with the visible, tangible truth behind the words. She wanted to make sure that the ghost they had heard crying at night, would become a spirit that was heard laughing on some nights instead.

The End

Dear Reader,

Are you wondering who the mysterious Lady Annabell Carlisle is, whom the duke called an "adventurous and imaginative young lady"? Then you might look forward to the next suspenseful Regency novel by Audrey Ashwood: "The Cold Earl's Bride", to be released in early 2020.

In the meanwhile, I am delighted to inform you about another publication: Please make the acquaintance of Grace Curtis in "To Steal a Duke's Heart" and follow her exciting search for happiness and love. Grace sets her sights on handsome George Blackmore, the newly appointed Duke of Cromford. However, fate seems intent on keeping them apart. When the duke's younger brother develops an interest in Grace's friend, Grace is determined to bring the pair together so that she might see the Duke again – and steal his heart...

Find a short reading sample of both books on the next pages.

Would you like to stay informed about upcoming books in this series? Then please sign up for Audrey Ashwood's release notifications here. You will receive a short message via email, as soon as the next book is available on Amazon. Perfect for everyone who doesn't want to miss the next new publication. Subscribers will receive a chance to read them for free.

Yours,

Audrey Ashwood

SNEAK PEEK – THE COLD EARL'S BRIDE

TO BE RELEASED IN EARLY 2020

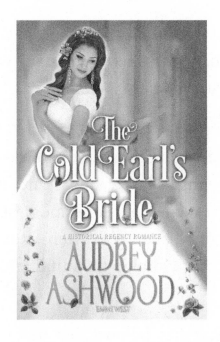

They took everything away from him.

His reputation as an honourable gentleman.

His hope for peace.

His faith in love.

Nevertheless, there is one thing that nobody can take from the merciless Marcus St. John, Earl of Grandover – his desire to take revenge on the men who wish for his demise. He is so very close to identifying the mysterious mastermind who is pulling all the strings in the background.

But then he stumbles into a cleverly designed trap, where he is suddenly forced to marry a woman who is clearly an instrument of his enemy.

The longer the ruthless earl has to watch this foe in his own house, the greater his doubts become about the role she is playing. She is smart and beautiful, and somehow, she touches his innermost being in a way that had long since been forgotten. Is it possible that she has completely clouded his mind and confused his heart?

Just when he starts to believe that he can see through her clever little game, the cards are shuffled anew...

Mysterious – emotional – magical. The new ro-

mance novel by Audrey Ashwood is yet another book that takes place in the midst of the colourful Regency era. An ideal read for anyone who loves sentimental but courageous heroines, as well as confident and strong heroes.

Reading Sample

This was not good.

The two of them had plotted something. But what was it? The movement of the palm leaves across the room steered her attention back to Marcus St. John. He had stepped out from behind the leaves. Since Felicity and her viscount had distanced themselves from him a little, he had been forced to give up his hiding spot, if he did not want to lose sight of them. Just for a split second, her gaze met his. His piercing blue eyes sent a chill down Annabell's spine. This man was cold, ruthless, and he was up to no good. But why was he so very interested in her sister? And why had nobody else noticed the Earl of Grandover's rather strange behaviour?

Had Felicity secretly entranced St. John, who was now

consumed by jealousy because he saw her dancing with the viscount? Annabell knew that her sister could be somewhat reckless, but she did not believe that Felicity would dally with two suitors at the same time. Then again, what did she know about the art of finding a husband?

Before she could think about it anymore, the musicians stopped their piece. The dance partners stopped moving and bowed towards each other. Normally, the viscount would have accompanied Felicity back to her mother's care, but he did not do that. Annabell's heart started to beat heavily within her chest as she saw Viscount Greywood manoeuvre her sister skilfully past all the other guests. He also managed to escape every single attempt to strike up a conversation. She stretched her neck to follow their path, but it would not be long before they would both be out of her sight.

Annabell looked over towards her mother, who was still engaged in a seemingly engrossing conversation with the vicomte. Where was her father? She definitely did not wish her father's anger to be directed at her sister, but... *thank goodness!* Annabell thought in frustration, he was nowhere to be seen. She tried everything she could to not lose the two conspirators

– which is what they undoubtedly were in her eyes – from her sight. If she were to go over to her mother and wait patiently until the duchess deemed it appropriate to interrupt her conversation with the vicomte, Felicity and the viscount would be long gone.

Her eyes darted towards her left. The darkly-dressed figure of St. John seemed to melt into the shadows. If it had not been for his light-coloured and slightly too long hair, she most certainly would not have seen him. The earl had also taken it upon himself to follow the two.

Annabell ducked her head towards a servant, who was offering refreshments. Her throat felt as dry as the desert, but she had no time to down a glass of expensive champagne. Apart from the fact that it was not very becoming for a lady at a social gathering such as this to drink like a drunk in a tavern, she also did not dare to drink even one drop of alcohol. Especially not now that she needed a clear head to save her sister from making a huge mistake.

This she was absolutely certain of: Felicity did not have anything intelligent on her mind right now and the viscount even less so than her.

Annabell pushed through the throng, almost relentlessly, which would have caused her mother to reprimand her, but at this point, she did not care about that. Her stomach was in knots as she saw the viscount's dark hair and her sister's reddish-blonde curls disappearing towards the garden. In hindsight, Annabell was even angrier at herself, than at her sister. The signs had been obvious. Tonight, Felicity had chosen her most boring and practical dress. It also happened to be the darkest coloured dress she could find. That way it would be so much easier to disappear into the night with the viscount. Annabell's heart raced. She simply had to prevent her sister from making a grave mistake!

Outside on the terrace, the cold of the British spring evening embraced her. In one spot, where there was a small piece of bare skin between the dress and the glove, unsightly goose bumps were immediately raised. How could she have been so stupid! While running down the stairs from the terrace, and stumbling after the eloping love birds, she remembered her sister's mood swings over the last few weeks. Felicity had been either overly happy or extremely sad, which Annabell now decided were the typical signs of seriously falling in love, even though she had never experienced it herself. It was thus – *if* the poets were to be believed. Annabell turned around to face the gradually dimming sound of voices in the house, but nobody seemed to have noticed her hasty exit into the garden. At least that was one thing that had not gone wrong. On the other hand, who would even care if her reputation was ruined? Annabell herself did not even care that much.

The two figures before her seemed to melt more and more into the darkness in the centre of the garden with each step. Annabell did not even try to mute her steps behind them, and she saw that her sister had hesitated and turned around. Annabell was almost certain that she saw a silent plea in Felicity's eyes or at least doubt, but that was, of course, nonsense and nothing other than wishful thinking on her behalf. With this much distance between them, and in the dark, it was impossible for her to make out more than just general movements. The viscount slowed his steps and spoke insistently to Felicity. Her sister's posture expressed hesitation. Then Rupert Greywood stepped so close to her that both of them blurred into a seemingly single shapeless figure right before Annabell's eyes. She thought that she could see the viscount looking in her direction, and it was almost as if he needed to assure himself that she was still there, before they continued on their way.

She was extremely relieved that she was not wearing voluminous skirts or a tightly laced corset, which would have made the pursuit even more difficult. Obviously, fate decided to quite literally throw a stone into her path at that moment, because Annabell stumbled and almost fell onto her knees. She stood up and looked in the direction where she had last seen the pair.

Felicity and the viscount had disappeared as if they had fallen through the face of the earth.

St. John cursed silently as he watched Greywood with this young woman, who seemed to have just stumbled out of her nursery, as they disappeared into the garden. Even in his thoughts, he refused him his noble title, which was obviously wasted on such a worthless fellow as Greywood, at least as far as he was concerned. This damned man was his only lead, and he had hoped that tonight he would be able to follow him to one of his meetings. However, at this moment,

Greywood seemed more interested in seducing this girl than working on his other, much darker plans. One day his lawlessness would lead to Greywood's demise.

An idea shot through Marcus's head, but he did not have enough time right now, and all he could do was memorise it for later. The bastard was attempting to disappear. The chance that Marcus would achieve his goal tonight was out of the question, thanks to this girl, but he wanted to make sure nonetheless. He decided to follow them unobtrusively anyway. Maybe he would see or hear something that he would be able to use later. He could still feel the gaze of the young woman who had also been hiding and watching the two lovebirds from a distance. The shock he had felt when he first saw her was still vibrating through his body. For a split second, he had thought that he was seeing a ghost, sent to him by some vengeful god. Her hair, her mannerisms, and the way she observed her surroundings so attentively and with barely noticeable amazement – even her controlled gestures reminded him of the woman who... He shook his head, angry at himself, and it took everything in him to push those painful memories away.

If he had not known better, he would have believed that she had also come here to watch Greywood. But she was much too calm and collected for a potentially jealous former lover. In addition, although the muted colour of her dress and her young pale face were extremely attractive, this rather noticeable contrast would not be something a secret observer would have chosen. Only when he noticed the worry written all over her face, did he realise that it was the young girl whom she was most interested in. For a moment, Marcus was distracted by his pity for this woman. The girl on Greywood's arm was as good as lost, even if she and her female guardian did not know it yet.

He watched her, as her chestnut brown hair, which was styled slightly out of fashion, finally disappeared into the massive crowd of heads, and then he continued his pursuit of the viscount. To his left, he saw Lady Wetherby almost running towards him, with her two daughters in tow. Without hesitation, Marcus took a sharp turn, nodded towards the Duke of Titchfield, and then followed Greywood out onto the terrace. The restless flickering of the outside torches made it almost impossible to focus on anything, but he managed to make out the waving seam of the dress before its wearer once again disappeared into the shadows.

Just as he had suspected, Greywood was leading the girl towards the stables. This suggested two conclusions, Marcus thought, as he followed as silently as he could. Greywood either wanted to seduce the girl right there, or he planned to take her to one of his doss houses and take his time with her. He was not a man who cared much about discretion. If he felt like it, he would simply find a corner somewhere inside the stables, and if someone were watching, then he would not care less. Whatever the case, it was not his – St. John's – task to prevent any of it, nor was there anything he was able to do without giving up his hiding spot.

Some leaves rustled behind him, but when he turned around, he could not see anything that could have caused the noise. *Calm down,* he told himself. It was impossible that one of his enemies had followed him here. He had taken every possible precaution to remain unnoticed.

A subtle movement showed him the way to continue. However, instead of moving towards the stables, away from the main house, as he had suspected, the two turned right and made their way deeper into the garden. One of his friends had once called him "overly cautious to an almost absurd magnitude," but tonight this caution would serve him well. He had memorised the floor plan of the house and its surrounding parks, just to be prepared for any situation. This was the reason that he now suspected that he knew where Greywood was going. In the centre of the garden was a pavilion, which was perfect for what he was planning to do.

Marcus stood still. Now that he was almost sure that Greywood was only interested in an amorous pursuit, he knew that he might as well just turn around and wait for the bastard to come back. So, what was it that made him follow the pair even further? Up until now, it had always served him well to trust his instincts, and he decided again, this time, to do just that. After a short moment of internal debate, he stepped from the gravel path onto the grass to dampen the sound of his steps. The moonlight broke through the clouds only sporadically, which worked as much in his favour as it worked against him. However, since he did not change old habits easily, he had dressed once again in rather dark clothing, which made him virtually invisible.

He started to move forward. In moments like these, his long years of experience of working in the shadows was an enormous advantage, since it allowed him to separate his body and his mind. Searching his surroundings for anything unusual, while making cold-blooded, quick decisions had always helped him to survive. Once more he thought he heard a noise that did not seem to fit with this night and his surroundings. Still, his eyes did not see anything that would have made him feel uneasy.

Finally, he could make out the shape of the pavilion in the darkness. Only a few steps separated him from his target. While he was thinking about how close he would be able to get to these two, and also about how odd it was that the woman in Greywood's arms did not make a sound at all, the hairs on his neck stood up. But it was already too late. He bounced against something soft, which he immediately recognised as female breasts that had been laced up only scandalously loosely. Before Marcus could wonder about the reason for his displeasure, he felt a burning sensation on his cheek. A tender hand in a white glove pulled back, but not fast enough for him.

His fingers enclosed the tiny wrist, and he ignored the

protesting and the painful scream as he pulled the woman towards him. "What have you done with my sister? Where is Felicity?" a voice, which under normal circumstances could have sounded rather pleasant, hissed into his ear. Now, under the vibrating alto, he could hear only two things: fury and fear.

Once more the memories hit him with full force. What he heard was a similar sounding female voice, which belonged to a different time and a different place.

"Be still," he ordered as he listened to the darkness. Most likely, her scream had already alerted Greywood, but he still wanted to avoid any extra attention. He knew that all the gossip and the stories about his transgressions, as well as the rumours about his past, had given him a rather dubious reputation. However, an attentive observer would almost certainly ask the question why Marcus had run out into the gardens at all.

"I do not think so," the strange woman replied defiantly. "Not until you have told me where Felicity is."

"I do not know, and I do not care," he answered harshly. He thought he saw the dark dress he had followed all the way out here, from the corner of his eye. "Be still, or I shall see to it that you will keep your mouth shut."

He was close to losing his patience with her. For a moment he was hoping that this strange woman in his arms would behave like a normal person, but she proved him wrong. She did something no well-behaved young Englishwoman would ever have considered doing. She opened her mouth and vociferously spewed a flood of insults towards him. In all his life, Marcus had heard much worse accusations than being called a "monster" which, given the situation they were in, seemed almost laughable, but her lack of reasoning and sheer disobedience angered him.

A short while later, when he was able to think again, he would struggle to find a logical explanation for his behaviour. In this particular moment, it had seemed like the only option he had, to silence this strange woman.

Maybe the mild spring air had played a part in it as well, or perhaps it was because of the delicious scent of her soft body in his arms, and the fact that her appearance reminded him of the happiest time in his life, but... he had pressed his lips against hers and closed her mouth with a kiss.

She smelled of almonds and something tart, which aroused thoughts of a hot summer's day in the country. Besides the scent of her perfume, he also smelled her soap, undoubtedly some expensive French concoction, which more than likely had been smuggled here. However, the most tantalising were her lips, as she opened them for him without hesitation. At first, he assumed that she was a very experienced kisser, but then her posture gave away the fact that she was simply overwhelmed. Obviously, such physical closeness was an entirely new experience for her. By now he should have realised that this woman was a complete stranger to him and not the beloved and dead woman of his dreams.

But for a moment, Marcus St. John, Earl of Grandover, a man with a bad reputation and a well-known love of the female form, forgot to study this situation carefully, and instead lost himself in this innocent but passionate kiss with this young woman.

It was the moment that cost him his freedom.

As the moon finally showed her pale face from behind

dark clouds, he finally saw who was about to rob him of his sanity, and it was already too late to deny that this kiss had ever happened.

Behind the woman with the chestnut brown hair, which threatened to fall into complete disarray, he saw three men rushing towards them with hasty steps. The first man he recognised as the Duke of Evesham, a fanatic royalist and a hater of Catholics. He was one of the most conservative peers in the country.

He looked at the woman he had just kissed. Her eyes darted from his face over to the duke and back to him. For a short moment, he thought that she would open her mouth and explain to the duke what had happened. That she had mistaken him for someone else, that nothing had happened that could not be forgotten, as long as all involved would swear to absolute silence in this matter, but she said nothing. Not even when the Duke of Evesham let loose a tirade of angry accusations. Her eyes, the colour of which he was unable to distinguish in the flickering light of the torches, widened in fear.

...

End of the Reading Sample.

"The Cold Earl's Bride" will be available on Amazon soon.

Sign up for Audrey Ashwood's release notifications. You will receive a short message via email, as soon as the book is available on Amazon.

SNEAK PEEK – TO STEAL A DUKE'S HEART

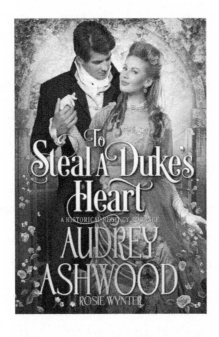

A disgraced young woman with nothing to lose.

A handsome, newly appointed duke, bound by his honour.

Her one opportunity to steal his heart.

Disowned by her parents for helping her sister elope to the Americas, Grace Curtis never expected to capture the attention of the witty and bold George Blackmore, the Duke of Cromford. After the sudden death of his father leaves him with the responsibilities of his elevated station, he has little time for romance... not even with the beautiful Grace.

When Cromford's younger brother, Edmund, takes an interest in her best friend, Grace encourages the relationship, in the hope of seeing the duke again – and stealing his heart.

However, Edmund divulges some unexpectedly worrying truths about his older brother, and Grace soon finds herself questioning her attraction to the newly appointed Duke of Cromford.

As she finds herself embroiled in a bitter war between two brothers, Grace must choose carefully where to place her trust. Will she be able to fathom the duke's true colours and find happiness?

Reading Sample

Grace moved to the corner of the room where wines and spirits had been laid out. She nodded towards a fine amber-coloured brandy and saw the valet who was charged with serving the drinks, perform a double-take. She could tell that she had put him in a quandary – should he serve spirits to a young lady? She met his eye.

"I assure you, I am in dire need of something a little stronger than punch, after dancing in that crowd all evening." She lifted her eyes slightly in what was meant to be a gesture of amused determination. It worked – either that or he did not dare to contradict her. She watched as he decanted a generous amount into a glass. It was true that brandy was not deemed a drink fit for a lady of refinement, but Grace liked the strong and full-bodied flavour. If her taste offended others, that was their own business. However, as Grace surveyed the room, drink in hand, she was a little curious to see if anyone might notice her and cast a glare of judgement in her direction.

Only one pair of eyes seemed to have noticed Grace's actions.

A man of striking aspect glanced her way for all of a moment. It was a quick analytical gaze, and Grace could not be sure exactly what type of impression she had made on him. He quickly looked at her face, down at her glass, and then took in the rest of her: a clean sweep of her profile. Grace could not even hazard a guess as to whether the man was impressed with her or appalled. His face was like the waters of a great lake – striking and beautiful, yet fathomless and un-knowable.

With such mastery over his own emotions and tells, Grace imagined the man would be a natural for cards. It seemed odd, then, that he was not playing. He stood as passive as a statue at the side of another seated gentleman and seemed to be acting as some kind of judge or councillor to his companion, who kept glancing up to the gentleman, and showing his cards, which suggested that the man's opinion was highly valued. However, the standing gentleman made only brief remarks to his friend, never allowing himself to be drawn completely into his friend's game.

As she studied him, Grace was pleased with the man's appearance. She allowed her gaze to linger on the subtle waves of his dark, neatly-cut hair and the line of his square jaw. She could not make out the colour of his eyes, at such a distance, but she fancied they were green like a forest. What impressed her most, was the sheer weight of his presence. It was a presence that was almost unaccountable, and she could not decide what it was that gave him such a powerful air – certainly compared to his friend. He dressed well. He wore an elegant black suit with a silver brocade waistcoat and matching cravat. It was smart, and most certainly the finest tailoring in the city. The gentleman exuded presence, and finally, Grace decided to attribute the man's attraction to his greater than average height, which was further accentuated by the way he held himself, his spine as straight as a ramrod.

Grace had no qualms about enjoying the view of the unknown man and was pleased to note that she had made some sort of impression on him as well. His gaze returned to her twice during the time she studied him. However, she did not seem to be distracting him from his cool observation of his friend's game. Grace might have worried about her own looks, were it not for the advances of the boy from whom she had so recently retreated.

Polite applause rose from the table signalling the end

of the round. The gentleman Grace had been admiring, patted his friend's shoulder in congratulations, and began to steer himself away from the players. His departure earned a round of disappointed groans, and the player who had sought his assistance looked a shade more cautious going into his next hand.

Meanwhile, the mysterious gentleman navigated his way straight towards her. The direct manner in which he moved, and the singular nature of his enterprise, sent a thrill through her, as she realised that she was his goal.

"Would you mind if I took advantage of your company while we enjoy a drink?"

A most direct question. Grace did not know what to make of it, but her curiosity was piqued.

"I believe the traditional custom is to seek an introduction through a third party, before imposing yourself in such a way."

The gentleman sucked his cheeks in just a little. He gave a confident bow.

"You are quite right. Forgive me for intruding." As

quickly as he had made his way to her, he turned to leave.

"No, please think nothing of it. It was merely my poor attempt at humour." Grace cursed herself for having nearly driven away the only interesting man at the party. She had not expected him to treat her playful chiding with such seriousness.

The gentleman turned back with the merest hint of a smile playing on his lips, and as the valet approached, he glanced at Grace's glass. "Can I bring something else for you too? Perhaps you could recommend the one that you are drinking?"

"Thank you, but I will have no more," Grace replied. "I can, however, say that it is oaken and has a definite tang of orange to the flavour. I have certainly tasted worse."

Grace smiled at her attractive companion as the valet poured him a glass from the same bottle as he had chosen for her a little earlier – only this time without hesitation. She brought the amber liquid to her lips again and reflected that this was the first time a man had sought her opinion on brandy. He watched her without saying anything – his delicate half-smile still in evidence – pleasant but not obnoxious, nor overly pleased.

"So then, shall we see to the introductions ourselves, or do you wish to wait until a mutual acquaintance can introduce us?" The gentleman raised his glass to Grace in salute and then took a sip. She found her eyes transfixed on the way his Adam's apple moved as the liquid coursed down his throat. Men did not usually drink with such finesse. He did not make a show of sloshing the brandy elaborately in his glass, nor did he play the part of the over wise connoisseur. His refinement came wholly from his lack of pretension while drinking.

"Perhaps... it may be more convenient for us to converse without names," Grace offered. "As soon as we bring names into this pleasing interlude, we open ourselves to a whole swathe of barriers to good conversation."

"How so?" He lowered his voice so she was forced to lean a little closer.

"Well, as soon as a gentleman introduces himself as, let's say, the son of a duke, some ladies might feel compelled to put on all sorts of feminine airs, and laugh in a practised fashion at his jokes."

"If that were the case, I certainly would not wish for that," he said.

"You would not? Does the thought of my trying to charm you not appeal?" Grace spoke teasingly but could not detect anything in the gentleman's expression or tone that suggested to her that he was joking.

"*Are* you the type of woman who acts differently depending on a man's rank?"

"I like to think I am not." Grace replied. "But who would not wish to appear more attractive in certain circumstances?"

"I appreciate your honest nature. I find that London is full of people who put on false faces to draw notice of a title or rank in *any* circumstances. And… as for whether or not your charming me would hold any appeal – perhaps that question can be asked again, at a later time."

"As relieved as I am to know that you see me as an honest woman, you do seem very certain in your assessment of me."

The gentleman shrugged. "No woman seeking to impress a man would choose to cloister herself in the gaming room, nor to be seen drinking, what I am bound to say, is a rather generously filled brandy glass."

Grace paused with a playful smirk flickering across her lips as she baited the intriguing stranger. "You seem to be telling me that I do not impress you."

"On the contrary, I'm quite certain that you must turn the heads of men, both single and otherwise, without even meaning to."

"You are bold, Sir!" Grace's voice had taken on a husky tone, and she absentmindedly began to curl a lock of her blonde hair about her finger.

"I would call it openness rather than boldness. I can assure you, however, that it was the potential of your character that drew me to you and not your looks, fine as they may be."

"You covet a woman's character but are not afraid to acknowledge physical beauty." Grace could feel a knot beginning to tie itself in the pit of her stomach, and her entire body seemed to be prickling with every passing second. She took a moment to look into the eyes she had wondered over from a distance. They were green, as she had hoped, but not the green of soft grasses and forests. His eyes were the green of precious gemstones – sharp and solid like the rest of his face – sharp jaw, sharp cheekbones, and sharp eyes. His visage was almost intimidating, but thrillingly so!

"Seeing as this conversation has nothing at all of the typical about it, should I take it you do not intend to ask me for a dance?" Grace hoped she did not sound wanton, but she could not deny herself the opportunity of standing with this man in a set.

"I had not intended to," he answered. "You have barely begun on your glass, and good brandy should neither be hurried nor left unfinished. Besides, you have expressed a wish to maintain anonymity during our time together. Were we to stand together in a dance, I'm sure there would be those known to us both, who would spoil our little game here."

Grace felt a little disappointed. Her own words and actions had conspired against her. There was never a man she wished to know more, and yet the whimsical suggestion of remaining strangers, now threatened to leave the man an eternal stranger to her. To this disappointment was added a further sting, as she realised that her mysterious companion appeared truly unin-terested in learning her name. Other than that, the man was refreshingly candid in his conversation, and she found her thoughts and opinions aligned with his on many of the matters that they covered. Despite the agreeable time they were having, something was obvi-ously playing on his mind. There was some resistance in his manner that she felt was keeping him from com-mitting wholly to their conversation.

"Tell me... if you could choose between dancing with me or knowing my name, which would be your choice – or maybe you desire neither?" The man's voice was confident as ever, and his emerald eyes studied Grace, as he asked her this playful question.

"You need not fear my being indifferent to you, Sir. May I enquire why I must *choose* between the two? Is there no chance of my learning your name *and* stealing a dance with you?" Grace cocked her head slightly, swaying a little, which she hoped would entice the man.

"I suppose I am interested to see what your intentions are. If you learn my name and perhaps my address here in London, we might have occasion to know one another better. Dare I say that you might even dare to employ those feminine charms that you mentioned hitherto, against me – even though you did not own up to them directly." He smiled to soften his words. "If, however, you truly would prefer us to enjoy a brief moment as strangers, destined never to see one another again, then I would wish to at least share one dance with you."

Grace felt a thrill run through her entire body, and she could not stop herself from biting her bottom lip in anticipation. She tried to imagine what it would be like to dance with the man. He was not built like the other gentlemen of the city. Most of them tended to have either round fattened stomachs that betrayed a lifetime of overindulgence, or they were willowy stick figures with atrophied muscles who were never compelled to physical labour. This man was broad-shoul-dered, and Grace could almost see his muscles straining under his gentlemanly attire. He seemed like a man accustomed to hard labour, much like the farmers in the fields near her family home in Bradford on Avon. The thought of being led by him, and held by him, sent a definite rush through her. Still, she knew her answer.

"I think, Sir, as tempting as a dance might be, I would

prefer to take your name, if you are offering it to me."

"Of course," The man added briskly. "I shall expect your name in return." He had a business-like air about him now, as though he were negotiating some treatise or loan.

"I shall oblige you with such, do not fear." Grace continued to smile, but the edge of her lip quavered just a little. For the first time, she found herself unwilling to own her identity.

"Very well. If I am to go first, may I present myself as George Blackmore, Marquess of Cromford."

Grace blinked twice. She knew the name. She did not concern herself much with memorising the names of London's elite, but the name Blackmore was inescapable. "It's a pleasure to make your acquaintance, Lord Cromford."

Based on his easy conversation, Grace had not expected the gentleman to have such a high rank, and if she was honest, this evidence of her own prejudice, shook her slightly. However, she immediately sought to regain her composure.

"Now we come to the matter of your own name." The

marquess's chest swelled then, perhaps in anticipation.

"I am Miss Curtis, Miss Grace Curtis." Grace's eyes scrutinised Lord Cromford's expression for any tell. Although she was no duchess, there was reason for the man to have heard of her or her family, and she expected their conversation to come to a disappointing close, if he were indeed aware of her past.

"Miss Curtis." The marquess repeated her name to himself. "It is a pleasure to meet you. I hope, despite all we vowed at the start of this interlude, that we shall have a chance to further this acquaintance."

"I should like that very much, my Lord."

So, Lord Cromford knew nothing of her. This was a relief to Grace, in the short term, although she knew the truth would out sooner or later.

"I am in London for the next month on business," the marquess informed her. "I hope we might have a chance to meet again, perhaps at Lord Rutherford's party on Tuesday next?"

"I believe my aunt will have received an invitation to that particular party. I shall gladly look for you there." Grace could feel an end to their conversation coming.

"I shall look forward to meeting you again, there." Lord Cromford gave a quick bow, which may even have been indifferent, and then looked back to the card tables. "Now, if you will excuse me, I must attend to my friend. He is a poor fit for cards, and I fear he may be goaded into gambling away his hard-won earnings, if I am not there to counsel caution."

"Good evening, my Lord."

Grace let out a sigh once the marquess was out of earshot. She had hoped that the man might glance back at her from the card tables. She had also hoped that his eyes might betray him, and that she would catch him gazing longingly at her. No such looks were afforded her. Once Lord Cromford returned to his friend's side, he seemed totally dedicated to the cause he had set himself.

It ought not to have been so, but the man's ability to not be driven to distraction by her, rather made him more worth knowing.

...

End of the Reading Sample.

"To Steal a Duke's Heart" is available on Amazon.

THE AUTHOR

Audrey Ashwood

Author of Traditional Historical Romance

Audrey Ashwood hails from London, the city where she was born and raised. At a young age, she began diving into the world of literature, a world full of fairytales and Prince Charmings. Writing came later – no longer was she a spectator of fantasies; she was now a creator of them.

In her books, the villains get their just desserts – her stories are known for happy and deserved endings. Love, of course, plays a major role, even if it's not the initial star of the show. With each written word, Audrey hopes to remind people that love transcends oceans and generations.

Don't miss out on exciting offers and new releases.

Sign up for her newsletter and the exclusive Reader's Circle:

www.audreyashwood.com/releases

More Books by Audrey Ashwood:

www.audreyashwood.com/books

INFORMATION, LEGAL AND IMPRINT

Miss Honeyfield and the Dark Duke

(Large Print Edition);

Originally Titled *The Dark Duke*

A Historical Romance Novel

by Audrey Ashwood;

Published by:

ARP 5519, 1732 1st Ave #25519 New York, NY 10128

Contact: info@allromancepublishing.com

1. Edition (Version 1.0); November 5th, 2019

© 2019

Image Rights:

© Period Images

© Depositphotos.com

Made in the USA
Monee, IL
06 December 2020